It was like that scene in *Dangerous Liaisons* where John Malkovich – as some count or other – tells Michelle Pfeiffer – as some duchess or other – that he must finish their affair, and the only explanation he gives is that it is beyond his "control".

She dies of a broken heart soon after.

It was the same for me, not dying of a broken heart or anything, well not yet, but there were no explanations.

No tears, except from me.

No 'let's talk about it.'

No cutsie brown-eyed smirk as his even features broke into a smile and he said, 'I'm only joking, you eee-jit.'

He was from Limerick, they say that kind of thing there.

About the author

Joan Conway lives in Dublin, Ireland. She works in film as a freelance location and production manager, and as a freelance script editor. She has had poetry published and has been short-listed for radio and screenplay awards. This is her first novel.

Cereal Lover

Joan Conway

CORONET BOOKS

Hodder & Stoughton

First published in Great Britain in 1999
by Hodder and Stoughton
First published in paperback in 2000
by Hodder and Stoughton
A division of Hodder Headline

A Coronet Paperback

10 9 8 7 6 5 4 3 2

A CIP catalogue record for this title is available
from the British Library.

ISBN 0 340 76625 5

Typeset by Avocet Typeset, Brill, Aylesbury, Bucks

Printed and bound in Great Britain

Hodder and Stoughton
A division of Hodder Headline
338 Euston Road
London NW1 3BH

For Howard, the paragon
Berni, the perspicacious
and
Jim, the patron

Now, don't get me wrong,
I left him

Chapter One

It was my birthday. I was thirty and there was a dead German in my garden. It wasn't really a garden, more a patch of neglected wasteland that I rented along with the house.

I knew he was dead because I held a mirror in front of his nose and it didn't steam up.

Come on, would you touch the dead body of a complete stranger that you had found just lying about? None of that American cop stuff for me. I had intended to use a feather – you know, to see if it moved when I held it under his nose – I remembered that from some play we did in school. But I couldn't find a feather; even the pillows in that house were made of some sort of foam stuff. I knew he was German because he had tannable skin and soft fair hair and he was wearing all the right labels on the outside of his clothes. And besides there was one of those tourist-guide-to-Ireland books lying beside him with 'Die Farben von Irland' written on the cover.

A dead giveaway, if you'll excuse the pun.

I was thirty. I wanted to wallow. I didn't want to

contact anybody about this visitor. I mean, he was fine where he was. I had no idea how long he'd been there. When I'd arrived the night before it had been too dark to see anything, especially a dead body, and I'd been gone for four days.

Maybe when I left he'd been just a baby corpse, a sapling rooting shyly in the corner, too small to be seen, and in my absence he had sprouted into a fully fledged adult corpse, flaunting his deadness at me.

OK, so it had been a bit of a shock, but that's just because when I first saw him I thought he was alive. When I knew he was dead – well . . .

But who do you contact when you find a dead body in your garden? Usually I would phone my mother when the world presents me with difficult universal questions. I didn't see any reason to startle her with this, though. The dead-body scenario would be just the type of thing she'd get off on. You see, it wouldn't be a regular occurrence in her part of suburban Dublin. She'd probably have driven straight here just to be party to it. She'd be found fumbling through his pockets for identification so that she could get the death notice into the next day's paper. First, of course, she'd phone his family, ostensibly to find out which papers they wanted it in, but really she would just need to be the first to break the news so that later she could say how terrible it had been.

I dialled 999.

The nice woman who answered figured that I probably needed to speak to the guards so she connected me to the local number. They didn't answer for ages because there was nobody in the nearest station. Rural Ireland is now manned by green boxes, which are inset into the outside walls of the police stations. They are a sort of long-distance intercom. If nobody's there when you visit you can whisper your desires and troubles into this box. It's just what you need on a dark night when violent cursing thugs are ripping your mattress apart and screaming blue murder for your life's savings – a nice, solid, comforting green box.

Anyway I got through to a guard thirty miles away and he assured me that there would be someone with me within an hour. Lucky it wasn't an emergency or anything. I suppose he figured that if the guy was dead he was going to remain that way. The guard told me to stay where I was and not to move anything. Undoubtedly he had mental images of me hiding the murder weapon, or giving the corpse a quick change of clothes so that he would look presentable for the day of inspection that lay ahead. He didn't seem to believe me when I said I wasn't acquainted with the corpse.

I suppose he had a point.

A couple of weeks before I found the body I had rented a house in a large, flat, rocky bit of the Burren. My nearest neighbour lived half a mile away. One of the reasons I moved, I tell myself (but not the main reason, I hasten to add), was that I was tired of cities. Tired of sitting in my car or standing on the street watching these people going by and wondering what on earth they all did and where they could possibly be going! So I'd moved to "the country" where I was determined to know everybody who passed, what they did and where they were going.

To date nobody had passed; my house was very remote.

I'd gone back to Dublin for a few days to collect some of my life, and when I returned to my new home, I discovered . . . well, that it was quite likely that nobody had passed since I'd left, but that there was this dead . . . You know the rest.

I wondered if maybe the house was bewitched or something, that you weren't supposed to pass it and if you attempted to you died. That's probably why none of the locals went by, but this foreigner had no way of knowing so he had fallen foul of the spell. Well, I wasn't going to research it: if it were true then I just wouldn't live to tell the tale.

While I waited for the guards to arrive all the other things that the dead German had pushed to the outside of my mind started to jostle for space in that tiny cell allocated to them somewhere at the back of my head.

They leapt forward, their short red cloaks horizontal with speed. "It's bad enough being thirty," they shouted, "but you're alone as well, couldn't even keep your boyfriend. And you're broke. Where's your big career now? And weren't you supposed to own a house by the time you were thirty, eh? Not live in some poxy rented place with somebody else's furniture. And let's really stand back and have a good look shall we? Shouldn't you be married now and have two point four children?"

"Hey, hey, hang on a minute." I stepped in and took what little control I could. "That's below the belt. Let's stick to the facts here, not supposition. We released the two point four children and the husband a long time ago:

they are no longer part of this negotiation. The rest, OK, I'll concede."

I had to.

I didn't own a house, my career was in a shambles and, yes, the hardest thing of all to admit – I was alone.

I had recently broken up with my boyfriend. "Boyfriend" wasn't exactly the right title, lover for the past four years more like. "Broken up" was another questionable description, not so much broken, really, as cracked, fallen apart, tinkling harshly to earth in so many pieces it couldn't possibly be put back together. Even if I wanted to. And I did.

Now, don't get me wrong, I left him.

Oh, yeah.

I'm not one of those obsessive women who stands by her man through all evils, weathering all abuse, fighting off anybody who might cast a glance in his direction.

Oh, no, I'd left him.

I certainly had the strength; conviction was my problem. One day I was happily and unquestioningly living with Niall – that was his name – and the next day, I wasn't. I'd been joking. It was Saturday morning. Niall had eaten the last piece of toast. But he hadn't done the "last Rolo" routine – we always did the "last Rolo" routine with the last everything: sweets, potatoes, suntan lotion. He'd just forgotten or something. So I said to him, joking and in an appropriately childlike voice, "Don't you love me anymore, Sugarplum?"

God it's so embarrassing when you have to repeat this stuff. I couldn't even tell my friends the exact circumstances of our breaking up, it was so embarrassing to admit that I, an adult soon-to-be-thirty woman, spoke to my lover like that.

But I did.

Niall, still munching the last piece of toast looked up at me and said, "You know, Val – I don't think I do."

Now I don't want you to think for one moment that he didn't do baby talk, too, he did. Just not that morning.

"What?" I said, in a normal voice.

"You heard me," he said, flatly, lowering his eyes, probably to see if there was any more toast left.

"Are you serious?" I gave a half-laugh of disbelief, my eyebrows, like they do, forming a huge puzzle on my forehead.

"Yes," he replied, deadpan.

"But that's silly," I argued, still not believing him. "You can't have loved me . . . last month" (yes, it had been a month since he had told me he loved me), "and not love me this month. It doesn't make sense."

He shrugged his shoulders, still not looking up.

"Is there somebody else?" I asked in panic, already smelling her perfume. How could I have been so blind!

He looked straight at me and shook his head slowly.

And, really, if I go on recounting the conversation it'll get repetitious because Niall refused to elaborate. This was very unlike Niall: he was known by our friends as the most articulate computer engineer they had ever met – I don't think they had met many but that never prevented generalisation among my peers.

He froze me out.

It was like that scene in *Dangerous Liaisons* where John Malkovitch – as some count or other – tells Michelle

Pfeiffer – as some duchess or other – that he must finish their affair, and the only explanation he gives is that it is beyond his "control". She dies of a broken heart soon after.

It was the same for me, not dying of a broken heart or anything, well not yet, but there were no explanations.

No tears, except from me.

No 'let's talk about it.'

No cutsie brown-eyed little smirk as his even features broke into a smile and he said, "I'm only joking, you eee-jit."

He was from Limerick, they say that kind of thing there.

He wasn't.

Joking, that is.

I tried arguing.

I tried silence.

I tried bullying.

I even cried myself to sleep, but he never reached over to comfort me. It was as if my warm comfortable Niall had been stolen by the body-snatchers and a changeling put in his place. A cold, monosyllabic changeling.

Next morning the bed was very unfriendly. Even the bedclothes had taken his side. I awoke clutching the sheet, still trying to fend off his indifference. In the chilly light of a new-year morning I decided that I had to make a stand. If I made a stand he'd see how strong I was and decide that he really did love me, want me, need me and wouldn't we forget all about it and wasn't he just being silly.

"I'm leaving," I said determinedly.

He met my gaze steadily. "I think that's a very good idea." He could be very frank: it was one of his many qualities that I admired.

Usually.

So I left.

I must have closed my eyes to hold back the tears at the painful memory, because when I opened them, two guards, set against a backdrop of Burren limestone, were staring at me suspiciously through the window. I suppose they were wondering why I was so upset about the death of somebody I didn't even know. I decided not to tell them about my failed relationship. It didn't seem like an appropriate time. Instead we talked about the Dead German. This distracted me from crying but I knew I was still thirty and I didn't feel that this business was making me any younger.

The guards were very nice, though. After they'd established that I wasn't armed or insane or anything. They said that they had to wait for the doctor's opinion before they could say if the German was dead or not. Well, officially, anyway.

They asked if I was sure that we hadn't had a lovers' tiff – it was Valentine's Day you see, so I expect they thought that he hadn't sent me a card or something so I'd killed him. I would have, if he had been and he hadn't, but of course he wasn't, if you get my drift.

Yes, I know what you're saying, it was Valentine's Day and it was my birthday.

And, yes, my name is Valentina. Believe me when I say everybody, and I mean everybody, on pain of death, calls me Val.

But I admit the birthday does have its uses. Because of all the cards I get on Valentine's day the postman thinks I am the most popular girl in the world. Except on my thirtieth birthday, of course, because nobody knew where I was – that's my excuse. My mother knew but she had given up sending cards because she had decided that they were commercial exploitation. She sent me a brown envelope containing a congratulatory letter written on my father's headed paper and a fifty-pound note. It had been in the house when I'd arrived the night before. She likes to get things done on time. I made tea for the guards, who politely tried not to grimace as they drank it black and sugarless. Housekeeping hadn't been uppermost on my mind that week.

"So, how long have you lived here then, ah, er, Val?" asked the younger of the two – not bad-looking, really, in a guardish sort of way. Short dark wavy hair, ears that stuck out just far enough to keep his hat from falling into his eyes, and he'd obviously joined up before they had started allowing the guards to be really short. "Two weeks," I said, with what I thought was a shy smile. I had decided that, in the circumstances the less like a hard-faced city blow-in I sounded the better. "Give or take," I added hastily as the older guard gave me a sceptical look. He must have been the "local" guard and had all my movements monitored. He'd probably taken my smile to be a seductive smirk calculated to lure the younger guard into whatever treachery I was hatching. Maybe he even knew something about myself and the German that I didn't know!

Before we could begin to discuss this, the doctor

11

arrived and unsurprisingly declared the corpse dead. By the time I had provided him with a rented blanket I'd decided that perhaps this incident was not such a bad thing after all. I mean, in one morning I'd increased the number of people I knew in the area by one hundred per cent. I now knew the local doctor and the local guard. Two less people to wonder about in the future.

After the doctor had arrived things started to speed up: the ambulance came with forensics and the pathologist. The place became positively crowded. Even some neighbours arrived. I didn't notice any of them passing the house, though.

I resigned myself to the fact that I wasn't going to get an opportunity to step back into the tepid depression with which I had started my day. I was staring gloomily into the sink at the ever growing mound of used mugs when Séan, the younger guard – first-name terms by now – blushed deeply to the tips of his supportive ears and asked hesitantly if I would accompany him to the police station.

Well he didn't so much ask as say, "Would you . . . would you mind coming along to the station with us, Val, to fill out a few forms and the like?"

And the like?

Did that mean I was a suspect or something? I didn't like the sound of that. After all I'd been through and now I was as good as being accused of murder!

I smiled at Séan, whose colour deepened to an exotic purple as he sank his head into the stiff collar of his uniform. "Of course," I said calmly. "Let me just get a coat. I'll be with you in a minute."

As I got my coat, and scarf, I looked at my face in the mirror. Was this the face of a criminal? I asked myself.

Could someone with this face kill somebody?

Could someone with this face be thirty?

Don't answer that.

Mirrors are so depressing. My eyes were red rimmed from days of crying, my skin was blotchy from lack of care, there were dark roots showing in my 'naturally' blonde hair and I didn't really care enough to put on lipstick.

God, I was falling to pieces.

Val O'Hara – the Brixton one

Chapter Two

In the guards' car on the way to the village I suddenly
remembered when I had last been in a police station. It
was in London soon after I'd met Niall. Everything was
perfect then: the sun was warmer, people were friendlier,
even the police horses looked happy. I must have been in
love.

We were living in Brixton – well, the Oval, really but I
always preferred to take the bus to Brixton on my days
off: it was more colourful. One of those days on my way
back to the bus stop I was approached by a man waving
an ID card at me. He was a plain-clothes policeman who
asked me if I would care to accompany him to the police
station. And he was asking, not telling. He explained that
they were looking for participants for a line-up – I'm sure
he didn't call it that, an ID parade probably. I was a bit
taken aback: despite how it seems, I do not look like a
criminal – I mean, I never even get stopped coming
through Customs or anything. Then, the plain-clothes
policeman, as though to encourage me, added in his best
Cockney, "You'll get four pounds for doing it."

Four pounds! My, don't the public services pay well! But my curiosity had already taken hold so off I went to the police station, accompanied by three other 'blonde Caucasian females'. It was not until I was seated in the line-up room behind the reflective glass removing all my jewellery that I began to question the situation. I didn't look like the other women in the room: yes, we were all white and fair-haired and two of us were Irish but that was where the similarities stopped.

I wondered which one of us was guilty – did I say us? I meant them, of course. I could certainly remember no crime that I had committed that would connect me to Brixton police station. I looked suspiciously at my companions. Suddenly the door burst open and a cursing, kicking – yes you've guessed – 'blonde' – on crutches propelled herself into the room. She took the last vacant seat, protesting loudly and in her frenzy promptly swallowed her nose stud while trying to remove it. I deduced that she must be the woman who had committed whatever heinous crime we were now all implicated in.

But how had she managed it on crutches? Perhaps that is where she'd gone wrong: she'd forgotten about the getaway! Or maybe, just maybe she was a victim of police brutality; though having been in the room with her for five minutes as she raged and slammed I thought it more probable that she had brutalised the police.

It was when we were all staring in front of us being identified that I panicked. What if whoever was on the other side of the glass chose me? What if they just did not have a clue and pointed me out? I could see it now, the headline:

VAL O'HARA – THE BRIXTON ONE

I envisaged a prison life of bodybuilding and lesbianism as learned lawyers heroically fought my case. Then, after about twenty years or so, my parents and a few other old dears – and, of course, some rowdy spectators attracted by the media – would stand waiting outside the prison with banners and amplified cheering to welcome me, grey-haired and masculated, to freedom. What had I let myself in for?

Nothing, obviously.

The lights went down and we all left by the way we had come in, except the woman on crutches who was ushered out of another door. As we passed Reception we were each given four pound coins and told that if we wished to participate there was to be another ID parade on the twenty-eighth of the month.

What did they want us to do, make a profession of it? Travel around the country doing ID parades until finally after years of scheduled venues we would qualify to make guest appearances at select, exclusive stations?

I didn't go back on the twenty-eighth, I was busy.

And even if I hadn't been, Niall wouldn't have let me. He claimed that one tiny misunderstanding in that line-up could have destroyed my life. I thought this a little melodramatic. But, then, Niall was a bit of a fatalist. A small fault, and the only one. Until recently.

When Séan, Fergus – that's the other guard – and I reached the station at Ballinacarrig (that was the nearest station to my cottage), we found that it was very quiet and very cold – it didn't usually open on Wednesdays.

The only sound breaking its sturdy silence was a post-apocalyptic whistle coming from the green box. Maybe it was a special wavelength devised by police headquarters to pacify rural unrest. Anyway, there didn't seem to be any big crime wave in North Clare that day.

"Come in, come in," Séan said, with as much enthusiasm as he could muster in the circumstances. "Sit down, I'll turn on the gas fire for you." He swept his hand across the seat of a chair as though to clean it, then placed it near the heater.

"Would you mind waiting a little while? There's a couple of lads coming from Galway – they'd have more experience at this sort of thing than us. I'll get you a nice cup of tea while you're waiting."

His torrent of speech came to an end. He smiled, his ears pitching his cap higher on his head. He moved towards the door and paused, shifting nervously from one foot to the other, his face an anticipation of raised eyebrows. He expected me to say something. Hell, for a moment I expected me to say something. But nothing came. I couldn't gain access to the smalltalk-with-guards file that must have been somewhere in my brain. Instead I nodded and lowered my eyes to stare at the weak flame that struggled from the heater.

"Ah, right so," Séan mumbled uneasily, shuffling out and closing the door behind him.

I was alone, alone in a cold, barren room with nothing to distract me from my memories. That meant only one thing, I was alone with Niall thoughts.

Again.

Deprived of a reason not to cry, I felt tears well up in

my eyes at the painful memory of when I had last seen Niall.

"I'm going," I'd said, clutching a hastily packed bag as I peered around the kitchen door at him standing by the sink smoking a cigarette. Yes, OK, so he wasn't perfect, he did smoke, but I actually thought that it gave him a certain suave image, like Alec Guinness playing the aristocratic Englishman or Peter O'Toole being the emaciated hedonist. Not that Niall looked anything like Alec Guinness or Peter O'Toole. No, Niall was handsome in that dark straight-haired, brown-eyed, light-bodied-but-tall sort of way. Not that that's what attracted me to him. And I'd love to claim that it had been his personality, but it wasn't.

It was his smile.

Like the curtains opening for one of those 1940s Broadway musicals, it dazzled and drew you in, no matter how much you tried to resist. He'd first smiled at me in an Irish pub in Elephant and Castle – see I know all the best spots in London. And don't think that I'm one of those sad Irish people who go to a foreign country and immediately find the nearest Irish bar in which to drown my sorrows. It was my first night in London after I had decided to 'emigrate', I was staying with friends who lived locally and who had arranged to meet some other friends in the bar. And, no, I don't know if they are the sort of sad Irish people who only drink in Irish pubs when they are abroad.

Niall was there and the minute we were introduced he drew me in, so to speak. He said it was mutual. I believed him. It was love at first sight.

I'd like to say that this was rare for me but it wasn't. It was love at first sight all the time with me, it just wasn't usually reciprocated. I was always falling madly in love, a fleeting smile, a glance, a passing BMW, a charming waiter invariably looking for a larger tip rather than a lifetime commitment. I suppose it's just as well that they usually came to nothing: I wouldn't have had time to do anything normal – like eat.

The funny thing was that after Niall and I started to see each other, which we did every night after we met, I sort of lost interest in all those other men. It didn't mean that I closed my eyes and never saw a cute buttock again. And, no, I'm not reducing men to objects. My opinion is based purely on the aesthetic. Now, however, it was more like window-shopping – you know, if you don't go into the shop you have no serious intentions, you're just looking because it's good to know what's in fashion.

Anyway, this relative disinterest all came as quite a relief because I had been afraid that I was going to be man-crazed for the rest of my life. I could see myself in the confines of some geriatric unit rasping my last breaths, leaning on my zimmer frame, drooling and squinting at nubile young nurses. You see, by the time I get to the nursing home there will be loads of male nurses. And if there aren't I'm not going.

So being in love with Niall was great, even after we first made love, which was days after I met him – you know the old rule: never do it on the first date. I met him, the next night we had a date and after that, well . . . And there was no awkward stuff. No waking up the next day wondering what on earth you ever saw in the guy and suddenly inventing a job so that you can dash off to it. Even though it's Sunday.

I hate those ones who are like that cartoon of the pussycat and the French skunk. He, the skunk, believes he has found his soulmate and keeps following the cat around amorously, kissing and hugging her at every opportunity. She spends all her time and energy trying to escape from the suffocating smell. You know the sort I mean – can't take a hint. And you're traumatised because you thought you really liked him, and now you feel so shallow that you end up going out with him for a whole month just because you're so guilty.

With Niall it was perfect. Two months after we met we moved in together. I had to find somewhere to live, as all my friends were tired of having my clothes piled in the corner of their living rooms. I had a job and Niall had got a promotion – in fact, he'd been out celebrating it the night I first met him – he could afford a better place to live. So we got a place together. It was great. We could even agree on the décor; for a computer geek from Limerick he had really good taste.

I suppose you think I'm heartless for not thinking of the Dead German for ages.

It's not that I didn't care, it's just that, well I didn't know him or anything. It's like hearing that your second cousin's husband's sister has died and you've never even met the second cousin, never mind her in-laws. So you're sorry but . . . And, no, I don't like dead bodies, but he looked very peaceful, really. He wasn't cut or anything – no blood. His head was at a funny angle, so I assumed his neck was broken. I've seen enough undercover-agent films to work that one out. I didn't say that to the guards, though, because they would probably have asked me how I'd done it.

And that's another thing. I was upset at being the chief suspect. Not because anyone would assume that I was capable of killing. I was upset because they thought that I would be stupid enough to leave the body at the back gate of the house in which I was staying and then phone the guards.

I should have just stayed in Dublin when I'd gone there the week before, pretended to everybody that I'd been on a ten-day holiday and that I was back. But I couldn't. I'd told anybody who would listen that I was off to make a new life for myself, that Niall and I had run our course – God, it killed me to say that – and that I'd always wanted to live in the country anyway.

I'd immersed myself in a river of lies on the current of which I bobbed right back to my country seat.

I'd gone to Dublin in the hope that Niall might have repented. I hadn't seen him since the day I had said that I was leaving. I'd gone straight to Suzy's house: we'd been friends since we were seventeen. She was very verbally supportive, muttering, "Bastard," at all the significant sobbing pauses. She loyally defended my decision to leave and said that I could stay with her for as long as I wanted.

I didn't want to stay long. Sharing what was in effect a cosmetically enhanced bedsit with Suzy was like trying to keep the Incredible Hulk in his normal clothes after he had lost his temper. It was impossible. Our life together was just bursting at the seams. I mean, don't get me wrong, Suzy and I got on great. She was my best friend, sort of. I say sort of because Suzy had loads of best friends. She was one of those warm, bubbly people who gets invited everywhere and always gives really sound advice when you cry on her shoulder. We'd meet at parties and occasionally arrange to go for coffee together, but she'd never come out with me if Niall was going to be there. Niall claimed that she didn't like him, he said that any time she heard that he was going to be out with me she made an excuse not to come along. I didn't think that was true. I'd always just assumed that Suzy was more a woman's woman who, when she was single as Suzy usually was, preferred not to go out with couples.

Anyway, she was really sweet to me but her place was just too small for two. I was in a homeless pickle.

The idea of going back to my parents' place to be molly-coddled, manipulated and I-told-you-so'ed was out of the question. So, as my mother's insistence grew, I blurted out that what I really wanted to do was go far away and live in the country. This was greeted with silence. Not the astonished Mother-of-God! type of silence, more the Oh-my-God-she's-at-it-again, teeth-gritted type of silence.

I may as well point out at this stage that my mother took a very dim view of my living with Niall. It wasn't so much Niall, though she didn't think him good enough, it was more us living together. She believed it to be complete folly. Yes, she acknowledged everybody did it, but she still couldn't see how a woman wasn't going to lose on the deal. She believed that any man 'getting his oats' should also get lots of red tape, responsibility and commitment. Maybe she had a point. I couldn't work out what it was but she had stated it so often that I had to concede, if only because of her tenacity.

My mother didn't have a very high opinion of men in general. She seemed to think that her husband, my father was OK – very limited, but OK. But when it came to 'men' as an abstract generalization, she believed them to be self-centred, manipulative, perverted sex fiends. That was with the exception of Bill Clinton. I'm sure it wasn't because he didn't fit into any of her usual man descriptions. He just seemed to have been granted amnesty. Nobody understood it. I suspect that she inherited an adoration of American presidents from her mother, who was renowned for her devotion to JFK. Yes, it was definitely hereditary.

It's my guess that my mother also inherited the silence on the phone that greeted my latest idea to go and live in the country. It was one of those silences that suddenly makes you start to think about your phone bill. Then it goes on so long that you start trying to work out if you can get the undertaker round to your parents' house to prise the receiver out of your mother's hand before rigor mortis sets in. It took a few carefully muffled sobs from me to get her back to life.

She was very helpful in the end. She said that she had friends, the Johnstons, who owned a summer house in County Clare and who weren't using it – not surprising, really, as it was the middle of winter. She said that she would borrow the key. While she didn't approve of Niall she didn't like to see me unhappy.

Cereal Lover

And so it was that the following Sunday I was lost on the back roads of North Clare looking for my new home. When I got there, however, it turned out to be not so much a home as an icebox. It was obviously a very small cottage that had been converted into a 'chalet' suitable for the city-dweller who wanted their holiday house to look like an Italian villa. Even if it is four miles from the sea on the west coast of Ireland.

This splendid open-plan structure was purely a tunnel for the bitter little North Clare winds that ran scowling, shoulders hunched, heads covered in dark shawls, through every draughty orifice of the house. And the storage heaters, while I'm sure they did a very good job storing, seemed more than reluctant to share any of their heat with me. The one small fireplace that had been retained in the living area was definitely more decorative than utilitarian as it spat viciously at the damp wood I'd found at the back of the house.

The cottage did, however, have a wonderful view. I had been gazing self-pityingly at this view when I'd found the Dead German.

There I am, back to the Dead German again. Was he going to be a permanent fixture in my head from now on, always lying about in there, dead, ready to pop up at the merest association? Well, I didn't want to think about the German.

I wanted to fume at Niall.

I had thought that when he heard I was coming back from the country to pick up some stuff he would want to see me. Yes, I needed some more of my belongings but what I really wanted was to give Niall an opportunity to meet me. Maybe he was too embarrassed and ashamed to contact me.

I left a message on the machine – our machine – saying that I would be by. He hadn't taken my voice off it: surely that was a good sign. I even arranged to go there when I knew he'd be in – Saturday morning. Niall was always at home on Saturday mornings, washing his clothes, checking his e-mail, making calls. I wasn't even putting him out: he would have to go to no bother to see me. I was sure that I would find him at the bottom of the stairs, a basketful of washed clothes in his arms, his mouth a grin of pleasure, a stray strand of dark hair falling over his eyes. "Val," he'd say. "God, I've missed you. This place is so empty without you. You're back to stay aren't you? I mean, if you need to go to the country you can go and stay with my family in Limerick." And he'd put down the basket of clothes, some of which I would notice were mine – the sweetheart – and put his arms around me and . . .

He wasn't there. My heart was thumping as I turned my key in the lock. When I stepped inside I was holding my breath. The moment I closed the door behind me I knew the flat was empty. That great big empty that shouts rudely and tauntingly at you in a deep voice. "You're such a fool, Val, you're such a sap, you really thought he'd be here. Well, tough, he's not, there's only me. Why don't you and me go upstairs and get to know each other a bit better, eh, luv? What do you say?"

I choked back my tears in angry fury and slammed about the flat stuffing my life with Niall into Dunnes Stores plastic bags, not caring what toppled or broke as I swept my belongings out of my home.

My former home.

How had it happened that I was the one doing all the moving, having all the upheaval, when he was the one who had changed?

Oh, yes, I could kill if I had to, I didn't mind anyone believing that. It's just, that day Niall didn't care enough about me to stay around to let me kill him.

I'm sure Guard Séan saw the fury on my face when he came back into the room clutching a cup of lukewarm tea. He looked taken aback, his face immediately lost some of the complacent composure he had attained while he'd been out of the room and his ears allowed his hat to move forward on his forehead.

"Am, the lads are here from Galway now, Val, if you'd care to talk to them." He looked at me cautiously then with hardly a pause rushed into one of his seemingly endless sentences. "They want to know if you have a solicitor or if you'd like to have one, you know if you don't have one yourself and you'd like to we could arrange one for you – 'Twouldn't be any bother at all, really."

A solicitor? You only needed those if you had done something wrong, or wanted to sue someone or make a will or something. I knew that much because my brother was one – of course, he did it in America where you had to do something really bad before they took you to the cop station. This was ridiculous: what if they did decide that I had done it? What if by some strange, alien series of freak circumstances I was found guilty?

In my imagination I had already gone to trial. Me, in the dock holding gloves and handbag looking earnest and distraught. Above me, the judge, sporting his death-sentence wig declares me guilty . . . to be hanged by the neck . . . The scene changes to me being dragged from the dock kicking and screaming. Next day in the cold morning light – this is all in black and white, by the way – having made peace with my God, I am led from my tiny cell. Then we see the man who loves me, standing at his living-room window, clutching my glove – I'd left it behind in the dock in my struggle. He is staring tragically across the dawn city. A church clock, standing conveniently near his house, strikes the hour of my execution. He lowers his head. The credits roll up the screen to the sound of the theme music.

Maybe I did need a solicitor.

I knew from watching police dramas on television that I was entitled to one phone call. I'm sure that as I hadn't been arrested I could have made as many as I wanted but I felt a bit bad about having to borrow the money from the guards. But who would I call? I was a single woman now, thrown out on the cruel world with no one to care about me or bother if I lived or died. On top of that I was thirty and nobody loved me enough to send me a Valentine card.

I rang my mother.

"Hi, Mum, it's Val."

"Oh, hello, dear. Happy birthday."

She was great, she always remembered my birthday – I mean even after all these years she remembered. She always said that she would never forget because I came into the world screaming and I didn't stop for three years. So I rang her on my birthday because I knew it was a day that inspired traumatic memories for her.

"Thanks, Mum. Look, I have a bit of a problem here," I said.

"Oh, is it the house, dear? Is something broken? You're all right, aren't you, love?" She always tried to guess what the problem was before you could tell her – it was like some sort of competition.

"No, Mum, I'm fine and the house is fine."

"Is it the car, dear, has it broken down? Where are you? I'm sure I can get the number of a mechanic for you. I told you that you should have joined the AA with a car that age."

"No, Mum, it's not that either. Will you listen a minute, I'm in the police station in Ballinacarrig."

My raised voice was attracting the attention of Seán who was shuffling some papers at a desk further down the hall.

"Oh, Mother of God what have you done?" There was a quiver of hysteria in her voice.

I've always thought that my mother suffered from a startlingly low level of parental trust, frighteningly low, in fact, when you consider that none of her children are murderers or pickpockets or anything.

I explained the situation to her. She thought it was very serious. She had obviously decided that if I wasn't guilty I was being framed for a murder. She said she would phone one of my brother Mark's friends who was a solicitor in Dublin and he'd be bound to have a cousin who was a solicitor down the country who could help. Are all solicitors related?

"Now, you're to sit tight and don't answer any questions and cover your face when the press starts taking your picture. Your father doesn't need this sort of publicity."

My father is a dentist: what sort of publicity would have an adverse effect on him? My teeth were in excellent condition: he had no worries there. And if *Hello!* magazine did want my story they would have to pay for it and wait until I had put on some make-up. I understood how careful management of your self-image can take years off you even if you are thirty.

The 'lads' from Galway didn't look too impressed at the delay; in fact, even before the suggestion of a delay they hadn't looked too impressed. They both wore raincoats. I really thought that only Colombo wore that sort of coat or, OK, maybe the US President's bodyguards, but not a couple of guys from Galway! Whatever happened to 'plain clothes'? And they were armed: I saw the shape under their coats. Obviously bottom-of-the-range raincoats if they didn't disguise the gun bulge.

We all sat silently in a small room for ages, as though they were afraid that I was going to disappear if they took their eyes off me – like a leprechaun from whom you are trying to get the crock of gold. You ask him where the gold is, he points at a distant hill, you look in the direction in which he is pointing and, hey presto!, when you look back he has disappeared. And it's not really possible to dig up the whole hill. Besides, I'd missed lunch. Come to that I'd missed breakfast but I'd had a lot of tea. I was hungry but I wasn't going to eat anything: that would look like I approved of my detention and I didn't. It did serve as a mild distraction from my miserable life but I still objected to sitting in a small room for ages with two sullen armed men. In good old Irish tradition I was on hunger strike!

Séan came in smiling. "Your mother rang to know if you're all right. She says that your solicitor is on his way. He'll be here by four o'clock."

I grinned in embarrassment. I was surprised that she hadn't demanded to speak to me just to determine that they hadn't done away with me in an elaborate cover-up. And I loved the easy way that now, magically, 'the' solicitor was 'your' solicitor. Despite the obvious disadvantages there is a great deal to be said for relatives, really.

My solicitor, when he arrived, declared that he was not really my solicitor but that somebody else would be handling the case later. "Terry O'Neill," he said smiling his fifty-something-well-established-well-suited-just-a-hint-of-cheeriness-about-the-tie smile as he extended a clean, outdoor hand.

"Hi," I replied, feeling very grubby in my I-don't-care-anyway two pullovers and leggings. Then I realised with surprise that I did care: he made me feel like a little girl who had been caught with the juice of stolen strawberries still on her chin. I'd thought that I'd managed to purge all my middle-class social conditioning but all along I'd just been hanging out with the wrong crowd.

Or maybe the right crowd, if they guaranteed that the worst aspects of my personality remained hidden.

I'm a huge advocate of escapism. Never try to solve a problem if you can more easily run away from it.

With much raincoat-rearranging and throat-clearing the interview got under way. After all the waiting the questions were amazingly easy. It was as though I was not really a suspect at all. I might have been doing an exercise in a language class using the past tense: What time? Where? How? Not the big how of 'how did he die?' just the littler hows of how did I find him? How did I know he was dead? They even asked me how did I know he was German. Terry O'Neill took a particular interest in that question. So I had to explain that I didn't really know, that it had just been the book lying beside him. He seemed surprised about the book. I suppose because you don't expect a corpse to need a tourist guidebook.

Terry O'Neill took notes all through the interview. He and the Special Branch guys made jokes, harmless ones, but it was all very buddy-buddy, very 'we'll have a good laugh and a pint out of this when it's all over, won't we, lads.' But I didn't have a chance to feel ostracised because Terry O'Neill kept drawing me into our own little conspiracy which excluded the 'lads'. He'd obviously done this sort of thing before. Maybe not a Dead German case, but certainly the questioning in a potentially-harmful-to-the-witness case. I felt taken care of: thanks, Mum.

As soon as I felt safe I discovered I was starving. Not just hungry, but that enormous grasping desire for food that would have led me to pull up whole plants in the hope that they were harbouring an edible root below ground. There weren't, of course, any plants in the tiny room in which the four of us sat but the noise from my stomach as I fantasised about food broadcast my longing.

Eventually the interview broke up and I left the room with Terry. It's very easy to get on first-name terms in

Clare, especially when you may just have committed the only murder in the area this decade – well, why limit it? – this century perhaps. When we reached the corridor Terry hung back to talk to the detectives. I was left standing in the cold hallway wondering what was supposed to happen next. Memories of Niall were just starting to nudge gently at the curtain I'd pulled to hide them when Terry came down the corridor smiling comfortingly.

"Well, that's about it for us, really," he said cheerily. "You should pop into the office tomorrow to meet Mary Reilly, your brief – she'll fill you in on anything you might need to know. It's only a formality, really."

"Oh, great," I said, suddenly feeling deflated. I was at a complete loss as to what to do next, it was such an anti-climax. I just wasn't that important anymore, nobody was interested in me. It's amazing how quickly we can get used to attention and when it is taken away Ego junior stamps his foot and screams for it back. Besides, I had no way of getting home, and even if I had I would just be delivered back to a life of rejection. He must have noticed my bewilderment.

"Do you have a way of getting home?" He was half smiling.

"Well, no," I replied, adding quickly, "I came in the guards' car," just in case he thought that I had one of those beam-me-up machines, 'To Boldly Go Where No Man . . .' and all the rest.

"It's on my way," he said. "Why don't I give you a lift?"

I didn't think for one moment that my house was on anyone's way, but sometimes, depending on the circumstances, I'm prepared to overlook facts. "Yes please," I simpered – well, my interpretation of simpering anyway.

I said goodbye to Séan the guard, who was moving aimlessly around inside the front door rattling a bunch of keys. He cleared his throat and swallowed, his eyes darting from me to the floor then briefly to Terry before he fixed his gaze on my scarf.

"Are you, that is, have you, amm, are you all right for getting home? It's just that I have to drop a summons to a house out beyond you so I could leave you off at your place without any bother."

He stopped abruptly, his gaze shooting anxiously to my face in an effort to pre-empt my reaction. I was stunned that the road to my house would be so busy. After all, I'd been there for weeks and nobody had passed. Before I had a chance to speak Terry interrupted, as he proprietorially ushered me towards the door, "Val will be taking a little lift with me, Séan, isn't that right, Val?"

As we stepped into the cold winter evening I turned to give a small wave to Séan. He was standing in the bright glare of office lights, his hat pushed well back on his head, glowering at Terry O'Neill's back. Perhaps he had thought that if he could get me alone he would have coaxed the truth about the Dead German from me and win himself a promotion. Terry O'Neill was ruining his career. Terry, oblivious to any damage he might have done, opened the passenger door of his very prosperous-looking car for me, then settled himself in the driver's seat. As he reached for the ignition he turned and said, "I don't suppose you've eaten?"

"No." I shook my head, trying not to salivate too noticeably. Not this year.

"Well," he said, as though he had just discovered gravity, "I haven't either, so why don't we get a little bit to eat before I drop you home?"

Suddenly I knew. It came to me in a blinding flash.

Inside this pompous rural solicitor there was a fairy godmother, gold dress, plump red cheeks, magic wand, the lot, and with one gesture of her enchanted stick she could solve all my problems. I wondered if she could do anything about Niall. That might be pushing it. Still, food would be good. And maybe a drink.

Yes, definitely a drink.

Now, I don't want you to think that I'm a substance abuser or anything. I didn't need a drink. Well, maybe I didn't need a drink.

I just knew that I really, really, really wanted one.

Aren't men great all the same?

Chapter Three

There aren't that many restaurants in small towns in rural Ireland and the one that Terry decided to go to had not yet opened for the evening. The dining room adjoined a pub and the barman assured us that we could sit at the bar and read the menu until the restaurant opened. Having greeted Terry by name he looked knowingly at me and pushed a plate of heart-shaped nibbles in my direction.

For a moment I thought it was because he knew that I was ravenous but then I realised the significance of the hearts: it was Valentine's Day and he assumed that I was Terry's 'companion'. He must have been a believer that only courting couples went out on Valentine's night. I wondered indignantly what age he thought I was if I was Terry's date. The stresses and strains of the day must have been showing on my face.

"Would we care for a little drink?" Terry asked.

I had by now worked out that he was one of those patronising diminutisers who believed that anything to do with anyone he perceived as being less than him was

referred to as being 'little'. No doubt had he inadvertently run me over with his car he would have come and
leaned over me lying on the road and said, in what he
believed to be a kindly tone, "Had a little accident, then,
have we?"

"Yes," I replied to the drink invitation, deciding not to
comment on the verbal nuances of a man who was, after
all, a total stranger.

The barman presented us with the menu: it was surprisingly elaborate for a restaurant in the middle of
nowhere. I considered eating it. I probably would have if
it had been illustrated. Did you ever do that when you
were a child? Cut out pictures of food from shiny cookery
magazines and eat them? It always looked so delicious. It
can't have been that I was hungry. I don't ever remember
being hungry as a child, but our diet was so disgustingly
healthy. Crisps were rationed: they were in the bad-for-
you food category. So on crispless days when our longing
became too much we would cut up an onion and some
cheese and eat them together to simulate cheese and onion
crisps. I don't do that anymore.

By the time we got to our table a couple-of-drinks-on-
an-empty-stomach later, I was feeling much . . . well, it's
not happier, is it? It's more numbed.

Terry was very easy company and had managed to
waffle on about a local vet who had succeeded in inject-
ing himself instead of his patient, a bull, with a sedative.
The farmer who claimed to have been injured by the bull
while the vet slept was suing him. There were, of course,
no witnesses. It all sounded a bit far-fetched to me but it
certainly took my mind off things.

We were well into the main course before Terry raised the subject of the Dead German. "You know your German was moved," he said lightly, looking at me without raising his head.

My German, indeed!

"Oh, thank God," I replied, waving my knife in the air in a manner that always infuriated my mother. "I was just dreading having to spend the night in that house if he was still lying about in the garden."

"No, no," said Terry, with just a touch of exasperation. "He was moved to your garden after he died. Before you found him."

"From where?" I asked, through a mouthful of food. I was determined that the German would not come between my dinner and me.

"I don't know," said Terry. "The detectives told me about it before we left the station. They had no further information, at least not that they were giving me."

"But how do they know he was moved? Were there drag marks or what?" I was querulous now and for some unknown reason feeling quite defensive. Oh, no! I'd become possessive about a corpse. What an empty life I must have.

"No," replied Terry patiently, ignoring my tone. "They figure that he may have been thrown out of a car or something. His neck was broken, you know, and his body was at all the wrong angles not to have been moved. But they won't have any more detailed information until there is a thorough examination."

Great dinner conversation! Here I was, my first time out with a man since I had broken up with my boyfriend and we were talking about dead bodies. I mean, don't misunderstand me, it wasn't a date or anything and Terry was ancient and I didn't fancy him. But he was a man. It was Valentine's Day, and my birthday, and considering how the rest of the day had gone I counted myself very fortunate to be out to dinner at all. Especially with a man.

OK, so he was old enough to be my father but at least he was male. I was thirty, after all, so how could I complain about anybody being old? And, for somebody who was ancient, Terry was quite entertaining. A bit patronising maybe, but I put that down to the older-men-in-the-professions syndrome. Besides, I didn't expect to have a lot in common with a middle-aged solicitor.

Not like Niall.

From the moment we met we'd discovered that we had loads in common. The fact that he was three years younger than me didn't seem to make any difference. He'd even read a lot of the books I'd read, which wasn't bad for someone who had studied computers. That he was from the country didn't make a difference either: he'd gone to university in Dublin and moved to London straight away after graduating so he had some carbon monoxide in his lungs.

We agreed that we both wanted to go back to live in Ireland. We didn't want to be emigrants for ever, even if it was only in London. So Niall started applying for jobs in Ireland and they loved him – no, honestly – whatever it was he did with those computers they all wanted him, so he just picked the one with the highest wage that he liked the best.

I hated my job in publishing in London, even though

the money was quite good – I decided I would much rather do a job I hated in Ireland. So I packed up and went along for the ride. My parents, of course, thought I was daft, giving up a good job to follow a man to whom I wasn't even married – well, that's it, really, isn't it? If I had been married to him they wouldn't have cared about my Good Job. Sanctity of marriage and all that.

Editing academic books wasn't a big business in Ireland but I had enough experience to get a job without too much trouble. It wasn't the same job I'd had in London. There, I'd worked directly with the writer on final drafts. In Ireland they didn't seem to do final drafts. I was editing the computer printout, looking for print errors; for the most part the grammar was abysmal but nobody seemed to care – responsibility for that had been lost somewhere in the chain of command. The pay was awful. I figured that, with time, I'd work my way up.

It was great to be back. We got a lovely apartment – on Niall's wages that was no problem – and immediately I picked up my social life where I'd left off before going to England.

Except it was better. Now I had Niall.

All my friends thought he was wonderful, we went everywhere together. That side of things had always been good. Work, on the other hand, hadn't panned out as well as I'd hoped. Don't get me wrong, I loved the people I worked with, they were great. But about eighteen months after I started, everybody in my section was asked to go individually to the regional manager's office. I decided that they had finally realised how invaluable I was and were giving me a promotion.

I was wrong. The regional manager was one of those guys who thought he was great because he made it to regional manager in an unheard-of publishing company. From the size of his beer belly, he'd been celebrating his promotion for a considerable time. He probably thought that the more of him there was the more of him there would be to appreciate. He was the sort who believed that working out was for gays, and women were for leering at. He stared pointedly at my chest every time we had a conversation; this time was no different.

"Val," he slimed, "we're making a few changes around here." His eyes travelled to my crotch and back up to my chest. "Some might call it downscaling, we prefer to call it restructuring."

Judging by his eyeline I wondered if it was my bosom that he wanted to downscale. It wasn't huge but, then, neither was my job, and I've always believed that there's nothing wrong with a bit of compromise.

"We have decided to initiate this with you and a few of the girls."

He threw a quick glance at my face to gauge my reaction. His eyes immediately relocated. I folded my arms. I managed to keep them folded for the rest of the conversation and as I got up and left the room. I can't wait until they introduce thought-monitors to the workplace so that people like him can be sued for mental sexual harassment.

What he'd really been saying was that the company had decided to put some of their workers on contract, working from home by Internet. I was one of them. It was a bit of a shock having no workplace to go to, no giggling group of conspirators at coffee breaks plotting the downfall of the stuffy floor manager. Nobody to admire the new top that I had just spent my entire week's wages on. Nobody to loan things to or cadge emotional support from in times of crisis. No casual cosy human contact.

I declared it would be great. Nobody breathing down my neck when I wanted a coffee break or a good stare out of the window. Nobody frowning if I decided I wanted to read my horoscope or an article on hair maintenance. Despite my claim, it took me a little while to get used to it. I went shopping in the morning on a weekday just to prove that I could if I wanted to, even though I had stayed up half the night before to get ahead of myself on work. I could even meet Niall for lunch because I wasn't stuck on some timed lunch break.

No, really, it was great.

Honest.

Soon after the restructuring my work allocation started to drop – some excuse about the new method being more efficient. It didn't feel more efficient to me as my already miniature income shrank. Of course I applied for other jobs, but now that I had spent the last while correcting computer errors, offers weren't flooding in. This meant that by the time I split up with Niall my savings were very depleted. I was in Clare, broke and not connected to the Internet.

I was very glad when Terry declined my offer to pay for dinner or, indeed, even half of it. He looked as though he could afford it better than I could. Anyway, I was sure I would be paying his firm a fee that would make the cost of dinner look like a price tag from a pound shop.

OK, OK, so I wasn't doing anything for the advancement of feminism but I hadn't noticed that poverty had ever helped emancipation.

And besides, well fed, I would live to fight another day.

Terry dropped me home – all the way to outside my gate. It was a very dark night. As we got near to the house I noticed that there was a light on in the living area. I didn't remember leaving a light on. My heart skipped. Maybe it was Niall: having heard from my mother what had happened he had decided to come and make sure that I was all right. On second thoughts, that didn't seem very likely.

But if it wasn't him, who was it? I supposed there could be any number of people who knew that the spare key was always in an old sock on the clothes-line. A flagrant abuse of security, I thought, especially with only a distant green box to look after me. I had no idea who it could be. What if it was the ghost of the Dead German who'd popped in to make himself a spot of dinner? Maybe the house really was haunted. It was perfectly situated for that sort of thing in the middle of nowhere. That would also explain why locals never passed by. I didn't like the idea of all that mystery associated with my house.

"There's a light on," I said nervously to Terry.

"So there is," he responded blandly, then seemed to sense my apprehension. "I take it you didn't leave a light on?" he added hurriedly.

His deductive reasoning was in good nick anyway, even if he was over the hill.

"Are you expecting anybody?" he enquired.

"No," I said wearily, wondering if the day was ever going to end.

"Well, don't worry," he said, with false heartiness. "I'll pop in with you and we'll see who it is. We'll sort out any little problem there might be."

Ah, so the fairy godmother was back, this time as a ghostbuster. Aren't men great all the same?

He drove his car very close to the house, pulling in behind mine and it was then that I saw another car parked at the side. I started to laugh. Terry looked at me self-consciously. "What's so funny?" he demanded.

"It's my mother," I snorted, "my mother's inside." I fumbled for the door-handle still laughing. "Thanks, Terry," I threw over my shoulder, as I clambered out of the car.

"Maybe I'll see you tomorrow," he half shouted, somewhat taken aback.

I suppose he'd been quite looking forward to leaping from the car beating his chest and roaring loudly as he frightened off all would-be predators lying in wait for the helpless lady. I'd ruined his performance opportunity.

"Sure, yeah, 'bye Terry," I called, running towards the house so that I could find the still unfamiliar keyhole while the car continued to provide light. As I struggled with the door, I wondered how long it had taken my mother to drive from Dublin. She must have left immediately after my phone call – well, as immediately as my mother can leave. She would have had to cook a meal and put it in the fridge for my father first. It wasn't that she ever cooked when she stayed at home. He did all his own cooking – unless there was a particularly exotic or popular recipe, which had to be attempted by my mother. These cooking forays were disastrous. She got extremely bad-tempered when she cooked. It only took a missing ingredient, a reluctant hollandaise or a particularly uncooperative piece of meat to turn her into one of Macbeth's witches. And it didn't matter how the dish turned out: anybody living in or visiting the house at the time had to eat it. I think that's why the entire family except my father had left the country.

She always did a basic meat-and-two-veg if she was going away. I think it stemmed from some subliminal wifely duty thing, and it was invariably still in the fridge when she returned.

Nobody dared ask her why she always did this. All it meant was that she drove very fast whenever she went away as she was always running late. But what was she doing in Clare? She hated 'the country'. In her view it was 'rough'. She found the odours distasteful, though she would never mention this in case she was seen as being rude.

Terry's car had pulled away, leaving me in darkness. The key refused to turn in the lock. I pushed my weight against the door and realised suddenly that it was locked and bolted from inside. There was no doorbell, of course, just a letterbox flap. Doorbells, like teacloths or parents, are one of those things that you never miss until they aren't there.

"Mum," I shouted, hammering on the bare wood with my key. "Come on, Mum, let me in." I heard a shuffle inside as she came to the door. I'd forgotten my mother's nervous distrust of the vast expanse of country darkness that blotted out everything at night. She simply couldn't understand why there weren't streetlights everywhere. She had been very relieved when my father's parents in Monaghan had died. It wasn't that she disliked them, it was simply that they lived in a big old house surrounded by trees that courted night darkness. She never explained why she hated the dark so much. All she would ever say was that it was full of 'things'. As a child this had always made me think of a jam-jar full of beetles.

I had only partially inherited her neurosis; nevertheless, it was seeping steadily into my system the longer I stood in the death-black outdoors. The Dead German, in a bad state of decomposition trailing himself across the garden, flashed into my mind. I shouted louder, "Come on, Mum, let me in. I'm freezing."

"Who is it?" she called out feebly from inside.

"It's me, Mum! Who do you think it is? Some nocturnal loony who believes you're her mother? Please let me in."

She opened the door a crack, then extended the opening wide enough for me to squeeze through as she scanned the darkness for – well, 'things', I suppose.

"That took you long enough," I snapped, when I was safely inside.

She shook her head emphatically and said, "You can't be too careful in the country, these days. I've removed the key from the sock. You mustn't leave it there – you've heard all those stories about people being robbed and beaten. It's very dangerous to be in an isolated place like this now."

"Yes, Mum, but nobody knows you're here so why should they try to molest you?" I spoke through gritted teeth.

She refused to be ruffled. "Well, I've never seen any place as dark as this and somebody's turned the heat off in this house. I was just about to call the police station to see if they had kept you in for the night." She deftly turned the conversation on to me in a tone that suggested I had been in hospital rather than at a murder inquiry.

"No, Mum, they didn't," I said, with a sigh. "I went for something to eat with the solicitor. He's not actually covering the case, some woman in his office is. Mary Reilly, I think."

"Ah, yes, Mary Reilly," my mother said ponderously, a little smile of approval playing on her lips. "She was in university with your brother. Shame you didn't study something useful like that."

Oh-ho, she was on to the dangerous topic of my career! Time to change the subject.

"What on earth are you doing here, Mum?" I asked abruptly.

"Well, dear," she said, taking the bait, "all I could think of was you here on your own, especially when you phoned from the police station, and . . . Are you sure that you didn't know the poor man?"

Such a trusting woman, my mother. Where was all this unconditional love we're supposed to get from parents? The only unconditional thing about our relationship was the patience I needed when I was with her. I expect she thought I was going to confess to using my breaking up with Niall as a cover for running away to my little country haunt with the Dead German. She'd probably come to the conclusion that he'd died of cold while staying in the house and that I'd covered it up by dumping him in the back garden.

"Mum!"

"It must have been terrible for you, just finding him like that," she probed. "Was he, was he, well . . . dead when you found him?"

"Oh, Mum, of course he was. It's got nothing to do with me, they've taken him away, he didn't even die here." I'd blurted it out before I remembered that I was talking to the most inquisitive person in the world. Well-meaning, but inquisitive.

"What? What do you mean by that? How do you know?" she demanded. I sighed and resigned myself to the inquisition, knowing that on about the hundredth question I'd lose my temper. Then she'd get into a huff. I'd spend the next hour trying to mollify her. We'd get her back to asking questions. Then I'd lose my temper again. And this would go on until one of us died.

Now, I hope you're not getting the impression that I have a mother thing, what I mean is an apron-string thing. For a start my mother would not be seen dead in an apron – that was her women's-lib statement in the sixties. As far as I know it was her only women's-lib statement. And she probably only refused to wear aprons because they were unflattering. Since I'd moved back from London I had spent two nights in my parents' house and they were at Christmas (the other one we'd spent with Niall's parents in Limerick). I would visit them once a month, if I had not dropped by in the meantime, and occasionally I met my mother in town for coffee if she was having difficulty making up her mind about a pair of shoes or a handbag or something. I must admit, though, that she was very useful in the type of crisis I had just experienced – no matter where you were, my mother, using the telephone, could form a human chain of contacts to anchor you. In the past few years she'd even developed a very efficient international network. I was the only one of her four children now living in Ireland. My mother believed that her children lived abroad so that she could have convenient foreign holidays when my father was too busy to travel. When she had received my call from Clare she was probably sorely disappointed that I didn't live in Bangkok or some other exotic place so that she could have flown to my rescue.

It's not that I wasn't grateful to her. It was really nice to see her. But she was going to stay. Like a cuckoo in a nest, she would evict all the comfortable safe silences that I had surrounded myself with to ease the hurt, humiliation and heartache of the last few weeks. Even as I thought this she threw the first carefully nurtured little birdie out of its haven.

"Any word from that Niall chap?" she asked.

'Chap', I think, was her word for bastard.

"No," I mumbled, through the knot in my throat.

"He's responsible for this, you know," she said dogmatically.

I looked at her in astonishment. What was she talking about now?

"He is, you know," she reiterated. "If he had sorted this thing out you wouldn't be here now, would you? You wouldn't have been here all alone this morning."

I stared at her through a foggy window of reawakened pain and tried to work out the logic of her statement. I got a vague sense of it. But all I could think of saying was 'Does a tree make a noise when it falls in the forest and nobody's listening?'

I didn't say it. There were enough dead bodies about already. For a woman who was essentially practical my mother had little sense of reality but, then, she probably didn't need it on what my father earned.

"Will you be staying long, Mum?" I asked finally, trying to calculate how I should ration my sanity to make it last.

"As long as you need me, dear," she said, smiling maternally.

Great!

What had the universe ever
done for me?

Chapter Four

The next day was the second day of my thirty-first year. I decided that, from now on, I was going to wear make-up anytime I went out in public. I don't know why I made that decision. I'd been wearing make-up every day for years. I'd only stopped when Niall and I had broken up. I was probably determined to make myself as unattractive as I felt by his rejection of me. I couldn't find any make-up, so I decided that maybe I'd start my new regime the next day. I put on some mascara, even though it ran every time I cried – and I was doing a lot of that. How can they advertise mascara as 'non-smudge'? Who do they test it on? Shop mannequins? So far I'd cried my way through most brands, none of which hadn't run.

I never used to cry; in fact, I used to laugh quite a lot. It was one of the things Niall said he liked about me, my laugh. We'd spent a lot of time laughing together – we had the same sense of humour: I believe it's called 'wacky'. We laughed at things like people walking into poles or glass doors. We termed it 'banana-skin-type humour'. There was one incident shortly after we moved back to Dublin. We'd gone out to dinner. The meal had been dreadful and I couldn't wait to get out of the restaurant and go for a drink somewhere decent. We were getting up to leave when Niall lost his balance – still almost in a sitting position, he just keeled right over. He grabbed the cloth on our table and pulled half-full plates, wineglasses, candles, everything on to the floor with him. But that wasn't all: on the way down he crashed into the table beside him and that went flying with everything landing mostly on the laps of the three people sitting at it. We weren't even drunk. I just started to laugh – I couldn't stop. I didn't ask him if he was all right or anything and as soon as he'd stood up he started to laugh too. I mean, anybody else would have lost it and accused me of being heartless; not my Niall.

Oh, God, there goes my mascara again! We got on so well. Why didn't he love me anymore? What had I done? I hadn't changed, not in any dramatic sort of way. In fact, not at all that I could remember. And neither had he. Except that he didn't love me anymore.

My mother was opening and closing cupboards when I arrived in the kitchen. She peered from behind the fridge door and said fussily, "There's no food in this house, dear. You're not looking after yourself."

Oh, no. She'd decided that she was going to be a Good Mother. Usually she never mentioned eating unless it was about one of her exotic dinners. There was always food in her house because every month she would empty the shelves of whatever supermarket she happened to notice while out shopping or meeting her bridge friends. Sometimes this would happen every two months, but it didn't matter because she usually bought enough to last half the year.

She would have it delivered. It would never fit in the car even if she had been prepared to do some lifting and carrying. Breda, the woman who 'did' the house, unpacked everything on to shelves and, as the weeks passed, would look for signs of decay, throwing away anything dangerous. Gradually the food would disappear. Maybe what my mother didn't like was empty shelves. I had a lot of those. "There's a box of Sugar Puffs under the sink, Mum," I offered generously.

I bought Sugar Puffs when I was depressed – I always bought Sugar Puffs the day before my period and threw them out the next day. I'd bought Sugar Puffs every three days for the past two weeks. They were great – you didn't even need milk with them. I didn't trust myself around milk: I was either going to forget it was there, or turn it sour at one glance – either way it would be no good to me.

"No, thank you, dear," my mother replied, curling her lip. She evidently didn't like unaccompanied Sugar Puffs. I suppose they are an acquired taste. We decided to go into the village for breakfast.

As we left the house and moved towards the car a uniformed figure emerged rapidly from the back garden. It was Séan the guard. He must have been sent out for the day to do some further investigation. From the expression on his face he hadn't been expecting us to go out so early or, indeed, at all. He probably hadn't brought a flask of tea because he had been so confident of our hospitality. He stood at the corner of the house, the unfriendly wind

from the back garden whipping at his topcoat as he tried
to coax a greeting through his disappointment. "How're
ye? Off out, I see. I'm just doing a bit of a check here on
the garden to be sure that there's nothing left, you know,
in case we missed anything. Like, yesterday when we
were, you know . . ."

His voice trailed off as he realised that we weren't
responding in any way. We were just standing staring at
him, an attentive audience. He swallowed and blushed.
We waited politely for him to finish the sentence; this
made him blush even more. He lowered his eyes and
kicked the gravel gently with the toe of his shoe. My
mother looked at me with a puzzled expression.

I decided that it was probably time to get us out of this
situation. "Mum, this is Séan, Séan, this is my mother."

Séan shot me a look of grateful relief, the remainder of
which he turned on my mother. She fluttered a little at
what appeared to her to be appreciation, and Séan and
herself nodded and smiled at each other until I declared
in exasperation, "Come on, Mum, or we'll be late."

It was a lie but I was afraid that some strange, regional,
Medusan magic might freeze both of them and I would
have to spend the rest of my days visiting the grotto of
my mother and the local guard: locked for ever in
mutual appreciation. Séan looked bereft as the car pulled
away; no doubt he realised that whatever dreams he'd
had about cosy cups of tea had vanished. And the key
wasn't even in the sock anymore if he had wanted to
help himself.

My mother glanced in the rear-view mirror and shook
her head. "What a nice boy, so well-mannered. It's such

a shame he's only a guard. Even with promotion through the ranks they never really earn much."

I had to be in Mary Reilly's office for 11.30 a.m.

My mother said she could do some shopping while I was at the solicitors'. She seemed unaware that the village was little more than a T-junction and that collecting a few items at the village store, which offered no selection, was not what she called shopping. I suggested to her that maybe she could buy some Sugar Puffs as I was nearly out. I knew that there were a few packs left in the shop. Nobody else in the area ate Sugar Puffs, it seemed.

Mary Reilly was a pleasant, efficient woman a few years older than me. She ushered me into her office enquiring after my brother. She didn't seem to remember him very well and she rapidly got on to the case of the Dead German. She didn't tell me anything I couldn't have read in the newspaper. But, of course, I hadn't read anything in the newspaper. More importantly, I hadn't heard anything on the radio. In fact, I hadn't noticed any media attention. "I haven't seen any sign of any reporters or anything," I said. "Surely when there is a dead body found there would be some interest?"

"The guards wanted to be able to investigate a bit more without the *paparazzi*. You know, of course, that they have found no ID," she said, matter-of-factly. "They will be releasing a statement today after the state pathologist has done his job, so I'd expect a few calls." Then she added, with a note of concern, "Will you be all right? You don't have to say anything you know."

"Yes, no problem," I said dismissively.

At the back of my mind I pictured myself – in slow motion, of course – dramatically shrugging off the clamouring press as the camera flashes accentuated the highlights in my hair. I really would have to get something done with my hair. My imagination fast-forwarded. I was on the front page of the newspaper. Distraught and supported by my mother, I followed the coffin in slow procession to the graveyard. I was dressed in black – it really suits me when my roots are done. As soon as Niall saw this his heart would soften. He would want to come to me, comfort me, reassure me, hold me, tell me that everything would be all right, that I wouldn't have to go through this alone, that he still loved me and he was a fool to think otherwise and—

"So is that all right, then?"

Mary Reilly's voice broke through my reverie.

"Ah, eh, sorry what?" I stammered.

"You'll give us a call tomorrow when things are a bit clearer. Yes?"

Mary Reilly gestured efficiently.

"Oh, ah, OK." I scrambled to my feet. "Yeah, thank you." I couldn't remember a word she'd said to me.

As I left her office the receptionist beckoned to me. "Mr O'Neill would like to have a word with you," she said confidentially.

"Oh?" I looked around wondering where he was.

"If you could just wait a moment he'll be right out to you." She nodded reassuringly. And, sure enough, she had barely finished speaking when Terry emerged, smiling, from his office. He held out his hand and shook mine – well, actually, he more took my hand in his and squeezed it gently while gazing sympathetically into my face. I removed my hand from his grip in as short a time as was polite. "Are you all sorted out, then, Val?" he asked brusquely, with just the right amount of professional warmth.

Oh, if only.

"Yeah, thanks, Terry."

I glimpsed the receptionist giving a tight-lipped stare at our obvious familiarity. I wondered if Terry was a little 'warmer' with his female clients than was acceptable.

"I was wondering, Val," he said conspiratorially, drawing me towards the door and away from any interested ears, "are you free this evening? I mean, that is, have you time to go to a little concert?"

My face must have formed a 'why' because he quickly elaborated. "I'd like to talk to you some more about your little incident." It was beginning to sound more like a bad case of potty-training failure than a possible murder. "And the concert is for a good cause. I bought the tickets from a friend of mine a long time ago and it had completely slipped my mind that I had them. But I'm sure that it would be good if you were seen supporting a local affair – with you being new to the area and all." His face creased into a benign smile. He made me feel like a recently arrived spy who needed all available opportunities to integrate. He didn't think I was convinced because he went on, "It's not often that anything of the social kind happens around here in winter so you should really take the opportunity to socialise while you can."

What was it about this man? He seemed to believe that he was God's gift to conversation. He even had a bishop's I'm-so-important-you-will-listen-to-everything-I-say way of pausing for long periods in the middle of sentences. I supposed that it was so that the person listening could take time out for a quick trip to Barbados then nip back to catch the end of his sentence. The odd thing was that he was so secure in his pomposity you couldn't even get mad at him.

"OK," I found myself saying, half wondering who he'd have asked if I'd said no – but, then, I couldn't help thinking that not many people said no to this man. In fact, I suspect that if I had said no he wouldn't have heard, he'd have just said exactly what he did say. "Right, then, I'll meet you in the hotel at seven thirty. Goodbye, Val."

I had completely forgotten about my mother until I got back to the car. Well, that is until I got back to where the car had been. It was gone.

Had anybody else been driving I'd have assumed it had been stolen, but with my mother at the wheel I had no doubt that she had just thought of somewhere more interesting to go. I was right. I heard a loud hooting in the distance and turned to see her waving cheerily at me from the other end of the street. She was outside the shop with what must have been all of the staff loading her car with stuffed plastic bags. So she had 'shopped'. As I got nearer she strode over to me with a look of exasperation on her face. "They have no delivery service," she gasped in astonishment. "We have to carry all the groceries home ourselves! Amazing isn't it? You'd think when everybody lives so many miles away from the shop that they'd have a delivery service – I've suggested it to them."

I wondered if they had taken it as a suggestion or a command. As she returned to direct operations at the shop I remembered my appointment for that evening. Or, rather, I remembered that she hadn't been invited. I supposed I could just drag her along – maybe not, though. I could think of nothing more horrifying than going out for the evening with my mother – well, actually I could but I'm not prepared to go into that now. The problem in this instance would be going out with a man nearer to her age than mine. They'd probably have loads in common and I'd be left unattended at a gathering of strangers.

I wondered what approach I should take in telling her I was going to abandon her.

"Ah, look, Mum . . . I have to go out tonight to a concert with a man I met yesterday, and leave you all alone in a freezing house in the middle of nowhere outside which a dead body was found recently, hope you don't mind."

It really didn't sound ideal.

"Ah, Mum," I said, when I got near enough not to have to shout.

"Yes dear?" She looked up, her face flushed from the exertion of directing the car packing. I paused. This was going to be a difficult one. Suddenly a look of horror spread across her face and, clasping her open hand across her mouth, she stared past me down the street. "Oh, my God," she half mouthed, half gasped, "I completely forgot to tell you about Rachel."

Rachel? Who the hell was Rachel? I swung round to

follow my mother's gaze. Yes, she was right, it was Rachel. Rachel was a friend of mine from college, whom I had met through Suzy. We'd been friends for ages, but we'd sort of lost touch when I'd moved to London. After I got back we saw each other occasionally but we always seemed to be living in different parts of the country. Well, that's a lie, I lived in Dublin and Rachel moved about a lot. We didn't seem to have too much in common anymore: either she'd changed or I'd changed; I'd never sat down and worked it out. She'd become the type of person who left messages on her phone which went, "Hi, this is Rachel. Sorry I'm not able to take your call right now, but I'm sure the synchronicity of the universe will lead us to communicate soon. Till then, 'bye."

You get the picture. She was what I would term a bit cosmic, which was fine, it's just that I wasn't, and any time I'd spoken to her in the last few years she'd been trying to lead me into communing with trees and rocks and other inanimate objects.

Now, I love trees and rocks . . . on postcards or in magazines, and I've seen some really nice ones in films. It's just all that outdoor stuff sort of passes me by. You see, Rachel believed that if she hugged a tree and leaves fell off and hit her – what does she expect if she hugs a tree in autumn? – the tree was showering her with love. That's fine. But let's put it in another context. What if you hugged somebody and they covered you in pieces of dead skin, wouldn't you think them a little antisocial? I didn't get this cosmic stuff. Different tastes, I suppose.

"What's she doing here?" I demanded, turning back to my mother.

"She rang yesterday before you rang, dear, about, you know, the solicitor," explained my mother, unsure of what tone to use. "She rang and I said you had taken yourself off to the country because you and Niall had split up."

"Oh, Mum, there's no need to broadcast it," I snapped irritably.

"I'm not broadcasting it, dear," my mother said, breaking into a poor-little-me-I'm-just-your-mother tone. "She asked after you and I told her. What – I'm not supposed to talk to your friends now?"

"No, Mum, no, Mum," I said, in exasperation. "But what's she doing here?"

"Well, by coincidence she lives in the country now too." My mother made it sound like I'd just won a prize. She also seemed to be suggesting that 'the country' was some small social club where you went to meet like-minded people. She wandered on, "and she said that she'd come visit you today, that maybe you needed some support, though that's not what she actually said, but that's what I understood." Her expression changed to defiance. "You can't just ignore her now that she's here." She raised her arm and waved at Rachel who, not having noticed us, was gazing in a shop window. "Yoo hoo, Rachel, over here, hello."

Looking around and seeing us, Rachel waved back excitedly, moving towards us. "Hi, Val." She turned to my mother: "Hi, Mrs O'Hara. What are you doing here? I thought you were in Dublin – this is so weird. Val, how are you?"

"Fine, Rachel, how are you?"

She turned on me with loads of sympathy in her voice. "No, how are you really? Your mother told me about – you know – your hurt. I thought I'd come and let you know you're not alone, that the universe does care about you and that, if you want, it will replenish you and fill in all that pain. I've brought a remedy for you for self-hatred, it's probably what you're feeling right now."

Self-hatred! More like crowd-hatred, I thought. What a menagerie, me, my broken heart, my mother, Rachel, the universe and now my self-hatred as well! I should have rented a bigger house.

Niall used to love having a go at Rachel, not meanly or anything. Any time we'd see her she'd either met some new man who was totally fascinating or had abandoned some spiritually inadequate male who hadn't been allowing himself to 'do the will of the universe'. I don't think she slept with them. I always thought it was more anthropological. But Niall would attack with comments like, "Never mind the universe, Rachel, I take it that the earth didn't move for you on this one?" Or "Yes, no wonder he left you, Rachel. If all you were after was his inner child he probably thought you were some sort of paedophile."

Rachel didn't like Niall very much. She said he was repressed. Did that mean I was repressed as well for going out with such an undeveloped man for so long?

I didn't think he was repressed – the opposite, in fact: he didn't have any of those usual 'men' hang-ups. He could sew on his own buttons. He knew that even if you soak a saucepan for days you still had to wash it. He didn't wear a paper bag over his head when he was buying tampons. He didn't think that my driving his car was going to change the way it related to him for ever, and he didn't think he had to come every time we made love.

That being said, for the last few weeks before we broke up he didn't think I had to come either, so we'd stopped having sex. Had I been stupid to ignore this? I'd just thought it was because it was winter. I thought we should all be hibernating instead of carrying on as though the world wasn't at a standstill. You can just see it: Mother Earth sitting under a tree, scratching her head, wondering how to get the temperature to rise and the leaves to grow again; meanwhile everything comes to a grinding halt.

That wasn't it, though. After about a week of deprivation I concluded that maybe it wasn't because it was January. Maybe this was what happened after four years of a consistently flourishing sex life. Maybe it just slowed down for a bit. Or maybe Niall just needed a bit of coaxing and flattering like we all do sometimes. I never guessed that it was because he didn't love me anymore. I should have been angry. I had been angry – for minutes at a time – but it wore me out and I started to cry and then I was just sad again. Sad and bewildered.

And now Rachel wanted me to commune with the universe. What had the universe ever done for me?

"There's been a bit of a crisis since I spoke to you on the phone, Rachel," my mother said, in her I-don't-want-to-have-to-talk-about-this-but-you-really-ought-to-know tone. "Val has had a difficult couple of days."

She told Rachel about my Dead German. Rachel was very supportive. She said that it was the bad karma around me that had attracted this misfortune. That I had to learn to let go of all those negative feelings or else bad things would keep gathering around me. She made me sound like a disorientated magnet or a dog in heat.

I sighed in resignation. My mother just looked puzzled.

Back at the house as we were unloading the car I decided that I'd better break the news about my meeting with Terry that evening. I was relieved that my mother wouldn't be on her own, but I wasn't at all sure that she would feel the same way. Having quickly explained, I added that meeting solicitors was a necessary part of being a murder suspect. I intentionally played down the social aspect. My mother looked a bit desperate but nodded understandingly. Rachel gushed delightedly, saying she could play my mother the inspirational tape she had brought along to help me. We had something to eat and I decided I should change to go out – after all, it was my first social appearance since I had returned to the land of the singles.

Well, OK, there had been one other occasion when I had been staying with Suzy. But after that outing she'd given up, saying I was bad for her image, going around looking like I did. So this time I decided that maybe an effort was in order.

Not for Terry, more for Niall. Just because he didn't want me didn't mean I had to disappear.

Bastard.

There, I'd said it. Suzy had said it for me, my mother had tut-tutted in disapproval but I hadn't yet been able to get mad enough to say it.

Cereal Lover

BASTARD.

I stamped around my room pulling clothes out of my collection of supermarket bags. Of course, I'd really brought nothing with me. After all, I hadn't packed thinking that I would be flinging myself into the social whirl of North Clare. I found a skirt; it must have snuck in while I was crying into another plastic bag. There was nothing to wear with it. Having looked in the mirror I didn't think I could get away with bare legs. It wasn't just that it was February. It was more that there were two strips of pale hairy putty where my legs used to be. "Mum – Mum, have you got any tights?" I yelled, without moving from my critical pose in front of the mirror.

My mother appeared at my bedroom door. She raised a curious eyebrow but made no comment. "I do have a couple of pairs I haven't opened yet," she said, noncommittally.

"Not that horrible biscuit colour you usually wear, Mum," I whined – even to my ears it sounded like a whine. I glimpsed a fledgeling look of indignation crossing her face and added, "My skirt is black, see, so they'd never go with it."

She responded, in an arms-folded voice, "No, dear, I have a black pair."

A black pair! She only ever wore those to funerals. What was she expecting to find when she got to Clare – my dead body? "Poor Val couldn't take the pressure, hung herself with the belt of a bottom-of-the-range raincoat whilst being detained under suspicion of having killed her secret lover." I wondered about my mother sometimes.

The black tights weren't the thick, woolly sort I would have needed to disguise the forest of hair on my legs. I'd have to lose the growth. Last time I'd 'defoliated' I'd had my legs waxed. I'd had it done by somebody else. I could never justify inflicting that amount of pain on myself. At least when somebody else was doing it I could blame them for the agony. They also pulled when you least expected it. The first time I'd waxed myself I didn't finish the job because I could think of no reasonable argument to continue hurting myself that much. What I want to know is who first thought of it? I've read the jars: they promote stories of ancient Egypt or Greece or some other civilisation which held hairlessness above sanity. Imagine inventing a procedure that pulls each individual hair out of your body and refer to it casually as 'waxing'.

I decided I'd shave. Anyway I had no wax. I discovered I had no razor either. Neither had Rachel, nor my mother. I decided to wear my jeans. Oh, how I'd missed all this indecision in the last few weeks!

I dried my hair, giving it as much style as I could, then I moved on to the make-up. Oh, no, I'd forgotten I didn't have any. I searched all the bags again but only came up with some lipstick. So I raided my mother's cosmetics bag and pasted on something very expensive that I'm sure was a derivative of Polyfilla. Just what I needed now that I was thirty. I finished my preparation with a liberal, but I like to think tasteful, application of lipstick.

I preened in front of the mirror. I didn't look bad at all; for an ancient, recently deserted woman. All the fretting I had done over the past few weeks combined with a diet of

Sugar Puffs meant that I'd lost a few pounds and it suited me. Rachel said I looked amazing, and that she knew just by my appearance that my karma was changing – there would be no more dead bodies for me.

She made me sound like a recovering necrophiliac.

My mother just sighed sentimentally and I couldn't help thinking that she was wondering how old she looked if she had a daughter as old-looking as me – always trust her for the kind thought.

Even if she was gracious enough not to verbalise it.

And his body!

Chapter Five

When I arrived in the hotel Terry was standing at the bar. He was wearing a navy 'blazer' with silver buttons, which made him look as though he had parked his yacht outside. He beckoned as I came in, raising his hands towards me in what looked like a large embrace. "Can I get you a little drink?" he asked expansively.

I bit my tongue, I couldn't think of a remark about the 'little' that would be purely witty rather than downright cutting.

As he ordered the drinks he leaned across me, pressing almost the whole of his body against mine. I looked up at him sharply to see if he was joking – he seemed totally oblivious to having done any space invasion. Maybe I was just being sensitive now that I was a single woman. Or maybe he'd learned the knack of doing this on crowded suburban trains. You know the situation: men continue to lean against you, face expressionless, even when the train is swaying everybody in the opposite direction. I wondered how he'd learned the skill in an area of the country devoid of trains, suburban or otherwise.

Maybe he had a simulator. Yeah, maybe he had a special machine in a room off his office where he and other like-minded local cronies went to practise the art of frottage. It could catch on.

We moved away from the bar and I placed myself at the other side of the table to Terry in case he was inclined to continue our physical intimacy – he showed as little sign of noticing the distance between us as he had the proximity.

"So," I said, deciding to take control of the situation rather than let myself be put off-balance by what must have been just a lack of distance judgement, "any news of the, ah, the dead man?"

"Well," he said, presenting me with one of his endless pauses, "it would appear that the man is a veritable John Doe."

It was lucky that I watched so many American cop movies: I knew what a 'John Doe' was. "Oh, really? Well, I—"

"Yes," he interrupted, before I could present my theory – he'd really only been having another long pause. "You didn't see anything on the ground or anywhere when you found him, did you?"

"No." I was puzzled by the question. "All I saw was the guidebook."

"Umm," Terry mused, giving me a searching look. "But that doesn't necessarily mean anything. They need a passport or some sort of ID. They'll just have to keep cross-checking the missing-persons' lists in Europe or hope that the airline comes up with something." He then launched into a never-ending monologue on the bad effect that murdering our tourists would have on the local community. He even knew how much local revenue was made through tourism. I nodded at appropriate intervals, hoping he wouldn't notice my eyes glazing over in boredom.

After a while I figured that a change of subject might stop the invasion of the monster yawn. I'd read somewhere that pompous men like to talk about themselves – well, actually it didn't just say pompous, it said all men. I decided to see if this was true. At his next pause I pitched in a question. "Have you lived in the area long, Terry?"

He looked a little surprised at the force of my enthusiasm but answered, quite genially, "All my life, I'm from Clare originally, really only moved away to do my training. I knew that I could do well here, I more or less stepped into my father's practice. I go to America quite a bit, I like the children to see as much of their relatives as possible – their mother is American, you see."

Wow, I'd really set him off. Which question should I try next? If I asked about his wife he'd think I was fishing or else he'd give me the my-wife-doesn't-understand-me-and-I'm-thinking-of-leaving-her line. I decided to ask about the children.

"How many children do you have?" I said casually.

"Two," he replied, "a boy and a girl. My wife and I divorced seventeen years ago so they haven't lived with me for some time except for visits."

He said it so matter-of-factly I wondered if he cared or if he regarded it as just one of those things that happens. I certainly wasn't going to ask. I also couldn't help wondering if his wife had left him because he rubbed himself against other women.

So what was I supposed to say now? We'd just covered about a thousand years in a few sentences.

Maybe if I got on to something more cheery. I could ask him if he had remarried, even though he wasn't behaving as though he had. But, no, that would sound like I was interested. God, how the rules of conversation change when you become single again! How nice it had been up until very recently to be able to drop 'my boyfriend' or 'my partner' into the conversation whenever I thought things might need a bit of clarification. I suppose I could lie but I never was very creative that way. Besides, I guessed that, between my mother and Rachel, word of my emotional bereavement would soon be part of the local gossip. In fact, I'm sure from the way the shopworkers had looked pityingly at me while they were packing the car that my mother had already told them all about it. So the whole area knew by now, including Terry.

I decided to go for a complete change of subject. "Have the guards questioned anybody else besides me about the, ah, the dead man?" I doubled back to our former topic.

"No, not that I've heard," he said and sipped his drink, quite unperturbed at the rapid change of subject. "They only released a statement to the press this evening," he continued. "That's a very long delay, really, but maybe now with the publicity they will be able to piece together his movements."

He paused, a different sort of pause from his usual

eternal-wait pause. "They're still determined to say that the cause of death was a broken neck. Foul play, of course, is most probable, but it very well may have been an accident and someone panicked and dumped the body."

He waited for my reaction to that theory.

I didn't see why anybody would want to move a dead body if they hadn't caused it to be dead in the first place. I had to confess, though, that I hadn't thought of what Terry had said, mostly, I suppose, because I'd decided that the entire affair was a frame-up to get me into prison; that I was the central reason for everything that was happening. It made no difference that I didn't know anybody who might want to frame me. I'm a great believer in any conspiracy theory.

For example, I'm very much taken by articles claiming that Princess Di was murdered and that an elaborate web was woven to cover the truth. And I warmly embrace the theory that man didn't actually land on the moon, but that all that flag-planting stuff was filmed in a studio and that the whole world has been duped. When it was popular to do so I also believed that John Major was a life-sized puppet fashioned on Rupert Bear.

It was therefore my belief that somehow, unknown to me, I was far more important to the grand scheme of things than I realised. I was surrounded by clues and messages that, if deciphered, would guide me to playing a leading role in saving the world from some evil intrigue. It didn't help at all that I couldn't work out the plot.

Terry's voice interrupted my thoughts, "The big

question I guess really is, where did he die?"

He was sitting with his eyebrow raised after making this statement when a voice broke across our conversation. "Hey, hello, what are you doing here? I didn't think this was your kind of show. In fact, didn't you say that you definitely weren't coming when I spoke to you yesterday?"

Startled, I'd turned round assuming I was being spoken to. I wasn't and it was just as well because when I saw the speaker I realised that some criminal word-fairy had broken into my brain and stolen all my sentences. I was speechless. Standing over the table was a very attractive man. I say that in controlled tones so that you can get the picture before I fall into inarticulate fawning and salivating.

He was twenty-something but his age didn't matter: at any age he would be just as stunning. He had fair hair – you know, that really soft hair – and his eyes were a vivid, striking green. He had what could only be termed a 'strong jaw' in which were set the brightest teeth this side of dentures. And his body . . . Descriptions spring easily to mind, but let's just say that when they were making him they got a pair of jeans and cut this man to an exact fit. Even his broad shoulders, which I know in theory should have nothing to do with jeans, fitted them perfectly.

And this Adonis was standing expectantly by my table.

"Ah, Dara," Terry said, looking a little taken aback – caught out, even – but not for long. "And I thought you were far too busy to go out this early in the evening."

Dara smiled a dazzling smile. "Oh, I just got fed up with papers and figures," he said, then turned his attention to me. "Hi," he said, "I'm Dara." He held out a big square hand.

Terry leaned forward and said, in a somewhat resigned voice, "Val, my son Dara. Dara, Val."

His son! He had just said that he had children but this was no child, and if he was, I was certainly going to have to get some serious therapy for my inclinations. Dara didn't look in the least bit like his father, except perhaps for the shape of his eyes. He must have taken after his American mother. There's obviously a lot to be said for the benefits of a hamburger diet!

"Hi, Dara," I breathed, flustered, a current of something like electricity rushing through me as we shook hands. This 'child' was setting off not just bells but fully harmonised concertos in my head. I hadn't experienced anything like it since, well, since Niall, and would you believe?, I hadn't thought of Niall for a whole thirty seconds!

Terry, oblivious to the bell-pealing, drum-rolling, cymbal-clashing and other orchestral cacophonies, said, "Do you want to join us for a drink, Dara?"

My heart stopped.

"No, Dad, thanks, I'm with a guy. I'll join you later when Ashling gets here."

Damn! Who was Ashling? And why had he looked pointedly at me when he had said he would join us later? Maybe the one thing that he had inherited from his father was a propensity for womanising.

Dara walked away and I tried not to look at the

magnificent cut of his jeans. Mostly because I knew Terry
was watching me. I think I could get very resentful if I
had a child who constantly upstaged me. Self-flattery
aside, I had by now decided that Terry had asked me out
for reasons other than my legal predicament. I wondered
if he often went for women who were so much nearer his
son's age than his own. I guess North Clare in the winter
wasn't the most lively place and the singles of the area
were probably always on the lookout for some new
blood. It might just be a matter of getting as far as he
could before his young women met Dara. A bit nerve-
racking for the old lad.

I turned back to Terry, smiling what I hoped was my
most disarming smile. I wanted to know everything
there was to know about Dara, what he did, where he
lived, what he ate, but, most importantly, who was
Ashling and what was the fastest way I could get her out
of the country.

Now, don't start getting any ideas, I still loved Niall,
he had my heart completely held hostage, but the paral-
ysis had eased for those few moments when I had met
Dara and I could feel myself getting easily addicted to
that pain relief.

"Does your son work around here then?" I tried to
make it sound like a casual question.

Terry nodded. "Yes, not far from where I live. He
started an organic farm on some of my land last year.
He's a horticulturist."

"That's nice," I said, realising that this was a dead-end
conversation as I didn't know one end of a vegetable
from another. My family had, deliberately, I think, mis-

placed their peasant roots a couple of generations before.

Terry looked at me expectantly: he was evidently used to young – well, younger – women asking questions about his son. I resented the supposition that I was just another dizzy female panting after Dara. I wasn't panting, breathing heavily, perhaps, but not panting. My only problem was that I was just broken-hearted, upset and traumatised by recent events and therefore, invariably, volatile. "Would you like another drink?" I almost snarled.

"Ah, yes," he replied, a little perplexed. "Tell you what, I'll get them, you go on in where the music is. I'll be in in a few minutes."

With a quick, confirming shake of his head, more to himself than to me, he disappeared towards the bar. With his right hand in his trousers pocket he swung his way confidently through the crowd. What is it about short men and their walks? As though to make up for their lack of altitude they either swagger, strut or roll. Terry was swinging. Maybe they try to distract attention from their height by having people comment on their walk rather than their shortness.

Believe me when I say that I'm not shortist. I've even gone out with short men, never for very long, though. I think I make them feel insecure. I'm five foot seven in my stockinged feet, so in high heels I tend to overshadow most 'shorter' people.

I remember there was one short guy whom I had gone out with briefly before leaving Ireland. Niall and I met him in a bar one night after we got back from London. He was drunk and seemed to think he was still my boyfriend, don't know why – it had been years before and not very memorable. Anyway, he was what my mother calls 'bothering me'; so Niall explained the situation to him and strongly suggested that he leave. As the short guy stormed off in a fury, Niall started to laugh. He couldn't stop laughing even long enough to explain why he was laughing. Finally, snorting and gasping, he pointed out that the man wasn't angry at his 'advice' but rather he was furious because he knew that we were laughing at the length of time it was taking him to walk away because his legs were so short. I suppose Niall was a bit shortist. But it was a good laugh.

How was I supposed to get angry at Niall when I kept having all these loving memories about the good times we'd had together? I was starting to get upset. It was my first social outing as a single woman, I wasn't even halfway through the evening and I felt weepy. It obviously wasn't safe to leave me on my own. Last time I'd been left on my own I'd found a Dead German in my garden.

Oh, no, he was back. It seemed every time I thought of Niall the Dead German floated on to the scene.

I was being haunted!

I wanted to cry.

I decided that I had better take a detour to the ladies'. I looked around for the nearest toilet and having focused on the door I went blindly towards it. I was almost there when I collided with something immovable. Cold liquid poured down my back to the sound of breaking glass. I was covered in beer.

"Are you all right?" a male voice asked softly, as I stood gasping at the cold, wet shock. I couldn't answer.

"You walked straight into me," the voice continued. "Val, isn't it?"

The voice wasn't familiar so I was surprised to hear my name. I looked up sharply, straight into the concerned green eyes of Dara. I was tongue-tied, I stared back at him willing that this moment of his considerate and undivided attention would last for ever. Eventually, so that he wouldn't think I was a half-wit, I mumbled, "Yeah, I'm fine."

He reached out and felt my shirt. "You're absolutely soaked through. You need to get out of that shirt," he said, still in the most sympathetic voice in the world.

I just wanted to cry. Being soaked through had got my mind off Niall but the Dead German was still there. I was liable to lapse into an incoherent blubbing at any second.

He must have noticed the expression on my face – it would have been difficult not to as I was staring unblinkingly at him. "Oh, look, it's not that bad." He put his arm around me in as much as he could without getting really wet. "I have a sweatshirt here you can change into." He grabbed it and led me in the direction of the toilet as though I was blind.

The Dead German disappeared.

"Go on, I'll wait here for you."

He pushed me gently towards the door. I wish there had been a speediest-top-changer-in-the-world competition that evening because I'd have won it. In my head I could hear the sports commentary: "Val O'Hara, champion top-changer, has just broken the world record again. Let's have another look at that in slow motion. See the way her arms and head emerge simultaneously, with that effortless style that defines her as a true champion. Yes, she's done it again, Val O'Hara retains the title and wins another gold for Ireland."

Forty-five seconds later, top changed and face checked – the Polyfilla hadn't cracked and I'd forgotten my lipstick – I was standing in the bar smiling and blushing at Dara.

What was this blushing business? I never blushed!

"How do you feel now, all right?" he asked, still gratifyingly concerned.

"I'm fine," I replied, and then, without knowing why, I added, "I think I'll go home now."

He looked surprised, which was a bit disappointing, really, because I wanted him to go on looking concerned for ever.

"But you'll miss the – "

I didn't even let him finish. "I know," I butted in, "but it's been a rough couple of days, I'm a bit wrecked." I smiled bravely – you know, the way they smile in *Little House on the Prairie* when the blind girl's family have all died to save her but the pet puppy has been spared and licks her tears away.

"Oh, yeah, that body and everything, that was tough."

If anybody else had said that it would have sounded as if they were talking about a puncture, or some other inconveniencing minor incident. He made it sound like it was really serious. He just had the knack.

"You heard about that?" I said, surprised that someone besides those of us immediately involved knew about it.

"It's a small place, Val. There aren't any secrets here. Besides, it was on the news earlier." He laughed.

My blush deepened when he said that. I wondered what rumour was saying about his father and me, now that we had been seen together in public. Maybe he was just being nice to me because he saw me as a potential stepmother. I had a sudden flash of the evil stepmother in *Snow White*, plotting to be rid of the product of the previous marriage by whatever means. I'd have to grow my nails longer, maybe get a facial wart or two, let my hair grow out. Damn, it wouldn't take much, would it?

I decided I simply had to go. "Well, bye," I said despondently.

"How're you getting home?" he asked, all concern again.

"My car."

"May I walk you to it?" He sounded genuine. I no longer cared why he was being so nice to me, I was just going to enjoy his company. I nodded and he smiled as though I'd just told him I was going to pay his phone bill for the next year.

"Let me just tell my friends," he said, heading towards the bar. I watched his handsome back as he worked his way through the crowd. I couldn't help noticing the admiring looks he got from the other women in the room. I resented them. I didn't want him to go and talk to other people. I wanted him to stay and concentrate solely on me. I wasn't handling this very well, was I? Maybe I was genetically unsuited to being a single person.

As Dara reached the bar a girl grabbed his arm in a familiar embrace and kissed him affectionately. Ashling, maybe? I was clutched by a consuming jealousy. I had no doubt that women did this sort of thing to him all the time. I just wished they wouldn't while I was watching. I looked on helplessly as he smiled down at her, laughing and talking and pointing towards me and the exit. I supposed he was telling her that he had to be polite because I was his father's 'girlfriend' and he'd just poured a pint down me. She turned to look towards me and I saw her face: she was beautiful, not good-looking or attractive or anything like that, but downright beautiful. She had just the right-sized mouth, large by Elizabethan standards but very popular now. Her eyes were the sort that turn up at the outside corners, all cute and kitten-like. Her skin was that sheer plastic skin with no cracks or freckles or anything. And when she smiled, which she did as she looked over, her face didn't crinkle up into smile mode. It was one of those hydraulically engineered faces that allowed the different sections of the face to slide under one another so that there were no creases. This worked for frowning too but it didn't appear as if she did much of that. Looking as beautiful as she did she probably didn't have anything to frown about. And I have to mention her nose. That was really the 'centrepiece' of the whole arrangement. It was one of those look-at-me-I'm-such-a-cute-little-nose-and-I'm-sitting-here-right-in-the-middle-of-this-face-and-I-never-get-in-the-way-of-kissing-or-anything-so-just-adore-me noses. I was relieved to notice that her hair was obviously dyed blonde, but it was cut daringly short and still looked great. My father would have been so proud to have her as a client: a perfectly straight line of white teeth showed shyly as she smiled. And there was another

thing, she was far too young – not a day over twenty –
way too young to be let out without a health warning.

I turned away as Dara leaned to kiss her goodbye. I
didn't want him to see my jealous scowl. I was also
aware from the strange stares I was getting that I must
look like an imbecile. My eyes were squinting, my
mouth, no doubt, was open, I was lost in a sweatshirt the
sleeves of which reached my knees, and I smelt like a
distillery. I could see people nudging each other and
commenting. They were, no doubt, deciding that as I
was the only stranger in the room and they all knew each
other, I must be the one who'd murdered the German.

What if they tried to lynch me? What if the little green
box wasn't pacifying them as much as it ought to and
they decided to take out their frightened aggression on
me? I smiled feebly into the crowd in the hope that I
would appear less criminal. I just didn't feel that I was
presenting myself at my best advantage to the crowded
room or to Dara, especially now that I had assessed the
competition. I definitely felt that I didn't want to play
anymore.

When Dara appeared at my side he was laughing.
After a few seconds I realised that he was laughing at
me. I felt I should be indignant but he was chuckling so
kindly that I couldn't get mad.

"What?" I demanded defensively.

"You," he replied. "Those sleeves are so long you look
like a child wearing an adult's pullover. Here, let me."
He leaned forward and proceeded to roll them up.
"There, that's great." He stood back to admire his work.

"Thanks," I mumbled, not knowing whether to be

embarrassed at having my clothes rearranged like a six-year-old or elated at being given such undivided and concentrated attention by the most attractive man in the room. Even if he had been kissing another woman moments before.

I was feeling baffled. I followed him through the crowded bar out of the hotel.

"Where are you parked?" he asked, taking my arm as if I was going to run away. I loved all this physical contact but I wasn't sure of its origins. I wanted to snuggle safely under his arm and forget the world. I wanted to hide from the painful memory of Niall and the nightmare of the Dead German. I wanted a sanctuary. I didn't lean closer or touch his arm with my cheek or even match my step to his but it was only because I knew I smelt revolting. I tried to convince myself that he was just being inappropriately friendly and made a mental note to stand at a safe distance from him in future. He was disturbing my heartbeat.

As we arrived at my car I suddenly remembered Terry. I'd completely forgotten him in my excitement. He was probably still wandering about aimlessly, drinks in hand looking for me.

"Oh, no, what about Terry?" I exclaimed.

"Don't worry, he'll be OK, I'll tell him. He knows a lot of people here anyway," Dara said, then stopped and stood looking at me, his eyes dark pools of light, his head tilted sideways as though he intended to say something else. I waited, thinking that he looked even more gorgeous in the soft yellow streetlight. He didn't say anything so I got embarrassed.

"Thank you, goodnight," I stammered.

"Goodnight, Val," he said quietly.

Rather too quietly, I thought, for a man who, up until half an hour ago, had been a prospective stepson.

I don't think my feet are
abnormally large

Chapter Six

"Val, you're back very early."

My mother's face was flushed from too much gin and tonic but she gave an uneasy sigh of relief when I came into the room. Then her face clouded: "I don't remember you wearing that . . . thing going out." She gestured at my sweatshirt. I mumbled something about the accident.

"You're still home very early," Rachel joined in garrulously.

"I didn't feel too good, Rachel."

"Did you take that remedy?" she demanded.

Drinking with my mother had made her bad-tempered. That was perfectly understandable, it made me bad-tempered, but I'd always thought it was just a family thing. "No, Rachel," I said, and rapidly changed the subject. "Any calls for me while I was out?"

Rachel and my mother looked at me pityingly and shook their heads. Eventually my mother broke the silence, "You see, dear, we unplugged the phone because some journalists started to call."

"What?" I shrieked, my heart contracting. "You

unplugged the phone? How am I supposed to know if N—?" I inhaled suddenly, stopping myself before I said his name. I started again with forced calmness. "How am I supposed to know if anyone calls for me?"

I mean, what did they think Niall was going to do now that the phone didn't work? Send smoke signals or something? Small as Ireland is, I didn't think you could see smoke patterns released on the other side of the country. Of course, he could try telepathy. Maybe not, though: my mother would either have me locked up because of the voices in my head or send me to Lourdes on the off-chance that they might be divinely inspired. And she would want to come with me just to make sure I didn't bypass the Pyrenees and go to worship at the sacred shrines of Cannes or Antibes or some other glamorous bikini-beckoning seaside resort. She could then for ever more refer to it as 'our trip to the south of France'.

They had no idea what they had just done. I glared at them furiously. Rachel gestured non-commitally while my mother looked into her empty glass. "If you're worried about Niall not being able to contact you, dear, he can always ring again tomorrow."

Tomorrow!

Tomorrow was a thousand years away!

Tomorrow was when the government mended potholes!

Tomorrow was when you never got that promised ice-cream when you were six.

Mañana!

Oh, yeah, I knew all about tomorrow!

"That's not the point," I snapped.

Then I stopped. What was the point? I wanted Niall to ring. I wanted us to get back together. I knew that if we did I could make everything all right again. I know the old theory that if a man mistreats a woman she is better off without him, but that's if he beats her or something. Niall had never hit me. He might have said he didn't love me, and he might have gone off for a couple of days now and again without letting me know when he'd be back. But sometimes he'd just needed some space. Of course he loved me, it was just that at the moment he thought he didn't. I'd probably said something that had hurt his feelings. He was never very good at talking about feelings. After the first few weeks of declaring undying love he'd always had difficulty telling me he loved me. But I knew he did. After all, he had always come back, hadn't he?

I sighed and poured myself a gin, then went to change out of the sweatshirt. Rachel and my mother looked relieved as I left the room.

In the hallway I stood for ages in front of the disconnected phone. The urge to plug it back in head-butted my thigh, cajoling and pleading with me to reach out and replace the connection. I resisted, sobbing my way quietly to my room, leaving the urge sulking darkly by the inert phone. The only reason I hadn't plugged it back in was because I knew that my mother and Rachel would simply unplug it immediately if I did.

I'd tried so hard to be sensible about the whole business. I'd even gone out for the evening, pretending everything was perfectly normal. People split up with their lovers every day. Why did I feel like someone had torn off one of my limbs? Well, it wasn't just one was it? It was all of them.

I was an emotional paraplegic. And I was so depraved that I had ogled a total stranger, somebody else's boyfriend (never mind son) into whose sweatshirt I was weeping bitter, frustrated tears. How could I possibly have thought that Dara was being anything more than polite to me? He was probably the type of sensationalist who wanted to be seen talking to me because I'd had a Dead German in my garden!

Niall and I always laughed about my luck with other men. He used to joke about how fortunate I was that he went out with me because nobody else would.

I remember once when we were driving to Niall's parents' place in Limerick we stopped at the end of a tailback caused by a police check point. I got into a complete panic because my tax had expired and I hadn't had a chance to renew it. Niall started to laugh and said, "This'll be awful bad publicity for the Dental Empire." That's what he usually called my parents. "They'll have to come and bust you out of prison – life sentence for tax fraud, you know."

"Damn," I said ignoring him. "Of all the bad luck."

Suddenly I had an idea. I pulled the tie out of my blonde hair, letting it fall about my shoulders, and proceeded to do some running repairs on my face using the rear-view mirror. During this frenzy Niall hooted with laughter, mumbling helpful things like, "Maybe if you show a bit of cleavage," and "Pity you're not wearing a skirt, you could pull it above your knees."

Anyway, by the time we got to the guard I figured

that I was glamorous enough to distract any man from his duty. I pulled the car to a halt at the checkpoint, wound down the window, flicked my hair and smiled straight into the face of a uniformed woman. I had to stop myself from laughing. Niall didn't even try, he'd been laughing the whole time so he just continued. As it turned out the guard was neither amused nor particularly interested in my recently lapsed tax. They were probably looking for more hardened criminals that day. She waved us on.

Niall snorted. "It's just as well it wasn't a man, you'd have frightened him. Isn't it lucky I go out with you, love? Nobody else would have you." He grinned at me sideways, his brown eyes hidden in laughter, his lashes catching the slanting evening light that bathed his face in gold.

I stifled a huge sob. He was never going to laugh at me like that again, never going to tell me how lucky I was that he was my boyfriend. And even if he wanted to he couldn't now because the bloody telephone was unplugged. I burst into a fresh flood of tears, almost howling at the pain of the memories. Better stop. All this crying was making the gin taste strange. I took some deep breaths. Just then there was a gentle knock on the door and my mother came unsteadily into the room. Sharing the living room with Rachel must have warranted another stiff drink.

"Are you all right, dear?" she asked, completely at a loss to know how to deal with this emotional situation. Tornadoes, war and murder she could take in her stride, but this uncharted suffering left her bewildered.

"Yes, I'm fine," I answered, rather too aggressively, and realised my mistake when I heard my mother's sharp intake of breath.

"Look, dear, I know you're going through a difficult period at the moment but I really don't think I deserve to be spoken to in that tone. I didn't come all this way to be insulted."

She stopped for breath and I sprang in to appease her before she could get on to the real mother-complex stuff. "I know, Mum, I'm sorry. I was upset. You're right, I'm very sorry."

She softened: "That's all right, dear, but it's not just me, there's poor Rachel as well. She is your guest, you know."

"Yes, Mum."

She led me out of the bedroom towards the living room. "Now, dear, you mustn't let things upset you so much. But you always were very volatile. Inherited my sensitive nature, I expect."

I closed my lips tightly, eyeing the useless telephone.

"Well, I'm sure there must be some hot water now," she said suddenly. "I'm quite exhausted from listening to that inspirational tape of Rachel's and I'm hoping that a bath will help me to thaw out a little. Really, Val, this house is just too cold." With a shiver, she disappeared into the bathroom and closed the door firmly, as though believing that even the cold wouldn't dare defy such an assertive gesture.

"Your mother's really great, Val," Rachel said, as she poured another drink. "Imagine coming all this way because she thought you might need help. Mine would never do that, even if she was still alive."

"Yeah," I said grudgingly.

Not getting anywhere on the mother subject, Rachel changed tack. "Would you like to listen to my tape now? It's very uplifting." She must have noticed the blotchy mess of my eyes and decided that 'uplifting' was the thing to cure it.

"Ah, no, thanks, Rach, I'm pretty tired," I mumbled ungraciously.

"Up early tomorrow, then," she persisted.

"What?" I asked, wondering what spirit of the morning she was going to ask me to worship.

"To go out and avoid the reporters," she answered, practically.

"Why?" I was bewildered.

"Your mother says there will be loads of press around tomorrow and that the family doesn't need that sort of publicity. She's decided we're all going shopping in Galway."

I sighed. Mother protecting her imaginary dynasty again.

"Seven o'clock reveille. You know, the morning is the best time to commune with the spirits of nature."

"How would you know?" I asked sarcastically, my conversation-tolerance wearing thin. Rachel had always missed her early lectures at college.

She sidestepped the sarcasm and explained enthusiastically, "Well, I've always felt it, but it wasn't until I went to Findhorn that it really hit home."

Oh, no, she was about to become Mystic Meg. She

hadn't stopped talking about her inspirational experiences with the fairies since she'd come back from a visit to Scotland almost five years ago. Somewhere in whatever bit of me was my middle-class upbringing I knew that I should now throw in another encouraging question so that she could 'share her experiences' with me. But I couldn't. I was exhausted. And I just didn't want to have this conversation. Talking with Rachel that evening felt like I was on the losing side of a mismatched tennis event. I decided to call game, set and match while I could still be civil. "Night, Rachel, talk to you tomorrow, OK?"

"Yeah, night, Val." Even she sounded relieved.

As I passed the phone in the hall I paused. The Urge dashed from its corner of the hallway giggling excitedly, grabbed me around the knees and pinned me to the spot. What if Niall was trying to ring? I was convinced that just because I was unreachable he would be attempting to contact me. Besides, I reckoned that the reporters, if there had been any, would have given up and gone to bed by now. I plugged in the phone. I hadn't even straightened up when it started to ring.

Wow!

I snatched up the receiver. "Hello."

"Hi, Val?" said a female voice.

"Yes."

"Val, hi, it's Suzy, belated happy birthday, sorry I didn't get to ring yesterday."

"Suzy, hi," I said, hoping she couldn't hear the disappointment in my voice.

"How's things?" she asked.

"Great. Mum's here," I said.

"Really? Are you OK?" She knew how I felt about living with my mother.

"Oh, yeah, fine," I answered.

"Look, Val, I actually just rang up to tell you that I saw Niall when I was out last night. I thought you should know," she said.

I tightened my grip on the phone. "So? I mean, I don't expect he'll sit at home for the rest of his life," I said defensively, secretly wishing that he would.

"Well," Suzy said awkwardly, "he was with someone. A girl."

"Probably just a friend," I choked abruptly, as a giant battering ram smashed into my chest, crushing its way to my heart.

"Val, he wasn't behaving like 'just a friend'. He was all over her."

The battering ram gave a final heavy swing and my heart stopped beating. I wondered vaguely if I was still alive.

I must be. Because if being dead hurt so much nobody would stay dead. They'd all picket the gates of eternal oblivion demanding the right to life. Even if the gods did turn a blind eye, there would be a huge revolution with billions of dead people all demanding the same thing.

A large blob of water fell from my face on to the phone. Yeah, I was alive.

"Val, are you still there?" asked Suzy anxiously. "Look, I'm sorry I just thought you should know."

"Yeah. Thanks, Suzy." I'd spoken – definitely not dead.

"Listen, Val, I've got to go, this isn't my phone. Talk to you soon; OK? 'Bye."

The line went dead. I held the receiver like it was a life-line, the steady buzz drowning my despair.

So that's why he didn't love me anymore. He loved somebody else. I clenched my teeth at the unbearable image of Niall with another woman. I even knew what she looked like. She looked like the girl Dara had kissed in the bar. Boy, she really got around.

I slammed the phone back in the cradle. It rang imme-diately. I snatched at it, knowing it would be Suzy telling me it wasn't true. It wasn't. Suzy, that is.

"Hello, is that Valentina O'Hara?" an efficient voice barked down the phone.

"Yes?"

"Hi, this is Ellen Ryan from the *Daily Press*. I—"

I didn't listen any further, I dropped the receiver, grabbed the connection cord and pulled violently, breathing hard to keep back the tears. The whole socket came out of the wall, crashing lightly but erratically across the floor. The phone went dead. I walked blindly to my room and threw myself on the bed, stifling my angry hurt with the pillow. I tightened my fists in fury. So he had lied to me. He had lied when I had asked him was there someone else. Of course there had been someone else. Otherwise why would he have been so uncaring when he told me he didn't love me anymore? I'd spent the last three weeks soul-searching, thinking up ways of changing my personality, giving him every opportunity to contact me, when all he had wanted was to get rid of me so that he could be with another woman.

I felt such a fool. So used. So disposable.

How come I hadn't noticed the signs? Was I so stupid that I thought this couldn't happen to us? That it only happened on television or to people I didn't know? I'd always believed that women with wandering lovers must have been aware of their partners' habits and chose to overlook them. Now I was one of them. I wondered how long it had been going on. How long I had been ignoring the facts.

I'd even convinced myself to believe Niall when he told me that there wasn't anyone else. How long had I been living in a threesome? I lay on my back staring at the ceiling, tears running into my ears, my trapped anger smothering my breathing as I fumed and raged. I heard Rachel and my mother go to bed. They had a whispered meeting about the broken phone but they didn't disturb me. When I was sure all was quiet I snuck to the living room and poured myself a large gin; a very large gin. Then, clutching the bottle under my arm, I went back to the warmth of my bed.

This time I really, really, really needed a drink.

"No comment, no comment," my mother's voice shrieked through my sleep. A door slammed and I started awake. I had an unbearable headache and my face felt swollen. Within seconds there was a rapid, agitated knocking on my bedroom door. "Come on, Val. Those reporters are here, it's time to go," my mother shouted through my door.

Then I remembered where I was. And I remembered the night before. I rolled over and spotted the nearly empty gin bottle. No wonder I felt as if a fleet of industrious and violent elves were restructuring my brain. But it wasn't only my brain. As the memory came flooding in, a heavy black monster of dread and grief eased itself on to my chest, pinning me to my bed. It was as if all the gravity in the world had decided to focus on me. I couldn't move. And it wasn't just that I couldn't move. I didn't want to. I didn't want to get involved in the world. There was more knocking on the front door, followed by a continuation of my mother's 'no comment' chant.

I was faced with a choice of insanities: either I get up and go shopping with my mother or I stay in bed and listen to her battle with the media for ever. I pulled myself out of bed. In the bathroom I almost revoked my decision. The swollen mass of puffy sunken ravines I was looking at in the mirror couldn't possibly be my face. And if it was, I wasn't going to appear in public with it. I wondered how those women in 1950s films managed to constantly throw themselves around weeping hysterically and never seemed to turn their faces into pulp. Maybe if you only do a short intense little weep it's OK. How come it's always on the day that you need a good face for the world that you're given a face that's been rejected by the manufacturers of those sponge faces you buy in jars? I think they're called potato heads and are sold to people who are tired of looking at their relatives.

I reached for my mother's cosmetic bag, grateful for her Polyfilla. Maybe a couple of coats of it would prevent strangers from stopping me in the street suggesting a detox programme. It seemed like a million years since I had last plastered my face. Back then, just over twelve hours ago, I had only been old and rejected.

Cereal Lover

Now I was old, rejected, face bloated, betrayed and a victim of the other-woman syndrome. It suddenly dawned on me that life was just a device for collecting descriptive adjectives. Adjectives that got worse as you got older.

Invariably.

I was toying uninterestedly with a bowl of Sugar Puffs when Rachel burst into the kitchen. "They're like vultures, those reporters. What a life, following people around and annoying them," she said, with suppressed excitement. They probably took classes from my mother, I thought bitterly, crushing the remaining cereal to dust at the bottom of the bowl.

My mother was standing inside the front door peering out at the reporters. She was dressed like a woman from one of those strict Muslim sects with nothing visible except her eyes. She probably thought that when the reporters saw her dressed like that they would think they were covering the wrong crime and leave in a scurry of scuffed shoes.

"Come on," she said, in a stage whisper, beckoning to us, "we can get to the car now."

We ducked out of the door and ran to the car like commandos running to a waiting helicopter. The reporters rushed forward. For some reason they thought Rachel was the one who had discovered the body. She did nothing to alter that impression. I felt sure she had spent the last hour slowly and mysteriously passing inside the windows clutching a hatchet or a large kitchen knife so that they would assume she was the 'murderer'. She probably hadn't been given enough attention as a child.

Even in my bereft condition I wasn't at all sure that I liked this transfer of attention – after all, I was the one who had gone through the trauma and distress. I stood in front of her while they were taking our picture.

My mother revved the engine in impatient protest and reversed back to us in a shower of gravel. We got into the car and she churned up the ground some more before shooting off. She must have been watching too many seventies private-detective shows on late-night television because we drove all the way to Galway like we were in a high-speed car chase.

Shopping with my mother when she doesn't know what to buy is like telling a five-year-old that he must give away one of his six sweets. He can't decide which so he licks all of them to make the extravagance of giving one away seem less of a wrench. My mother had to go to every department and try everything in each one that caught her eye, proclaiming all the time in a tut-tut voice, "Provincial towns have so little to offer, really."

I was dying.

Not only did my body feel that it had aged about fifty years, but the heat of the shops was melting the Polyfilla from my face. My head ached and my mind, without my authorisation, was harbouring a brutal image of Niall and some unknown other embracing intimately. The 'unknown other', by the way, was still blonde. Blonde and extremely attractive, even though they were snogging so hard I couldn't see her face. I hadn't spoken for hours. My inability to eat earlier had been replaced by a consuming phantom hunger. I say phantom because when I thought about normal food, like Sugar Puffs or anything, my stomach turned, but when I thought about a McDonald's Big Mac and fries great orchestras of romantic music played in my head and I practically drooled on Mother's latest fancy in the coat/shoe/blouse section. I wanted junk food like I wanted nothing else in this world.

Except maybe Niall dead.

Still, if I could just have a burger and chips maybe I could see my way to giving him an amnesty; for half an hour or so.

The problem was, I couldn't work out a way of getting a McDonald's. Perhaps it was that I had killed all my brain cells the night before or maybe I was just numbed with the shock of Niall's infidelity. Ideas weren't coming easily. You see, I couldn't just announce it. PC Rachel would break out in a rash of rainforest destruction and evil corporates while my mother would start an endless stream of little sayings like 'A moment on the lips, an inch on the hips', which would go on until my next offence. And, besides, I didn't want anyone to know that I ate junk food.

I did.

Eat junk food, that is. I had travelled miles from my North Clare haven just to get it. I had eaten enough junk food in the last three weeks personally to guarantee that the rainforests would never again have a normal ecosystem.

It was the perfect comfort food.

Tasty.

Destructive to the world.

Fattening.

And guaranteed to stay in the system long after death.

I wasn't going to confess to having anything to do with it. That's why I found myself agreeing with Rachel when she suggested we go to a restaurant called The Green Feast. I immediately felt nauseous at the thought of all the crisp, fresh lettuce I'd have to face. Besides, 'green' and 'feast' don't even belong in the same sentence. Believe me, I have sophisticated taste in food. Under normal circumstances I'll eat any nationality and race: Greek, Japanese, Indian, even English. Just not today.

Today I wanted to eat American.

I wanted to eat fried, fattening, forbidden, fast food.

I'd have to find a way of getting rid of Rachel and my mother.

Immediately.

Suddenly my mother broke across my scheming. She was very excited. "Look, it's a branch of my hairdresser's! Oh, I'll just have to see if Leonardo's about. I know he's here one day a week. The last couple of days have been so stressful that having my hair done is just what I need."

She disappeared into what looked like a pink cave, but was back in seconds. "You'll never guess," she said. "The only time they can take me is now. You two go and have lunch, I'll meet you here later."

Excellent!

One down and one to go.

Rachel wasn't small enough to be bundled against her will into confined spaces and imprisoned. Pushing her in front of a car would only delay eating longer with all the fuss it would cause. To get rid of her any other way I would have to confess to my fast-food fetish.

Couldn't do that.

There was nothing for it except to go to the Green Feast.

"Val, are you all right?" Rachel asked, in a concerned voice.

We were sitting in the Green Feast, which turned out to be a nice well-lit, roof-level restaurant. I was staring unhappily at my food. My couple of attempts at answering Rachel's well-meaning questions had been abysmal non-starters.

"Yeah," I sighed.

Sometime during the morning I had lost the energy to be angry with Niall. With the anger dissipated, all I felt was a huge sense of failure and disappointment. It was as though nothing really mattered anymore and conversation merely interrupted my misery.

Rachel however, was not easily put off. "Val look, I know this thing with Niall is difficult for you, but you were so much better yesterday."

Yesterday I wasn't the wrong end of the other-woman scenario.

Yesterday I could nearly convince myself I still had a boyfriend.

Yesterday I'd still had the Dead German to distract me.

Yesterday I hadn't had a ravaged, puffy face.

Yesterday had been heaven.

"Val?" said Rachel, even more concerned by my continued silence.

"I'm sorry I'm such awful company, Rach," I mumbled. "It's just that . . ." I paused, swallowing hard.

Oh, no! I was going to cry. And in a public place. A solitary tear escaped from the corner of my eye. It ran slowly at first, unsure if it should be out without its friends, and then with great speed, ecstatic at its freedom, down to my chin, where it dangled, delightedly, trying to catch the light on its best side.

Rachel silently put a clean napkin in front of me. I took a deep breath. "Niall is seeing another woman," I blurted out.

There it was; for such an earth-shattering event it fitted into quite a short sentence.

"You're sure?"

"Oh, yes, Rach. Suzy saw them."

Rachel sighed in agreement. She knew that if Suzy said so it was true. She and Suzy had grown up together somewhere in Kildare. They had become best friends in kindergarten and had remained that way right through school and university. It was through Suzy that I had got to know Rachel. Suzy was always introducing people to each other, mixing and matching from the different social groups into which she fitted with an ease I constantly envied. Strangely, for such a social butterfly she could always be depended on to tell the truth. That's why we both knew that if Suzy had said that Niall had been with another woman then he had been. I took a few more deep breaths so that the whole school of tears wouldn't dash out to join their pal. I was determined that there would be no more crying, no more pathetic self-pity. I fought to regain my anger.

However, as though she could mind-read, it was Rachel who presented the furious outburst. "He's just being such a little shit."

I looked at her in astonishment, completely forgetting my confused emotions. Rachel rarely used bad language and she never got angry or resentful. In fact, I'd never heard her call anyone that before. I tended to agree with her, though.

"You've got to just get him out of your head, let him go," she said, in a very determined tone.

What was going on with her? Where had all this at-one-with-the-world-and-universal-love stuff gone? How was I supposed to commune with my grief if I was to take this sort of Fascist approach to things?

"But, Rachel, I can't just do that, I love him," I bleated. "I mean, relationships aren't all just plain sailing, you know." I was getting a bit more aggressive. "There will be difficult patches – you can't just walk away."

"Yes, Val, OK, but the difficult patches should not be caused by one partner's complete indifference to the relationship."

She had a point. In fact, her point was so good that I got mad. "Well, I don't know about you," I said angrily, "I can't just cut my feelings dead like that."

"I'm not saying that," Rachel said conciliatorily, a glimmer of her pre-dogmatist-from-hell self showing through. "I'm just saying that if he doesn't care, let him go. You don't need that."

I wasn't appeased. I had been harbouring a deep hurt and what I didn't need was this sort of antiseptic practicality forced on it. It stung. It made me angry, and I was going to pour that anger, undiluted, on to what had provoked its release. Rachel was it. What did she know about relationships? I'd never seen her go out with a guy for more than three months. What would she know about long-term commitment? I attacked.

"I don't see that you are in any position to talk. When did we ever see you in a committed relationship?" I snarled.

I hadn't really meant to say it, I'd been thinking it and it had just sort of fallen out.

Rachel looked hurt and went quiet.

"Sorry," I said. "That was uncalled-for."

Rachel nodded and said nothing. She played with her fork. After about ten years she spoke. "One of the reasons I came to visit you yesterday was because I needed to get out of my place. I'm breaking up with my partner of the last two years and the house just wasn't big enough for both of us."

I was speechless. The thieving word-fairy was prowling about my brain again. I sat open-mouthed.

Two years!

She had never told me. I'd just thought she'd been living in the country growing vegetables and hugging trees in age-old Rachel fashion. I know I hadn't seen much of her but I assumed it was because she didn't like Niall. I had thought that, with time, they would just get used to each other, and eventually we would all be a bit closer. But all this time she had been living with somebody! Finally I found a few stray words that the word-fairy had overlooked. "I didn't know, Rach."

"I didn't tell anyone, except Suzy, but she doesn't

really count," she answered.

"So why is it . . ." I ventured.

"Breaking up?" She finished the sentence for me.

I nodded.

"Infidelity," she sighed. "Not like Niall, not a once-off thing. Sort of serial infidelity – there always seemed to be somebody else. Never as important as me you understand, just somebody different every six months or so."

"But you stayed in the relationship," I half asked, half stated.

"Yeah, I was in love. I am in love. I tried to convince myself that ours was a modern relationship, that we didn't need that exclusivity, that possessiveness I see in so many relationships." She snorted bitterly and paused for a moment, seemingly lost in thought. Then she went on: "Besides, I didn't think anybody else would have me. You know my track record on relationships." She refilled her glass. I said nothing. I didn't know what to say.

She shrugged and lowered her eyes. "Eventually I realised that I was really just a cushion while there was no one more exciting about. That I was always second best."

She looked up, the hurt in her eyes too painful for me to hold her gaze. "I've spent a lot of time recently telling myself that if my partner isn't prepared to stop doing something that really upsets me then I'm not getting what I need in the relationship. Talking didn't work. So I've left. The only way I've been able to do that is by being very angry."

I didn't know what to say. I didn't even know this version of Rachel I was talking to. I wanted my old Rachel back. I wanted the Rachel who talked about synchronicity and unity, bonding and the inner child. I didn't want this rational, determined creature who looked and spoke like she could take a seat, cheering and knitting, in the front row of a French guillotining frenzy. I wondered vaguely if she still hugged trees.

"Did I ever meet this guy?" I asked gently, awed by her having managed to keep him a secret all this time, even if he did sound like a total user.

Rachel looked at the table, then back at me. "Actually, she's a woman, her name is Jamie, she's Australian."

Great!

I don't think my feet are abnormally large, but I never knew that I could fit both of them in my mouth with such dexterity. I could taste the shoe leather.

Rachel was gay and I never knew! I mean, how was I to know if she never told me? It wasn't like she'd ever made a pass at me or anything, not that I'm saying she should have but, well, I mean . . . What? Women don't fancy me either? Where was I when they were dishing out sex appeal? What was wrong with me? My boyfriend went off with another woman and my gay girlfriend doesn't fancy me? What was the problem here?

Oh, my god, what was I thinking? Rachel was my friend: of course she didn't fancy me. How could I be so selfish? How was I going to react? All sorts of pennies were dropping noisily and painfully (my hangover – remember?) inside my head. I had to have known all along that Rachel was gay and just not bothered to acknowledge it. Rachel must have noticed how shocked I looked because she started to laugh. That made my shamefaced apology so much easier. Especially as she laughed the whole way through it.

When she was finally able to take a breath, she said, "Suzy told me about you and Niall splitting up and that you were living near me. It seemed to be just right that I come and stay with you till Jamie moves out at the end of the week. I hope you don't mind."

I shook my head.

She beamed at me, her faith in the world obviously restored, and said, "It's amazing how just when you need it the universe provides."

Rachel was back on track. I could feel she was heading towards an outburst of cosmic jubilation. I braced myself. Suddenly I felt a hand on my shoulder and a familiar voice said, "Mind if I join you? It's a bit crowded in here today."

It only took a millisecond to guess who it was. Seeing Rachel's mouth drop open as she stared over my shoulder was a good hint as well.

Dara.

I froze and felt flustered. How could this happen? How could I meet Dara on a face-day like this. I kept my head down, trying to hide my facial landscape of badly filled crevices. Why did we have to be in the brightest restaurant in the whole world? I was sure that the path made by the tear earlier was like a dried-up riverbed down my cheek. Still, I couldn't just sit there and not look at him, ever.

I turned round and curled my lips up at the corners in what I hoped was a smile, trying to minimise the crack factor. "Of course, Dara, please, yes, am, Rachel, this is

Dara, Dara, Rachel," I said, all in one breath.

"Hi." He beamed. No cracks there – his flawless smile illuminated her. Rachel's mouth dropped open even wider. He slid his body behind my chair and put his tray on the table. I tried to remember if I had put any of the Polyfilla around my ears. I came up with a no. That meant that my profile was probably worse than the front view. I promptly turned my chair around to face him. I instantly regretted it as he looked at me in surprise. He probably thought I was some sort of weirdo who got off on watching people eat. I curled my lips up at the corners a bit more, in what I thought to be an encouraging way. Now Dara looked puzzled but started to eat. In the circumstances I thought that very brave. After a couple of chews he must have noticed that neither Rachel nor I was capable of thinking of anything to say: Rachel because she didn't know him, and me because I had no idea how my Polyfilla would react under the strain of a whole sentence, face on. And, besides, I figured the less I drew attention to myself the less he would notice how old and creased I looked.

"You got home OK last night, then?" he asked pleasantly.

Last night! Had that only been last night? It felt like a thousand years ago.

"Yeah, thanks," I said, trying to be expressive with my eyes rather than the rest of my face, hoping for the least amount of disruption.

Rachel raised her eyebrows. I knew what she was thinking. Firstly she was thinking, Hey, not bad; she might, as I had just discovered, be a lesbian, but that didn't make her blind. Secondly, and I didn't mind her thinking it for a while, she thought that Dara was the solicitor I had gone out to see the night before. It would all seem less sordid if she didn't know the details.

"Have you any news about the body?" she asked Dara forthrightly, leaning across the table and confirming my thoughts.

He was back!

The Dead German was back in Technicolor, stomping with dead weight through my untouched salad. I had been so preoccupied with my Niall misery that I had hardly thought of him. I mean, don't get me wrong, he was still ruling my life. After all, I was having lunch in Galway with Rachel and now Dara because my house was infested with reporters who, no doubt, wanted to know if I had killed him.

Oh, no, I can guarantee, the Dead German had never gone away.

I had.

Into the dark, preoccupied, desolate land of Niall-with-another-woman.

"No, no news," Dara answered hesitantly, taken aback by the question.

"The place is crawling with reporters," Rachel said, enthusiastically starting a relaxed conversation during which I smiled gratefully. Not widely or anything but I think I appeared normal. Rachel even managed to get Dara to talk about himself. It wasn't difficult but I certainly couldn't have done it. I found out that he grew organic vegetables and delivered them to local restaurants and shops. The Green Feast was one of his best buyers.

I didn't suppose he supplied McDonald's.

I was glad I'd decided not to push Rachel under a car or anything. She did look a little puzzled at first with all the talk of vegetables. I watched as she tried to work out why a solicitor would have a sideline in organic gardening. Eventually she just shrugged her shoulders and collaborated. Lunch had become quite a pleasant experience. Dara was so ordinary. I don't mean ordinary-boring, I mean normal: he talked and laughed. He had that easy sense of humour that's not mocking or disparaging, just witty. His green eyes lit animatedly as he told us funny little vegetable stories. I even forgot to restrain my facial movement. It was just as well because it would have been very difficult to hide my shock if I hadn't been able to smile when he proposed calling around to my house that evening. I suppose it wasn't so much a proposal as a means of retrieving his sweatshirt. Bottom line was, he wanted to call by that evening!

"This evening . . ." I gasped, my mind going completely blank. I stared wildly at Rachel.

She must have understood because she smoothly finished my sentence for me. ". . . would be fine," she said, "maybe around eightish? Val's mother is going out with me, but Val will be there, won't you, Val?"

I nodded, my face still frozen in a smile. I wasn't breathing. My heart had stopped. This was happening so often, these days, it couldn't be healthy for me.

Help!

Dara got up to go, looking at me with a warm smile. "So, see you later, then," he said, sliding behind my chair to freedom. "'Bye, Rachel, nice to have met you."

He was gone.

Rachel started to laugh. "Nice one, Val, you're such a dark horse, you never told me."

"Told you what?" I demanded. There, I'd obviously started breathing again.

"About that gorgeous item! Here you are, weeping over a loser like Niall, and you have this guy panting so hard I could barely hear myself talk."

"That's not true, I hardly know him," I said defensively, secretly pleased.

"Not because he isn't making himself available to be known." She practically snorted. "He's keen."

"Do you think so?" I asked, wanting her to say it again.

"Yes," she said emphatically, "and he's just what you need right now."

"And you lied about you and Mum going out?" I said, trying to throw obstacles in my own path. Not that I didn't have a whole secret list already! I decided not to tell her about Dara being a prospective stepchild. Or about Ashling. Or about the very pretty blonde girl if she wasn't Ashling. Sometimes a lot of explaining kind of ruins things.

Rachel laughed. "Don't worry, your mother and I will be going out, I'll find something for us to do."

I looked sceptical.

"Don't worry," she repeated, "he's just what you need. He's in touch with the life force, he works with the earth, he'll help you to heal."

Yeah, right.

He might work with the earth but that didn't mean I

had to look like something that had just been dug up. I'd better buy some make-up. And tights. And get something to defuzz my legs.

I had so much to do.

If only to keep the panic at bay.

I was going to have a gentleman caller!

There is only ever one ex-girlfriend

Chapter Seven

"But why can't Val come?" my mother asked.

Rachel and I looked at her. She had been very pleased when Rachel had suggested going to a new vegetarian restaurant in Ennis. What my mother didn't understand was why I didn't seem to be going along.

"The guy who gave me that sweatshirt last night is probably calling by to pick it up," I said, in what I hoped was a casual voice.

She looked puzzled. "You're not going to stay in just because somebody you don't know might come to pick up a sweatshirt, are you?"

Oh, yes I was! A high-kicking chorus of 'yes' dancers was doing the Lyons Tea dance in my head. There wasn't one 'no' among them. I'd better not be too emphatic, though, or my mother would suspect that my determination was based on something more than social duty. It's not that she was anti-men or anything – that is, beyond her belief in their uselessness and immorality. It was more to do with my not wanting her to think me totally fickle. One day I was in floods of anxious tears over Niall, and the next I was organising my life around a stranger who had loaned me his sweatshirt.

Even I thought I was fickle.

Of course, I still wanted to kill Niall, and the next minute myself. But between these two desires there was a whole second when I thought of Dara with a nervous, excited feeling. I liked that feeling. It was distracting. Distracting was good. Besides, I took it as an indication that I was still alive.

I decided to play for the sympathy vote. "I'm not really that hungry, these days, Mum, I think I'd prefer to stay in."

She took the bait. I wasn't my mother's daughter for nothing. One tiny step into darkest emotion for me, one huge leap away from intimacy for my mother. The years of living with her had paid off. "All right, dear." She sighed. Then, not to be outdone, she added, "But I don't like leaving you alone in what is practically the scene of a murder."

"I'll be all right, Mum."

I guided her and the grinning Rachel towards the door.

"When did they say they would repair that phone?" my mother asked, frowning at the mutilated instrument as she passed it.

"As soon as possible, Mum," I repeated, for about the thousandth time since I'd contacted the phone company that morning.

She shook her head, mumbling, "And without a phone if anything happened."

"Nothing is going to happen, Mum. 'Bye."

I ushered them out of the door into the early night towards the car. Suddenly Rachel doubled back and pressed something round and hard into my hand. It was a stone. "That's a special crystal to bring luck in love," she whispered, and ran into the darkness after my mother. I stood at the door watching the car lights illuminate a sweeping tunnel of flat, rocky countryside. Just what I needed, I thought, fingering the stone, a love projectile! What was I supposed to do with it? Throw it at the guy and knock him out so that he couldn't escape? And, anyway, why was she giving it to me? It obviously hadn't worked for her.

As the car disappeared I closed the door rapidly on the winter darkness that stampeded towards me across the deserted garden. Maybe the stone was magic and would protect me against the Undead if the Dead German decided to go B movie. Better stay away from the windows just in case. I rushed around the house closing all the curtains so that I wouldn't frighten myself with my reflection in the windowpane every time I walked into a room. So OK: now I wouldn't really know if there was anything outside but maybe that was a good thing. I would be all right as long as I kept all the lights in the house on. If they went out it meant I was in big trouble. I pulled a chair in front of the main door to ward off my nervousness.

At the moment I had other troubles! I had so much to do: face, hair – what about my clothes? And, worst of all, where was Dara's sweatshirt? The last time I'd seen it had been that morning when, after sleeping in it for the night, I had thrown it, no doubt in a crumpled ball, on the floor of my room. I also had a dim memory of spilling gin on it. Well, come on, have you ever tried pouring a drink when you are inebriated, crying hysterically and lying down? I would have to wash it. I would have to find it first.

I eventually discovered it under a towel on the bathroom floor. It smelt very unpleasant. While I washed it in the basin I had plenty of time to contemplate the massive reconstruction job I needed to do on my face. Even the kindness of the slightly steamed mirror didn't disguise my discarded-paper-bag appearance.

There was no way to dry the sweatshirt so I hung it up over the bath to cool so that Dara would think I had washed it the night before. I didn't want him to know that I had been lying around in it all night in a drunken stupor crying over another man.

I wondered what Niall was doing at the moment.

Little Mr Infidelity!

Bastard!

I supposed he'd had the other woman sleeping in my bed since the second I'd left. When the door had closed behind me he'd probably dashed to the phone and rung her. "Come on over now, darling, she's gone. Let's show this bed some good times for a change."

The imprint of my head would still have been on the pillow! I wondered had he even changed the sheets. Maybe he got a perverse kick out of mingling our scents. Probably some pheromoney-stud thing.

By now he probably had her living in the flat with him. Inevitably she was using all the things I had chosen for my life with Niall. He'd probably given her my best clothes to wear while she was painting. I'm sure she did a bit of that, brilliantly, in her spare time. No doubt she criticised my taste in towels and cushions. Scorned my furry-face slippers. Had a successful career. And a car that wasn't unfashionably old.

She was probably twenty.

Cellulite free.

And naturally blonde.

Bitch.

All these resentful thoughts were doing nothing for my efforts at putting on my new make-up. Maybe I was being too ambitious and should have stuck with the Polyfilla. No amount of smoothing and filling in seemed to make any difference. In fact, it was making it worse. I moved on to the eye make-up. By the time I had smudged all around my eyes for the third time I was furious and ready to give up. Why all the fuss anyway? Dara was just going to come by and pick up the sweatshirt. He was probably going to stay on the doorstep for two seconds, take the sweatshirt, say, "I'm in a rush, got to meet my girlfriend," and disappear into the night. And I'd be left all on my own with my perfectly made-up face. I went and poured myself a drink as consolation and carried it back to the bathroom working through alternative I've-just-come-to-pick-up-my-sweatshirt scenarios. I was on to about my fifth enactment when there was a knock on the door.

Aaaaah!

I grabbed the sweatshirt from the side of the bath and bundled it into a plastic bag. I sucked in my stomach and straightened my skirt (I'd had to go with the thick woolly tights because I hadn't had time to do anything with my legs). I took one last look in the mirror at my ravaged face and hurried to answer the knock. In my frenzy I'd forgotten about the chair I'd wedged against the door and I slammed my shin painfully against it as I reached for the latch. It crashed on to the floor and I cursed loudly. I fumbled at the door, letting the wet sweatshirt fall out of the bag on to the none-too-clean lino. I rescued it, inhaled deeply and reached for the latch again. It took a huge effort to attain a slow dignity, while trying, at the same time, to keep my fluttering heart from escaping out of my mouth.

Believe me, there are few things more humiliating than opening your mouth to someone you hardly know and seeing your heart gallop away from you into the night. My face was set in a frozen smile that must have looked more like terror than hospitality. I opened the door and stopped dead.

It wasn't Dara.

It was Séan the guard, in uniform, his ears keeping his hat now in a tilted-back position. Possibly his evening-wear style. He looked a bit startled: I don't think he'd been expecting such a fervent welcome.

"Val. How are you?"

"Fine, Séan, how are you? Come in."

"Grand. I'm only staying a minute." He stepped into the hall taking in the crumpled plastic bag, the toppled chair and the dismantled phone. He glanced at me shyly. "You're looking well." He blushed.

Must have been the dim light in the hall. Maybe if I could find a few candles I could pretend there was a power failure when Dara arrived. I would put them all over the house and he would see me in soft, flattering tones. But that would probably mean I could be attacked more easily by the Undead . . . bad idea.

"Thanks." I scrunched my mouth into a smile. "Can I help you with anything?"

My smile must have been warmer than I had intended because even though his blush deepened a strange expression came into Séan's eyes. If I hadn't known better I would have sworn that it was a look of hopeless adoration but it was probably just the soft lighting in the hall. After all, if it made me look well it could have any effect! Still the long silence was getting out of hand so I pursed my lips and raised my eyebrows in an efficient, questioning gesture. Sean started, as though he had been suddenly and violently awakened from a pleasant dream. He opened his mouth and quietly gasped for air before he spoke. "Well, ye went away so quickly yesterday I thought it best if I looked in on ye again today. I noticed as well during the day that the phone doesn't seem to be working, so I thought I'd do a little check, you know, to see if you were all right." His tone was somewhat sheepish now.

"Oh, we're fine," I said, in my best I'm-such-a-nice-person voice. "The phone is, ah, broken but we have asked for it to be repaired."

I didn't want to get into explanations about what had happened to it. He would probably interpret my behaviour as being that of a person with violent tendencies and move me to the top of the suspect list – if I wasn't already there. I changed the subject. "Any news on the, you know, dead body?" I asked delicately.

"No," he replied, shaking his head, "nothing yet. Still no ID but I'm sure it won't be long now. A lot of media interest." He made it sound like a Dublin property sale.

"Yeah," I said, at a loss for conversation.

Séan shifted uneasily from one foot to the other as his eyes searched for something in the gloomy hall. He didn't seem to want to leave, yet he also appeared at a loss for something to say. I stared at him, willing him to go. The last thing I needed was the local guard lurking in the background when I opened the door to Dara. His eyes met mine for a shy moment.

"Well, I'll go again," he said abruptly, spinning around and walking out of the door. For no obvious reason he reminded me of Zebedee out of *The Magic Roundabout*.

"'Bye," I said, relieved but slightly puzzled. All the same I shut the door quickly so that 'things' couldn't get in as he moved away into the darkness.

Strange visit! Probably all part of the job, revisiting murder sites at the dead of night. Or maybe there was more to it than that, maybe he really believed that I had killed the Dead German! I wondered if he thought I'd done a runner. Unplugged the phone and gone on the run with my mother and my spacey friend, no doubt terrorising the country with an epidemic of Dead Germans. We'd be called 'The Aryan Activists'.

Or, rather, 'De-activists'.

Or maybe 'The Teutonic Plague', though they are very big words for the tabloids. They'd probably settle for 'Kraut Killing Trio' or something alliterative like that. It would be like that film *Thelma and Louise*. Only it would be Thelma, Louise and one of their mothers. And the authorities would be feverishly trying to stop us before we could reach Germany where we would have an entire country of targets.

Evidently Séan had a high opinion of me!

I had only just gone back to staring at myself in the mirror and bemoaning the obvious fact that Dara was not going to turn up when there was another knock at the door. Séan had probably forgotten to fingerprint me or something. I went to the door, bending to pick up the capsized chair as I did so. When I opened the door, with an amused 'what-now' expression on my face, Dara was standing there smiling, looking even more handsome than I remembered.

Oh, no, I'd forgotten to check if my skirt was straight!

"Hi, Dara," I said, surprised and confused but determined that I would be on top of this situation, even if I was clutching a chair and had an almost uncontrollable desire to look down at my skirt. "I have your sweatshirt here. Hang on a minute." I dashed back into the hall to grab the plastic bag. "I'm afraid it's still wet," I shouted over my shoulder. I swept up the bag. "There you are," I said triumphantly, presenting him with the heavy plastic which by now felt like a used disposable nappy.

He looked a little perturbed but accepted the bag as though it were a gift. "Thanks," he said and paused. "I thought I might pop in for a minute," he added hesitantly. I must have looked bewildered because he added hurriedly, "I mean, if it's inconvenient or anything . . ."

"Oh, no, I mean, oh, yes, I mean, please come in," I finished in a rush, stepping back to let him in.

In the dimly lit hallway he looked even more attractive, his green eyes shadowed by his hair, his face creased into a half-smile. Speechless, I led him into the living room towards the fireplace, the only relatively warm area in the house. He sat down, his well-built frame dwarfing the cheap armchair, the overhead light catching the shine of his fair hair. What was I supposed to say to him? I wasn't used to talking to amazingly good-looking men. Well, Niall was good-looking, I suppose, but I was used to talking to him. When we used to be on talking terms. "So, have the journalists stopped bothering you?" he asked conversationally.

He made it so easy: he just asked questions and I answered them – I even heard myself being witty a couple of times, nothing too risky, just a little bit of 'humour for beginners' in case we didn't find the same things funny. Eventually I even remembered to offer him a drink. Mostly because I thought I was going to die of nervous exhaustion if I didn't have one. I gulped mine greedily. Then I figured I'd better slow down or he might think I was an alcoholic. Of course, he got on to asking me about what I worked at, so without actually lying I gave the impression that I was just getting away for a while from a hectic career in the publishing business.

I didn't mention anything about Niall. I didn't want him to think I was the reject I now knew myself to be. At the same time I didn't want him to think I was some sad spinster who had never had a boyfriend, so I alluded to a relatively recent amicable break-up that could very well have been my decision. Well, that's not a complete lie. I was the one who'd decided to leave.

At that point I thought I should get on to the much more interesting subject of Dara before he asked me any really searching questions. "So your father told me that you spent some time in Holland . . ." I said, not sure if that was the right question to ask. Maybe he'd think I was doing a quick check to see if his father was a liar.

"Yes," he said, taking the bait like the good little conversationalist he was. "I went there just after I finished studying. It was the place to go after the horticulture course." Oh, no, another conversational dead-end. I still didn't know anything about gardening. Maybe I could ask him if he had grown cannabis while he was in Holland – after all, it's legal there, isn't it?

Maybe not.

Ask, that is.

"So," I said, going for the easy option, "did you like it there?"

"Oh, yeah," he smiled, "I mean, it was great for a while, it's a really together place, and it was the perfect excuse to get away from my father."

What? I'd asked one simple, innocuous question and, hey presto!, I was slap in the middle of some father-son thing that I wasn't sure I wanted to know anything about.

"Oh," I said, non-committally.

He must have seen the expression on my face because he started to laugh. "Oh, nothing like that. Dad wanted to set me up in business straight away, any business, really, but I just wanted to be sure that organic farming was something I could make a go of. By going to Holland

I got to do some research and escape Dad's insistence at the same time."

How horrible for him having to escape all that goodwill. Still, he didn't seem spoiled or anything. I wondered was I being biased. You see, he was just the kind of man who was so handsome that unless he tried to kill me I'd think he was great, no matter what he did. I was starting to stare. Better say something.

"Did you stay long in Holland?" I asked lightly.

His face darkened and he looked down at his drink. I did a quick check in case it was empty; it was fine. Had I said something wrong? I held my breath.

After a six-month pause, he said, "I was there for just over three years."

OK, so that wasn't difficult, was it? A simple answer to a very easy question. What was happening here? Now that I'd known him for a day he was turning weird on me? He looked like he was going to cry. Maybe it was because the house was so cold. Or maybe my crying had become a disease and he had contracted it. Whatever it was, he had gone very quiet again. Well, I wasn't going to interfere. If I couldn't say anything right – and it was obvious that I couldn't – then I wouldn't say anything at all. Anyway, not saying anything would give me an opportunity to gaze at him and that was fine by me.

"I . . ." he faltered.

Gosh, whatever he was trying to say must be heavy.

"I was going out with a girl . . . in Holland. Actually, we were living together."

He paused again. I didn't want to hear this bit but I couldn't very well tell him to shut up. I made a big fuss of fixing him another drink even though his glass still wasn't empty. I mixed it extra strong, hoping he'd forget and change the subject. I just hate men who talk about their ex-girlfriend. Talking about mothers runs a close second, but ex-girlfriends are grounds for a divorce even before the relationship has started. In fact, I would strongly recommend not starting a relationship at all if he as much as mentions his ex-girlfriend. I put it in the singular because even though he may have gone out with hundreds of women there is only ever one ex-girl-friend.

You will find yourself by his deathbed tenderly hold-ing his hand. By now he's about two hundred years old and you've been together for one hundred and fifty. His lips will curl into a little smile. His eyes will grow dim with memory as with his last breath – and not for the first time – he recounts the story of how they met. It was in the park. She'd been walking her dog. He'd been read-ing his favourite book given to him by his mother on her deathbed. The dog and the book didn't get along and the book lost. He was distraught but when he looked into her eyes he forgave her and . . . Life's too short for ex-girlfriend stories. I know that now. Niall used to have an ex-girlfriend. I mean, Niall had quite a number of ex-girl-friends, but he had this particular one he used to talk about all the time. He should have nominated her for canonisation, he certainly made her sound like saint material. Her name was Grace.

Amazing Grace.

See, she was already included in some song or other.

Niall was always telling me cutsie little anecdotes

about Grace. Each tale was designed to portray what a sweet, thoughtful, imaginative person she was. There was one story he told me several times about a surprise birthday party she organised for him. It was the summer after he left university, he was saving for his first car so he had intended having a very quiet, inexpensive birthday. A week before his birthday he had taken out the bank book of his specially opened car account and waved it at Grace. "Grace," he said, "I'm having a slim birthday this year because I want my Porsche-book to get fat."

'Porsche-book' was what he called the little bank book because he jokingly claimed that he was saving for his first Porsche. Grace, of course acquiesced demurely at this and blinked her adoring innocent eyes at him. One week later, on his birthday, she suggested that they should meet after work for a drink, only one because of the economising, and then they would go home together for their quiet evening in. Of course, when Niall got to the bar where they had arranged to meet he was greeted by an outburst of song as all his friends showered greetings on him. People he hadn't seen for months lined up to buy him a birthday drink and before he had time to grasp the situation the doors at the back of the bar were flung open and three people came in carrying a cake the size of a child's pedal car. Indeed, for a moment he thought it *was* a child's pedal car because if it hadn't had the candles on it that's exactly what it looked like. When he examined it more closely he realised that the cake was, in fact, a little red Porsche, right down to the fat little wheels, his very own miniature red Porsche that

Grace had ordered specially for him, along with organising that all his friends be there to eat it. Sweet, sensitive, thoughtful, imaginative Grace.

Blessed Grace!

Holy Grace!

I had a theory. I never mentioned it to Niall. He'd have got all indignant. I figured that if I ever met Grace I should kill her; kill her and hide the body. And then, after a few years, go back and check out if the corpse had rotted. We'd soon find out if Grace was a saint or not – wouldn't we?

You see, dead saints don't rot.

I wondered vaguely if there was any chance that the Dead German was a saint. Maybe they should have just left him in the garden and checked his condition in a few weeks.

It wasn't until I'd started to think about things during my exile in Clare that I'd worked out that Grace didn't really exist at all. Oh, yes, there had been a girl called Grace, but she wasn't that perfect. What I was getting was a sort of blanket version: all the qualities that Niall thought he wanted in a girl were now manifest in this mythical Grace person. It was probably all based on some Oedipal thing. Come to think of it, Niall's 'father' was actually his stepfather. His real father had died when he was ten. Maybe there was more to this than I thought. I wonder . . .

I must have squinted suspiciously because I suddenly realised that Dara had stopped talking and was looking at me inquisitively. "You OK, Val?"

"Oh, yeah, sure, just some smoke from the fire, I'm

fine." I coughed a bit to emphasise the point.

Dara glanced around the room for the invisible smoke.

"You were saying about your girlfriend in Holland," I said encouragingly.

I'd decided that perhaps I would let Dara off just this once. Maybe it was because he was so attractive to watch as he spoke, or maybe it was because I'd just had three strong drinks in succession. The jury was still out on that one when I somewhat drunkenly forgot about it. Besides, I needed a quick cover for my squint. He nodded despondently.

"What happened to that, then?" I asked. He wasn't exactly gushing with information. In fact, he looked downright uncomfortable.

Had I asked the wrong question? Again. Well, he'd brought the subject up, not me.

Still.

"I'm sorry," I said, "it's really none of my business."

"No, no, that's fine," he said ruefully. "You see, I don't know what happened."

"What do you mean?" I asked, still not wanting to have this conversation.

"Well, one day she just said she didn't love me anymore." He paused. "There was no warning, nothing, she just stonewalled me."

"But there must have been a reason," I said, more for something to say than conviction. But also because I couldn't imagine how anybody could stop loving him. They wouldn't even have to talk, they could just look at him.

"No," he shook his head slowly, "finally I decided that

it must be a Dutch thing, you know, some sort of cultural difference. Anyway that put me off relationships," he finished flatly.

"Yeah, I know what you mean," I said, laughing knowingly and somewhat too enthusiastically, just stopping myself from slapping my thigh.

Was he trying to tell me something? If he was so anti-relationship, what had he been doing with that girl the night before? That had looked very 'relationship' to me. He certainly hadn't seemed to be giving off many anti-relationship vibes. But, then, perhaps I was a bit desensitised, what with being traumatised and cheated on and everything. Maybe it was just me he wanted to impress with this 'off relationships' stuff. Well, don't worry, I could take a hint. Besides, I was 'off relationships' myself at the moment – thank you very much.

I was becoming bitter. I could feel them, the short little Bitters jumping excitedly at the walls of my tolerance. Some of them had managed to find footholds in the rugged face and were recklessly starting to scale its height. One had even managed to lasso the top of the wall and was tugging sharply to check the safety of the rope. I had to get them under control. Maybe it was time for another drink. Definitely time for another drink.

"None for me, please," Dara said, drawing his glass closer. "I'm driving."

I poured another for myself. I had obviously overcome my fear of being seen as an alcoholic. This was just typical, wasn't it? I'd managed to meet one of the most handsome men in the country – why limit it? probably the world – and he was wearing a huge 'unavailable' sign on his back. I know it was on his back because if it had been on his front I'd have seen it and I wouldn't even have spoken to him. Maybe.

Well now that I knew it was there I couldn't just stop talking to him. What was I going to talk about? Vegetables were out. So were ex-girlfriends – been there, didn't like the scenery. Social life? No, he'd think I was fishing for a date. His father? No, he'd still think I was fishing for a date, only with an older man.

There was always the Dead German.

Uuum.

The Dead German.

We'd said mostly all there was to say about the Dead German at lunchtime. Maybe I could tell some jokes. I'd never been any good at it before, but now I simply wanted the conversation with Dara to flow again. I mean, he was just sitting there looking really uncomfortable. I was busying myself chopping a lemon and trying to remember any joke that would liven things up when I heard the front door open. The voices of my mother and Rachel crossed the hall and they bustled into the room surrounded by a cold halo from outside.

"I thought I saw another car," my mother said triumphantly, as she swept towards the fireplace. Then she stopped and turned expectantly towards Dara. He smiled, stood up and introduced himself. My mother blushed gently as she shook his hand. So he had this effect on all women, no matter what their age or state of mental health! When she heard his name she immediately asked, "Are you related to Terry O'Neill?"

Oh, no, I could feel a lineage inquisition coming on.

"Yes, he's my father," Dara answered pleasantly. "Do you know him?"

"Well, no, we just met him. He was with Mary O'Reilly," she looked pointedly at me then turned back to Dara, "and he invited us to his birthday party tomorrow night. Isn't that very nice of him?" She extended the question to me.

I nodded. Why was she asking me? What assumption was she making? It had nothing to do with me, well, not like that, anyway. Had she been listening to gossip in the village? I glowered.

My mother moved towards the drinks. "Rachel, what would you like? Dara, something?"

"No, Mrs O'Hara, I was just about to leave," Dara said, and smiled towards me. "Thanks, Val." He turned to go.

Well, he was smooth, didn't miss an opportunity. There had been no mention of leaving a few minutes before. Oh, well, at least with his back turned I could read the 'unavailable' sign more clearly.

"'Bye," I said, disheartened, turning towards Rachel and my mother. They were glaring at me and making furious go-with-him gestures towards the door.

"Val will see you out," my mother said, in a calm voice that belied her feverish hand gestures.

"Great," Dara said, looking relieved.

What? He couldn't find his own way to the door? I threw a death-by-slow-torture look across the room as I followed him into the hall. At the door he turned to me, "Val," he said, "this party tomorrow . . ."

"Yeah?"

"I had wanted to ask you to that."

"Well, your father has invited us all, so it's OK," I said lightly, skipping on rapidly to avoid any misunderstandings.

"No," he persisted, "I wanted to ask you to go with me, as my . . . um guest, you understand."

I wasn't entirely sure I did, but I certainly wasn't going to start asking any awkward questions that might spoil what I thought he was saying. "Oh," I said.

"Will you?" He looked at me pleadingly, his eyes filled with some indefinable emotion that looked convincingly ardent. Was he saying what I thought he was saying? I didn't want time to move on in case I was wrong. I wanted to bask in that gaze like a cat in a sunny spot.

Better say something, though.

"Sure," I said, as shortly and as casually as I could, given that my heart was trying that kamikaze routine of leaping out of my body into the night again.

Sure.

Anytime.

Anyplace.

Anywhere.

But I'd have to do something about my legs.

I could do Sleeping Beauty

Chapter Eight

"But, Mum, you'll miss the party," I said, half-heartedly.

"I know, dear, I'd love to go but I really can't leave your father alone any longer, and it is my bridge evening this evening," she said.

"Dad can survive another day," I said, wondering why I was putting up such a fight when I really wanted her to leave. But it was all part of the game, wasn't it?

"You don't need me anymore. There's no charge against you, only three reporters have knocked today, and you are off to a party with a young man tonight," she said, and sniffed. "Besides, Rachel is here," she added, as though Rachel was the new saviour.

She'd won. When she could accuse me of potentially enjoying myself I hadn't a leg to stand on. I could let her go guiltlessly. All the same, I tried to look unhappy so that I wouldn't lose the sympathy vote completely.

By now my mother had begun to miss her social life in Dublin. She was probably also very fed up with being constantly cold. She had done her motherly duty and she had the basis for conversation for the next couple of weeks. She was returning to the metropolis. Eventually she was ready to go. As she stood in the hall she glanced at the defunct phone. "You are to ring me every day," she said. "I'll contact the newspaper that got the spelling of your name wrong with that hideous picture of you. Really, I just don't think these reporters care about professionalism anymore." She stopped for breath.

Briefly.

Then surged on, "I hope the phone people come to fix that phone today."

Since she had declared that she was leaving she had been barking instructions about food, heat, personal hygiene and controlling the press. In fact, she had covered most topics. I was beginning to feel like one of those nodding dogs that used to live in the back windows of cars. Every time she opened her mouth my head started to move up and down rhythmically. I had a feeling that this could go on for ever, but by three o'clock my mother had disappeared into the landscape. The house seemed curiously empty as I adjusted to the absence of constant chatter. The only noise now was in my head as I talked myself out of the guilty feeling that I should have been nicer to my mother and that I'd regret those squandered moments when she was dead. That went on for about a minute and was immediately lost in the mental effort involved in trying to work out how to get the temperature of the house up to a level at which I could remove unwanted hair without dying of exposure.

Rachel wasn't being much help: she had bought a hot-water bottle and was currently wrapped around it in bed, reading a book. I whined into her room. "I'm going to freeze to death if I have to leave this cream on for twenty minutes."

After an age of shopping indecisiveness I had finally decided to buy hair-removing cream, despite knowing how awful it would smell. Waxing just didn't seem worth the pain-to-hairlessness ratio required and I didn't trust myself with a razor, even one of those cute dinky little pink ones that swore to a safer, smoother shave. To be honest I had difficulty believing that they would do the job at all when their macho cousins in the men's toiletry section were twice the size to do a quarter the work. It had all been too baffling for me, so when Rachel in exasperation had thrust the cream into my hand and steered me towards the checkout, I had meekly acquiesced. But now, in the safety and warmth of her bed, Rachel wanted no part in the process. She peered impatiently from behind her book. "If you were meant to be hairless you would have been born that way."

What was she? My mother?

Well, actually, somebody else's mother because mine would have advocated whatever method got rid of unwanted hair fastest. And, anyway, I had been born 'that way': it's just that things had changed horribly and now I was hairy. Besides Rachel never wore anything but jeans and if my memory served me she'd always had very hairless legs. In college when the rest of us went into hysterics of insecurity and artificial tan at a day warm enough to wear shorts, Rachel would appear with naturally brown legs and no apparent unwanted hair problem. She wore shorts with the ease and confidence of a young village boy in one of those French Resistance films.

153

I groaned.

Rachel lowered her book. "If you must conform to that sort of thing, that collaboration with a patriarchal view that women are merely somewhat heavy-breasted pre-pubescent boys and therefore should have no body hair, why don't you have a very hot bath and when you're really warm stick your legs in the air and put the stuff on them, then hold them there until they're done?"

Yes! What a brilliant idea. I could continue topping up the bath with hot water to keep me warm – that is if I could reach the taps with my legs in the air. "You're a genius, Rach," I said, skipping from the room.

This process, of course, went on for hours, as heating enough water to fill the bath took ages. By the time I emerged, pink, steaming and hairless, I had only enough time to rush through the rest of my beautifying. Glancing at myself approvingly in the mirror for the last few touch-ups I noticed that I looked almost happy, well, excited, really.

I remembered that feeling from about a thousand years ago. I used to have it when I was meeting Niall, when we first started going out. Even for ages after we started living together I would have that rush of antici-patory excitement when we were going to a party or something. While I was getting ready, Niall would come and sit on the edge of the bath, drink in hand, smoking a cigarette and watching me. He never said much then, except when he thought I was taking too long. On those occasions he would start to mumble in a mock really thick country accent, "Come on, now, girl, aren't you grand? Sure who'll be looking at you, only me?"

Cereal Lover

If he'd had enough to drink he would even try to carry me off. Well, he would try to throw me over his shoulder. This never really worked because I'm not exactly a tiny, delicate creature and Niall was no Samson. We usually ended up on the floor, a laughing tangle of arms and legs.

In the mirror my freshly made-up face crumpled at the memory. Was I ever going to stop being an emotional yo-yo? I fought the urge to cry by thinking of Dara.

That didn't help: I still wanted to cry.

Suddenly Rachel thumped on the bathroom door shouting, "Hey, are you OK in there, Val?"

"Yes, yes, I'll be out in a minute," I answered, in as steady a voice as I could. Then I set about adding an extra layer of make-up to cover the new cracks and streaks. Rachel went back to humming loudly to herself in the living room into which she had moved after I had sealed myself in the bathroom. She'd obviously decided to hit the gin early. I took a deep breath and stood back from the mirror.

Uuum, not bad.

I didn't think I looked like a recently deserted woman – I mean, I didn't look too desperate or rejected. I even went as far as to think that I looked as though I could walk into a room and everyone there wouldn't turn around and mumble, "Oh, look, she's out without Niall, bet she's looking for another man, be on your guard."

And even if they did it wouldn't matter.

I had a date.

When Rachel and I got to Terry's place we had to stay in

the car for a little while, in awe.

Wow!

Everybody had said that the party was at Terry's, but what they hadn't said was that Terry's was a castle. And I don't mean one of those straight up and down tower castles, I mean a real castle like the Sheriff of Nottingham's, only with big windows. It had everything except the drawbridge and moat. It even had a basement – you could just see the tops of the windows above the ground. It was amazing. Being a solicitor in rural Ireland must be very profitable indeed.

The front door was ajar and bright yellow light spilled out to mingle with the red and blue light that illuminated the parking area. It looked like Sleeping Beauty's castle must have looked before she went to sleep for a hundred years and all the brambles grew up around it.

"Get a load of that," gasped Rachel. Now and again I thought that I could detect an Australian influence in her expressions.

"It's probably haunted," I muttered, wondering how Terry had managed to get divorced and keep the castle.

"Do you think so?" said Rachel, her eyes widening. "Even if it isn't, there should be major vibes here."

As she said this the front door opened wider and Dara appeared. Standing in the beam of yellow light he was the Handsome Prince. Maybe he was looking for his Sleeping Beauty. I was a good sleeper. If I wasn't traumatised, upset, deserted or haunted by Dead Germans. We could work on the beauty, perhaps turn the lights out or something.

Yes, I could do Sleeping Beauty.

Maybe not in the car, though, it didn't really go along with the conventions of the story.

Rachel nudged me. "Hot date or what, mate?" Maybe she was thinking of applying for citizenship of Australia.

Meanwhile the Prince looked around and when he saw our car he came towards it smiling. Rachel made *Jaws* music sounds until I pinched her, then she just giggled. I clambered out of the car. "Val, great of you to come, hi, Rachel, come on in, it's freezing out here."

"Hi, Dara," I said, suddenly giddy with excitement, just like Cinderella must have felt when the Prince asked her to dance at the ball. Gosh, it seemed like that evening I might get to star in all the popular fairy-tales! But that was OK if it meant that I was going to a party in a castle with a handsome man.

Now I'd like to point out that I had been to parties in castles with handsome men before. Well, one, actually, and it wasn't really in the castle, it was more in the grounds of the castle. When I first started going out with Niall he had asked me to a rave on the estate of one of the big houses outside London. I'd never been to a rave before. My friends in Ireland weren't 'ravers'. I was very excited: it seemed so cosmopolitan to be heading out of London on a Saturday afternoon to 'go party'. Niall was a devoted raver. Nothing made him happier than to do some E with his friends and head off to the Ministry of Sound. No wonder he'd stayed so slim.

Niall liked E. He said it was his kind of buzz, he didn't do it that often, just at weekends when he wanted to 'party'. And he hadn't even taken it every weekend since we'd come back to Ireland. He always wanted me to take some because he said sex was great on E. Before we left for that first party Niall had tried some subtle persuasion. "Go on, Val, just half a tab."

"No, thanks," I said, embarrassed, feeling prudish.

"Ah, go on, sure you won't have any fun without it."

"Nah, I'll just stick to a six-pack, thanks."

Niall laughed. "There's no alcohol at this, Val. It's a plastic-bottles-of-water-only type of gig – you know clean-living youth and all that."

"Oh, right." I was taken aback.

It wasn't that I didn't want to try the drug. I mean, everybody with us was taking it. It's just that I knew I'd be the one to get kidney failure or something. I'd keel over in the frenzied, dancing crowd and be trampled to death. My flattened body would only be found as the summer dawn broke and the last stragglers, dishevelled, disorientated and stranded in the middle of nowhere, left the park.

I could see my parents huddled around the radio, their handkerchiefs wrinkled and stained, listening to the report of my senseless death. They would be ashamed to be seen in public because their daughter in her mid-twenties had died from taking a teenage drug. People would point at them almost accusingly and say, "Look, it's Mr and Mrs O'Hara. Their daughter died of that dancing drug – you know, the one that makes you dance so much you dry up and die."

No, E definitely wasn't a good idea.

I stopped the car frequently at pubs on the way to West Sussex, ostensibly to go to the toilet but really so that I could down some very rapid, multiple shorts. I was quite drunk when I got to the rave. As it turned out, it was just as well because it soon became apparent that Niall had been invited by an ex-girlfriend who had been anticipating a reunion and was put out by my presence. I didn't really mind – after all, Niall was an attractive man and women were bound to ask him out. He assured me that he had no interest in her and we had a really great time.

We always did.

Now, of course, with hindsight, I wondered just how ex the girlfriend had been. Maybe I should have asked a few more questions.

I could feel my breath getting shallow with anger and hurt as the memory of Niall's more recent behaviour bubbled to the surface. I must have been glowering because Rachel sounded surprised as she asked, "Are you all right, Val? You're not sensing evil spirits are you?" I shook my head.

Yes, but not here.

Dara chuckled, gently took my arm and said reassuringly, "The only evil spirits in this house are the ones we'll give you inside and you needn't drink them if you don't want to."

Rachel laughed and I felt the gloom lifting as Dara led us into the castle.

"Val, so glad you could come, loved your picture in the paper." Terry swung his way down the hall, drink in one hand, the other outstretched in greeting. He kissed me lightly on the cheek making no other physical contact. Maybe he only did that sort of thing when you least expected it, or when he thought nobody was watching. He shook hands with Rachel mumbling something about her being in the paper also and that it was nice to see her again. Then he turned back to me, "Your mother decided not to come, then?"

"She had to go back to Dublin," I answered quickly, surprised that he had noticed her absence.

"Shame." He mumbled courteously, then spoke to his son. "You really should get our guests a little drink, what, Dara?"

We followed Dara into an enormous high-ceilinged room. It was full of people, most of them Terry's age, all of them shouting above very loud music. After we got our drinks we moved further down the room.

Rachel turned to me, raising her voice above the noise, "Everybody's a bit old, aren't they? And they don't look very Irish."

Before I could react Dara laughed. "You're right," he said. "They're all Dad's friends and most of them are foreigners who have moved to Ireland. Dad does all their property deals for them – it's a big part of his business. All the younger gang is in the kitchen. We'll go in there later but first let me show you a bit of the house. Dad won't mind, he's really quite proud of it."

As we passed through the room and out into the hall Dara shook hands and smiled at most of the guests, and we got the benefit of the approving glances and whispers that lapped in his wake. Rachel and I got a couple of odd looks probably because of our picture having been in the paper, but nobody said anything to us – perhaps they hadn't had enough to drink yet. Dara led us up the broad sweeping staircase away from the noise and smoke. Upstairs it was almost impossible to believe there was a party going on: we could only hear the faintest sound of music and then only if you stood quietly in the corridor. I had assumed that the first floor would be made up of whatever ridiculous number of bedrooms a house this size could hold and I was quite looking forward to seeing Dara's. It might be a little titillating, unspoken intimacy. As it turned out, upstairs was laid out in a smaller version of the rooms downstairs. There was a library, a drawing room and a dining room. At the end of one of the corridors, taking up what seemed to be the entire end of that wing, was a billiards room. I didn't suppose that this room had a twin downstairs but I made a mental note to check later, just in case!

The drawing room had a fire burning and Dara directed us to armchairs on either side. "Another drink perhaps, ladies?" he said, mimicking the formal bow of a butler. We laughed and handed him our glasses, which he carried to the well-stocked drinks table.

Rachel stretched her toes luxuriously towards the fire. "This is a great room, Dara, it's just the right size and shape."

"Yeah," Dara spoke as he continued to pour the drinks, "I prefer this to downstairs. Downstairs is just too big, I'd rather things a bit more homely. This is the get-away-from-the-party room for those of us in the know."

Ah, a prince who liked the homely: things were looking up. I didn't really have time to work through the advantages of this discovery because I was trying to settle myself in the soft chair so that my stomach wouldn't stick out too much. I was having some difficulty finding the most flattering position so I was glad that Rachel kept up an inquisitive banter.

"How come there seems to be two of everything in this house, two dining rooms, two drawing rooms? Did the builder forget he'd done downstairs and just start all over again when he got up here?"

Dara laughed warmly at her deduction and I had to stop my subtle wriggling to stare in appreciation.

"There isn't two of everything." He chuckled. "For example there's only one kitchen. No, what happened was, when my parents first split up they both wanted the house so they decided that my mother could have her life downstairs and my father should refurbish up here so that he had his own home within a home. They spent a small fortune on it and in the end they were even more unhappy as neighbours than they had been as husband and wife, so Mum left."

Dara crossed the room with our drinks and continued talking. "It was a bit rough on us kids but we were relieved not to have to listen to them fighting anymore."

Rachel and I looked at each other, unsure what to say next. I wasn't at all certain that princes were supposed to have dysfunctional families. Maybe that's why they left home and fell in love with women they had barely or never spoken to. On that premise I calculated that maybe it would be best if I spoke as little as possible to Dara. Before I could work out the logistics of this, Dara presented Rachel and me with a book each. "See, we're even in a couple of these coffee-table books, look."

Using our raised knees to support the large, hard-backed volumes he had handed to us, we flicked through the shiny pages, giving little appreciative gasps at the beautifully presented pictures. The house looked even better in them.

"It must be great for you to live in a place like this." I sighed wistfully.

"Oh, I don't live here," Dara said, as though it would have been the most unnatural thing in the world for him to live in his father's house. "I have my own house on the land I farm."

Ah! Could I get anything right? So much for the bedroom theory and the brief secret fantasy of casually visiting Dara in the castle once our relationship had developed. Well, a girl can dream, can't she, or is all that supposed to stop, too, when you reach thirty? Rachel must have noticed my discomfort because she smoothed things over by saying, "Next time it's the guided tour of your place, then."

Dara looked directly at me and said quietly, "You're more than welcome anytime, I'd love to have you visit."

I felt myself blush under his gaze as I struggled to find a way of ending what was now a tortured silence for me. I spoke the first words that came into my head. "Well, we should really be getting back to the party. Your father will think we've run away."

I sprang out of my chair, gulping down the rest of my drink. Dara looked a little surprised but graciously led the way as Rachel followed, giggling, behind us.

"I'll take you down the other stairs. It comes out right

in the kitchen," Dara said, leading us down a narrow staircase and back into the noise and bustle of the party.

'Kitchen' was far too modest a word to use on the room into which we arrived: it was more a large hall with a balcony running around three sides and it was full of young people. Very young people. Few of them looked older than twenty. I hadn't known there were this many young people in rural Ireland.

Rachel tugged my arm and stage-whispered, "I'm going to find the toilet, be back soon."

Following Dara's directions she disappeared through a low door on the other side of the room.

I was alone with Dara.

Well, that is, except for all the other people in the room. He smiled at me warmly and indicated his empty beer bottle. Leaning towards me so that I could feel his warm breath on my neck he said, "I'm just going to get another beer – there wasn't any upstairs. Can I get you anything?"

I shook my head then watched his back disappearing into the crowd. I had a sense of *déjà vu*. Again, just like in the bar the first time I'd met him, I was left in a crowded room on my own. Still, the disappearing back made a very pleasant view.

A number of people had waved to us when we'd come into the room but they weren't looking at me at all kindly now that I was without my escort. In fact, I was getting a few cold stares. They'd probably read the paper too. They were doubtlessly itching to come and ask me how I'd killed the German. Either that or they thought I was a chaperone. I felt very old in that room. Maybe if I wore a little sign that said, 'I'm with someone', I wouldn't feel so friendless.

I shuffled my feet and looked about me in what I thought was a self-confident manner. This only served to draw some mildly alarmed looks, so I gave up. About a week of staring at the floor later I decided I could justifiably glance nonchalantly around the room without feeling too uneasy. That's when I saw them. They were on the balcony, their heads bent close together, laughing and talking. She ran her fingers through her short blonde hair and he raised his head, throwing his laughter across the room below. It was Dara and the blonde girl from the pub.

So she was here. I wondered if he had invited her as well. He had probably asked both of us as some sort of guarantee, in case one of us didn't turn up. I must have looked horrified because people near me started to look curiously towards the balcony. I felt like an idiot. I felt even worse than I had in the pub because at least then I'd only bumped into him, I'd just happened to borrow his sweatshirt, I'd only been waiting for him because he had asked me to. Now I was his date and he had gone off with another woman.

Another woman!

My life was full of other women.

It had never been like that when I was with Niall. Well, not really. I mean, yes, at parties he would disappear for hours and eventually I would find him chatting enthusiastically to some girl or other. He would introduce us and say, "Well, I need a refill, anybody need anything?" And off he'd go leaving me to make small-talk with this stranger. I, of course, would escape as soon as I could, saying I had to go to the toilet or something – I mean, what was I going to say to a complete stranger? Besides, he wouldn't have left us alone if there was anything going on. Once he even pretended he had forgotten my name. We had a good laugh at that. He just needed to circulate a bit to reassure himself that he was still attractive to women, that was all. He would always turn up later with that irresistible glint in his eye. He'd smile at me and say something like, "Hi, I don't believe we've been introduced. Name's Bond, James Bond. I've been watching you all evening and, in the interest of Her Majesty the Queen I'm afraid I must insist on you leaving this party with me. Immediately. There are certain matters that must be uncovered, my dear, and I would very much like your full co-operation. Why don't we go somewhere a little more . . . secluded?" And I would pretend to be a German/Russian/French *femme fatale* type, fluttering my eyelashes and pouting. We would keep this charade going all the way home and right through our love making.

It was great. I really missed that fun and intimacy.

There had been only one occasion with Niall when I had been really worried.

He disappeared, or so I thought. It was in London and I figured anything could have happened to him. He was missing for two days. When he finally turned up he laughed at me. "Sure it was only the E," he'd said. "You've never taken it so you wouldn't know. It makes you want to go for ever. Myself and a few of the lads went on to the Fridge for a change of scene, and sure it went from there, we ended up at Mark's place fit for nothing." He put his arms around me and smiled meaningfully into my face. "I'll have heavy responsibilities for long enough. Sure you wouldn't deny me my bit of fun now, would you?"

And I knew he was referring to us getting married and having children and things, even though we'd never talked about it. I just smiled and agreed. I knew he loved me. I knew that I was the only one for him.

Until now, now that he'd been with another woman, he'd said he didn't love me and he wasn't coming back.

My throat tightened. I could feel resentment and anger trying to push past the knot.

I glared up at the balcony. Dara and the blonde were still there, their heads close together. How could he do this to me at a party where I knew absolutely nobody but where everybody had seen me come in with him? Now I was standing like a fool, staring about me, isolated and confused. As well as that a group of barely-old-enough-to-drink teenagers standing just in front of me were talking about me – I knew they were from the way they were deliberately not looking at me. I had to get out of there. And where was Rachel anyway? Even in a house that size it couldn't take so long to go to the toilet. As I fumed, somebody touched my arm. I swung round, my anger drowned by relief, thinking it was Dara.

It wasn't. It was a girl from the group who had been talking about me. "Excuse me," she smiled politely, "we were just talking and we wondered if you are the woman who found that dead body. You look very like the picture that was in the paper." She stopped expectantly. I glared at her. Was the party so boring that she had to go about asking strangers if they were, by any chance, murderers? I wanted to tell her to get a life or go murder someone herself but I knew that would be rude. I also felt very upset that anyone had recognised me from the hugely unflattering picture in the newspaper. Maybe if I smiled at her I would look like I had Dracula fangs and she would get frightened and run away.

I smiled. She looked encouraged.

Damn!

I was getting myself in deeper. How was I going to get out of there? I needed to find Rachel and leave. I nodded quickly, mumbling, "If you'd excuse me I have to, amm, I must, I think I left the lights on in my car."

I ran. I bumped and scrambled my way to the low door through which Rachel had disappeared. Once on the other side of it, and having slammed it firmly behind me, I ran down a long corridor, taking no account of the direction in which I was going. Soon I found myself in a labyrinth of corridors each of which got progressively gloomier and all of which seemed to lead nowhere. I was no longer passing snogging couples in shadowy alcoves, and all the doors I tried were locked. Dim lights hung at irregular intervals, too far apart to dispel the gloom. The carpet on the floor had stopped corridors ago and now my footsteps echoed eerily and noisily on the stone floor. I paused, panic-stricken, to catch my breath. I felt a sudden chill of apprehension. I wasn't alone. I stood completely still, not breathing, listening for a sound that would confirm my hunch.

There was nothing.

No gentle rattle of chains as whatever it was dragged

itself from the basement. No spine-chilling laugh reverberated through the deserted corridors. No thud of heavy, dragging rhythmic footsteps shattered the silence.

Then I knew what it must be. I knew with absolute certainty.

It was the Dead German.

What else could it be? He was finally seeking retribution. He obviously didn't know who'd killed him and had decided to pin it on me. He was following me. This whole thing had just been a set-up to get me alone in a dark, unfamiliar place so that he could reap whatever revenge it was that the Undead reap. I had no doubt that it would be a very slimy and disgusting reprisal.

But how had he known I'd be at the party? Oh, no! Maybe the whole village was infiltrated by the Undead and they were all plotting against me. They had already got Rachel – no wonder she'd never come back from the toilet. And now they were after me! I had to keep moving. Running my hand along the rough wall to keep my balance I stumbled on, I was almost whimpering with fear. I was so lost. Nothing around me looked in the least bit familiar so I gave in to the urge to run. I increased the pace of my stumble to a quick jog, taking the next corner very sharply in my effort to escape the Dead German. Immediately I crashed into someone who grunted in surprise as I knocked the wind out of him. I knew it was a man by the smell and texture. Even as I screamed a pair of strong arms wound themselves around my waist and a deep voice said into my ear, "Val, what on earth are you doing here? You'll catch a little chill running around this end of the house."

It was Terry.

Terry wearing his outdoor coat and scarf. I'd like to say that I was standing face to face with Terry, which in a sense I was because we were the same height. But to tell the truth it was more a case of my being in Terry's arms.

Yuck.

He was gazing into my eyes as if he was an astronomer and I was a telescope about to reveal an undiscovered galaxy. He was clutching me with the same fervour. I couldn't move and even when I tried I had to be very controlled or I would wriggle against him in a manner that would probably be described as 'provocative' if the case ever went to court. It was a bit of a tricky situation. The time when I could have suddenly burst from his grasp as we first collided was long since past and to stay in this position any longer could be hugely compromising. And I didn't want to offend him, he probably meant no harm.

Maybe.

I'd have to faint. That was the solution. I'd just have to pass out cold. I closed my eyes tightly, held my breath and let my whole body collapse, my head shooting backwards so that my mouth fell open. Terry cursed under the weight and floundered, but he managed to get me fairly gently to the ground. I know you'll think that I was taking a huge risk on the molestation-while-unconscious front but if he tried anything like that I could just miraculously come round. Anyway, I'm sure that I didn't look in the slightest bit appealing with my limbs and hair scattered everywhere and my mouth gaping.

Cereal Lover

"Val, Val, are you all right?" He patted me lightly on the cheek. I kept my eyes tightly shut. He checked my pulse and breathed a sigh of relief. He took off his scarf, folded it and put it under my head, then he straightened up and walked away. I listened as a nearby door opened and then there was silence for a few seconds until I heard water running. I almost started to giggle at the idea that he was going to mop my brow.

This fainting stunt was great – not that I'd used it often. In fact I'd really only used it once before with any great success. I'd been Inter-railing in Europe with Suzy when we were still students. We'd stopped off at some friends of my parents in Hamburg because we needed a shower and some food. When they heard we were coming they'd decided to arrange something they thought we would like so they had bought tickets to a Monsters of Rock concert. They had no children of their own and had been advised that we 'young people' would love this. It turned out to be really crowded. We were at the front of the standing-room-only section but there were spaces in the seated area. I had already made eye-contact with a couple of the bouncers and figured they would be fairly sympathetic. So I 'fainted', right into the arms of the handsomest. He immediately broke into Fraülein-in-distress mode and, lifting me over the barrier, placed me gently on one of the empty seats where I spent the rest of the concert in comfort. Suzy was furious but secretly impressed.

Nice things like that used to happen to me when I was young. Now I had to use my wits to escape from the fathers of men who leave me for another woman on our first date.

I heard Terry returning and lay still. Suddenly what felt like a bucket of cold water splashed across my face. I 'came to' gasping and spluttering as Terry, not wearing his coat now, clutching an empty plastic container in one hand and a wine bottle in the other, looked at me with an amused expression on his face. What was he playing at?

"Sorry about that, Val. I couldn't find a cloth but I thought a little water might do the trick. Do you feel well enough to walk?"

"Yes, Terry," I said weakly, then added, "I feel a bit queasy." I hoped that the threat of vomiting on his birthday clothes would prevent any further physical intimacy.

It did.

The Dead German had come back

Chapter Nine

"Where have you been?" Rachel demanded, as soon as I walked into the room. "Myself and Dara have been looking for you everywhere."

I glared at her, motioning towards the door with my eyes. She looked in that direction, puzzled, but before she could say anything Terry spoke. "She got lost, would you believe? I found her wandering about the corridor when I went to the cellar to get this particularly nice little Bordeaux. A St Estèphe ninety-two that I had been keeping, actually." He held up the bottle that he had brought from the basement.

Rachel glanced at Terry then turned to look at me, making a who-does-he-think-he-is-with-his-St Estèphe ninety-two face. At the same time, in a normal voice, she said, "But why is your hair all wet, Val?"

Terry, who seemed to have decided that I had lost the power of speech, interrupted before I could answer. "She took a bit of a turn, poor girl, nothing a little dash of brandy won't set right. Come along, sit down here, I'll be back in a moment."

"Val, what's going on? Have you got something going with that creep?" Rachel whispered furiously at me as soon as Terry was out of earshot.

"Me? No. Of course not, but I've got to get out of here, Rach," I whispered back urgently.

"What's the matter with you?" Rachel seemed a bit annoyed. "You can't go without saying goodbye to Dara. He's been frantic looking for you."

"That's exactly what . . ." I stopped talking as Terry plus brandy appeared.

He smiled, holding out two glasses. "I thought you might need a little glass as well, Rachel, to top up that one."

He indicated benevolently at the enormous measure of brandy that Rachel was already clutching and had been determinedly gulping down when we'd met her.

Suddenly his smile broadened. "Aha," he said, "the very couple. I'll leave you in safe hands. I must get back to the rest of my guests."

He nodded towards the room behind me, swung round and moved towards an attractive brunette, who looked about one-third his age. I twisted my neck to look behind me and confirmed my worst fears: Dara was feet away and rapidly nearing.

I exhaled in desperation.

My worst nightmare was coming true.

Walking beside Dara, smiling like some sort of happy-day face, was the blonde.

I suppose he was going to try to pass her off as a friend of the family. I clenched my fists. Rachel looked at me with concern, then looked back at Dara and his friend and waved. "Hi, I found her, well, it wasn't me, really, it was your father, he found her in the dungeon or some-where."

Rachel laughed up at Dara, her face flushed from too much brandy. By now Dara was beside us, I could feel the effect his proximity was having on me even though I now knew he was a cad.

"Where on earth did you get to, Val? You just disap-peared. I was afraid that after what we were talking about earlier you might have been spirited away." He laughed heartily at his own joke, as indeed did Rachel and the blonde.

The blonde.

She was miles better-looking close up than she was at a distance. She wasn't even wearing any make-up, her skin was flawless. Her neck attached to its petite little jawbone was like that of a delicate fawn. Her arms were long and slender and her breasts were just the right size for her minuscule short-sleeved top. And she was smil-ing at me! If I didn't know her better I'd have said she was smiling kindly. But it was probably just pity – if she was capable of that. Dara, noticing me staring at her, said, "I don't believe you two have met, have you?"

Oh, yeah, get yourself out of this one, I thought. Let's see what far-fetched story you can come up with to explain away this little beauty.

"Ashling, I'd like you to meet Val," Dara continued. "Val, this is my sister Ashling."

His sister!

A likely tale!

Just because I was new to the area he thought he could

get away with spinning a yarn like that. Better play along for the moment though. I inclined my head and smiled as Ashling reached out to shake my hand. Manicured – might have known.

"Hi," Ashling said with a slightly American accent. "Dara's told me a lot about you, it's great to meet you." She smiled. There was something about that smile. It reminded me of . . . well, of Dara, really. They even had the same eyes.

It couldn't be, could it? Maybe it was true, maybe she was his sister.

In my confusion I started to speak rapidly. "Hi, Ashling, lovely to meet you too, this is such a wonderful party, isn't it? Great to see so many people enjoying themselves, amazing of your father to, you know, have it, especially in such a brilliant house and all, does he have many parties?"

I stopped abruptly, baffled by my babble. Dara and Rachel were looking at me a little perplexed. Meanwhile Ashling, concentrating hard to keep up with me, said pleasantly, "Well, he, like, used to have some sort of birthday party every year and they seemed to get bigger and bigger as he got older. This is his first one for a while. It's probably to do with his getting older and trying to prove he's still up to it."

Ashling and Dara looked knowingly at one another and laughed uproariously. Rachel and I couldn't but be drawn into the mirth. It was such a relief to find a family that didn't take itself seriously. Mind you, it was an even bigger relief that Ashling and Dara were brother and sister.

And, no, I wasn't prepared even to consider the incest scenario. Smiling to myself at the idea, I gulped a mouthful of my brandy and felt its heat seeping into me. This meant that Dara really had asked me to the party and that there was no other woman. I looked across at him, and the warmth in his eyes as he looked back at me cruised through my veins with the alcohol. Ashling and Rachel exchanged glances and suddenly discovered that they had to dash off for refills. Rachel was really knocking it back! Still, at the moment I didn't care. I was alone with Dara. Even though the room was churning with drunken older foreigners, we were completely alone.

"I thought you'd run away," Dara said softly, removing the by now, suddenly and surprisingly enough, empty brandy glass from my grasp and taking my hand in his.

"I . . . aam. No, I just got a bit lost looking for the toilet," I said limply. Well, what was I supposed to say? "I had run away, actually, because I thought that you were shagging your sister but your father captured me and brought me back."

To tell the truth I was speechless. Dara was looking at me as though I was the only person in the world. Though that's not strictly true. I could be the only person in the world and he could hate me; then he wouldn't be looking at me like that. No, he was looking at me as though I was the most important, most perfect, most desirable person in the world.

Gosh!

That being said, it was all a bit too much for me. I burst into speech. "I wouldn't mind another drink. Would you like one?" I indicated his right hand in which he held my glass and a nearly empty beer bottle. I didn't want another drink – in fact, I didn't even really need one. I just needed to do something normal. You know that situation where something has happened, you've won the lotto or something wonderful like that, and you go and wash the dishes just to keep a hold on reality. That was me, plunging the depths for a bit of reality.

Dara didn't seem at all taken aback, he just laughed and said, "Sure," and, still holding my hand, he led me across the room towards the drinks.

It was sort of embarrassing.

Well, it wasn't, really. In fact, I felt very proud. I mean, he was the handsomest man in the castle, possibly in the world. And he was holding my hand. That would show all the people in the other room that they'd been wrong to look at me like I was some kind of deserted, chaperony type spinster person. I mean, if they were going to assume that I was a murderer I wanted them to assume that I was one who was desired by a handsome man.

This wasn't embarrassing, this was great.

I stared about defiantly, catching as many eyes as I could. We got our drinks – I had another brandy because it seemed to be bringing me luck – and beat our way to an alcove by the window.

"It's really crowded in here," I said, with a little gasp as somebody jostled my arm. I moved closer to Dara. I could feel the warmth of his body and smell the faint, lingering scent of his aftershave. Maybe crowded wasn't such a bad thing, after all. Dara looked across the room then turned, put his lips close to my ear and said, "It is a bit packed, isn't it? How about we go outside into the garden? We can put our coats on – it's really a lovely night."

"Yeah," I said, my voice calm. But that was the only thing that was calm. I was in the clutches of an emotional excitement equal only to what must have been felt by the children of Hamlyn when they first heard the mesmerising tunes of the Pied Piper.

I was following a magic tune.

I was entranced.

I was even more entranced when I saw the garden. It was amazing. It was like an exotic wonderland. Maybe I really had followed the Pied Piper to inside the mountain!

Even though it was winter the garden looked very alive. It was dimly lit by soft lights hidden in the shrubbery. It had been deliberately planted to look its best when it had grown a little wild. The effect was spellbinding. I oohed and aahed as Dara took my arm and led me gently down a side path. "Let me show you the best bit," he crooned, sending a shiver of pleasant anticipation down my spine. At the end of the path, picturesquely framed by creeper, a red wooden door was set in the wall. Dara pushed it open and led me into another garden.

This was where the real magic lived. It was just like the Secret Garden. It was completely enclosed by an old high wall, but a lamp was hidden in the overhanging growth at either end so that as we stepped into the enclosure we stood in a pool of gentle light. The rest of the garden was bathed in winter moonlight, the slightest suggestion of frost sharpening its edges. I knew fairies lived there because if they didn't they'd be very stupid. I mean, imagine if you were a fairy and you could live anywhere you wanted. You're given the choice between say, an old quarry and this splendid garden. Which would you pick? Correct! The garden.

"Whose is this? I mean, I know it's your father's but, you know, who plans it and minds it and stuff?" I asked, awestruck.

Dara paused for a moment, shyly, then said, "Well, I suppose it's mine, really. When I was sixteen I started it. The walls were here but it had grown very wild. Originally it would have been the vegetable garden, but that was so long ago there wasn't anything left."

He'd been here until he was sixteen and older? I'd got the impression from Terry that his children had left when he and his wife divorced. How to phrase this without Dara thinking I had been gossiping about him with his father?

"So did you spend a lot of time here?"

That was vague enough, wasn't it?

"Not a whole lot. When we were young, after the split-up, we used to do one summer here, the other in America," he explained. "Then when we got older my sister was almost full-time with my mum in Chicago and I was in boarding-school here so I would spend my holidays and weekends with Dad."

He looked around the garden happily. "This has always been my special place. A gardener does the rest of the garden but this is mine. I missed it a lot when I was in Holland. Sometimes I think it's what drew me back.

You probably think that's silly." He halted awkwardly.

Silly? No, silly's not the word, not even near it.

Silly doesn't make you want to cry.

Silly doesn't make you want to hug somebody.

Silly doesn't make your heart beat double time.

Silly isn't charming.

"Oh, no," I choked, "I think it's wonderful. It's just so . . . so . . ." I paused and swallowed. The old reliable word-seeker seemed to have become inoperable. Sirens were bellowing and technicians were scurrying everywhere in panic. There was a red alert on. A word had to be found. Any word. Now! Eventually they unearthed one and delivered it.

". . . beautiful," I breathed.

What a let-down! You just can't get good staff, these days! I supposed it could have been worse, it could have been something like 'spiffing'.

"I'm glad you like it," he said, taking my hand and leading me gently into the moonlight. "When I first met you I knew you'd like it, er, em . . ." he broke into a stammer ". . . I mean, I hoped you'd like it."

"I love it," I said emphatically, no longer sure whether the magic was the garden's or ours as he turned towards me and looked into my eyes. I remember hoping vaguely that my mascara hadn't run when Terry had tried to drown me earlier. Then Dara leaned towards me and gently kissed my lips.

I had a power failure.

Everything shut down. For two whole seconds my system went into shock, there was silence in my head. An amazing huge silence, punctuated only by the distant whistle of a post-nuclear-explosion wind. At least, that's what I thought it was. I was wrong. As it turned out, it was the whistle that came before the lust bomb struck. And strike it did, with a searing blast. Steam jetted out of my ears and I had to close my eyes because my eyeballs were about to burst out on springs. My temperature soared well beyond anything recordable and my genitals tightened into a knot any seafarer would have staked his life on. Now, I know my Home Guard was on duty that night: it had already protected me against Terry. But it was useless against this invasion. The casualties were countless. All my resistance had been wiped out. Dara didn't seem to notice. In fact, he didn't scream and run away or anything, he didn't even look shocked and horrified. He seemed to have liked kissing me because he kissed me again. And this time we even got our arms and everything involved. I could feel him getting hard as he leaned against me. I could feel my eyes getting lost somewhere down the back of my head with all the desire that was crashing through my system.

It was just like being fourteen again, snogging out the back of the school hall. Well, to be truthful it wasn't at all like that, except that we were kissing outside in the cold. Back then, I'd just thought that the boy had a very sturdy hip-bone. I'd had no idea what was going on until I was fourteen and a half.

It had all come as quite a shock. But I'd got over that and now I knew exactly what was going on and I was very excited about it. We were just reaching the point where I was seriously considering that maybe we should take the hedge-clippers to our clothes when I heard a voice in the distance calling my name. I tried to ignore it, pretending that my eardrums had been destroyed along with my willpower during the lust explosion.

"I think you're wanted," Dara mumbled into my hair, where his delicious lips had been taking a tiny little rest between kisses.

"No," I groaned, as the voice got louder and a small head of short blonde hair appeared around the red door.

"Sorry to interrupt," grinned Ashling. "Rachel seems to be, like, a little bombed and really wants to be taken home."

"Is she OK?" I asked, not giving a damn.

Dara started to laugh at my tone.

"I guess so," said Ashling, "she just needs to go home."

She made a sympathetic face and opened the door wider: she wasn't leaving without me. I tried to figure out a way of never having to leave the garden. Maybe if I could find one of the garden fairies I could get them to turn Ashling into an owl or something so that she would lose interest in us. Or, better still, I could get the fairy to put time back by half a minute and freeze it there so that the perfect moment could go on for ever.

The fairies were a bit scarce that evening.

Dara put his arm around me and led me from the garden. "Duty calls," he said, as we headed for the house.

"I'm sorry, Val," Rachel moaned, as she sat looking very pathetic in a cold blast of night air inside the front door. "It must have been that brandy. I never drink brandy."

Ashling gave a short laugh, "I'd say it was more like

those three cocktails you had. I've never seen anyone drink so fast."

Rachel looked sheepish and shrugged drunkenly. "Who needs friends?" She turned dolefully to me. "Can we go home now, Val?"

"Of course we can," I said, in the kind voice I use for dogs if I like them. Now don't get me wrong, I didn't like Rachel – at that moment – in fact I'd safely say that I hated her, but I wasn't going to start showing that side of my personality to Dara. Especially while I could still taste him on my lips.

This showing one's best side was obviously not the sort of thing that Rachel went for. As the three of us watched she started to turn a very strange shade of green and her expression changed from discomfort to distress. "Oh," she said, clutching her stomach, her face looking like something out of *The Exorcist*. I stared at her incredulously.

"I think you need the bathroom," Dara said, and helped her out of the chair.

"Here, I'll take her, we've been there before," Ashling said smiling, and led away the doubled-over Rachel.

Can I just comment on how great it is to see someone so pretty not afraid of a bit of sick? I mean, Ashling could just as easily have been terribly busy or unavailable, but no, she volunteered. I meant her no ill will now that I knew she wasn't Dara's girlfriend. But you have to admit there's always that niggling resentment against very pretty women, isn't there? You know, even if they're really sweet it's still nice to see them getting their hands dirty or, in this case, feet. It makes them almost lovable.

I stress 'almost'.

I must have been smiling slightly at the image of Ashling supporting Rachel as she got sick because Dara slipped his arm around my shoulder and said, "What's so funny?"

"Oh, nothing," I answered, blinking up at him, once again awed at how beautiful he was. The memory of the moonlight kiss flooded my mind and wreaked havoc with my sex organs. "Nothing important."

I inhaled deeply, filling my lungs with his scent, wishing I could stay safely under his arm for ever. He looked at me, then leaned down and gently kissed the tip of my nose. "Let's talk about some important things then, shall we?" he said.

"OK," I replied, puzzled. "Like what?"

"Like, when am I going to see you again?" he said lightly.

Hey presto! He'd done it. He'd just leapt right over that horrible hurdle between a casual snog and commitment. And he hadn't even batted an eyelid or got tongue-tied or mumbled or anything. This man was a real hero – why hold back? He was a god. And he wanted to see me again. Cue Alleluia chorus!

Usually at this point in a dating conversation, if I could remember back that long ago, I would drop my eyes, lean my head to one side, look at the ground and generally go all coy and bashful. Then I'd mumble, 'I don't know,' like it was nothing to me whether we ever saw each other again or not, even though all the yes banners stored in my brain were fluttering and dancing in the strong breeze of my desire. This time would be different.

I raised my chin, which was already plummeting towards the floor, looked him nearly in the eye and said flirtatiously, "When would you like to see me again?"

His eyes hunted for mine. "I thought tomorrow would be nice." He smiled slightly.

"Well, now," I said, playing along, "tomorrow sounds very nice to me too. Do you have any particular time in mind?"

He dropped the smile and looked at me seriously. "Would you come to my place for lunch?" he said. "I'll give you a map of how to get there. It's not difficult."

"Lunch at your place would be lovely," I echoed after him, more to convince myself that he had really said it than anything else. "One o'clock?"

"Perfect," he murmured, just as Rachel appeared back into view running her shoulder along the wall for support. Ashling was walking behind her, talking to Terry. Now that I had a clear view I could see as little family resemblance between the father and daughter as I had between father and son. I wondered if there is a special gene-buster you can get that excludes the genes of one parent over the other more attractive parent. I was, of course, assuming that Dara and Ashling's mother was beautiful because if she wasn't the O'Neills must have bought their offspring at a special beautiful-children outlet – might ask them for the address.

"I'm ready to go," Rachel said bravely, taking her coat from Dara.

"Me, too," I said brightly to the 'family'. "It's been a wonderful party, Terry, thank you."

"Yeah, thanks," said Rachel, like a slurring echo.

"Nice of you to come to my little do, wonderful to see you again," said Terry expansively, swaying at the hip. He'd obviously got well into the celebration. "If you need anything, anything, and I mean anything, don't hesitate to ask," he managed to articulate, clutching at my hand. The 'hesitate' got a bit lost. But, then, 'hesitate' is that sort of word, isn't it? Can't hold its alcohol.

Dara was grinning, his head bowed into his chest to hide his smile.

"Yes, of course, Terry. Well, thanks again and, ah, 'bye," I said, glancing at Dara, too shy to say anything about our arrangement and the map.

"I'll walk you to your car," Dara said.

As Rachel and I got in, Dara grabbed my hand and pressed a piece of paper into my palm. "It's the map," he said, "from one of my brochures."

Dara put his hand under my chin and brushed his lips lightly against mine. "Goodnight," he whispered.

Could it really get any better, I wondered, as I manoeuvred the car along the narrow roads home. Rachel held her head very near the dashboard and moaned, claiming that the road was going by too fast.

"Rachel, how come you got so drunk?" I demanded, puzzled. "I never remember you getting sick from drinking before."

It was true. When I first got to know her we were seventeen and just setting out on the new road of experimental drinking. Rachel had always been the one who could drink anything. She used to win all the drinking competitions and still be together enough to brag about it. This going-green business was most unusual, unless being involved in the cosmic world had altered things.

"I . . ." she started, then paused and sighed. "I met Jamie." Her head was bent towards the floor now.

"What?" I exclaimed. "Your ex was at the party? How? What was she doing there? How come I didn't see her?"

"It was just after we went back to the party, that time I went to the toilet. You see, she has a home-catering company called Cuntry Cuisine," she hesitated and then went on, "it's spelt 'C-u-n-t-r-y', you know. Of course, everybody thinks its just alliterative to go with the CU in cuisine, but she gets a great laugh out of it." She took a breath. "Anyway, she was doing the food for Terry's party so there she was."

"And," I said impatiently, "what happened?"

"We had a chat."

"Yeah, and what did Jamie have to say for herself?"

"She said that she missed me and that she needs to talk to me. She asked me to come by to see her tomorrow. Is there any chance I could borrow the car for a bit?" Rachel peered at me apprehensively.

"Of course," I replied, then remembered my date. "Well, I'll need it up to about late-afternoon, so anytime after that. But do you really think you should be talking to her? I mean, maybe meeting her isn't the best thing?"

"I know, I know it isn't, but seeing her tonight just messed everything up. Now I have to talk to her." Rachel started to cry noisily, only stopping to hiccup occasionally.

I reached over and patted her on the arm. What could I say? I knew exactly how she felt. If it weren't for my failed attempt to run away from Terry's party and the happy events that resulted from this, I'd be sobbing with her.

As I rounded the last bend before my house I was considering how my luck had changed, how much more pleasant the world seemed and how I wanted it to stay that way. Even as this thought was still in my mind I brought the car to an abrupt halt almost flinging Rachel through the windscreen.

"What the . . ." she muttered bad-temperedly, and then, following my gaze she just said, "Hey."

We were staring at my house. All the lights were on and the front door was wide open, the yellow glow streaming out on to the wasteland until it blended with the moonlight.

"Did we leave the door open?" she asked, as if it was a serious consideration.

"I really don't think so," I said sarcastically, as I pushed my foot on the accelerator, speeding the last few yards.

We got out of the car slowly and stood looking at the house, both of us suddenly afraid. We didn't know what to do now – I mean, what if whoever had done this was still in there?

What if whoever had done this wasn't a who but a what?

What if whoever had done this had escaped from the mortuary, or wherever they were keeping him, and was lurking inside waiting to get us?

I felt sick with fear.

It had finally happened, as I'd known it would.

The Dead German had come back.

Sugar Puff slush

Chapter Ten

"No, there's definitely nobody here," Rachel said in a normal if still slightly slurred voice.

"OK, I'm going to close the door now, and then we'll take one last look around," I ordered, pushing the door to and locking it, pulling the bolt across the bottom as well. Then both of us moved from room to room reassuring ourselves once more that we were alone in the house. The place was a mess, the furniture was overturned, drawers were pulled out, the cistern cover was off the toilet, even the lagging jacket had been torn from the boiler. The groceries that Rachel and my mother had stacked on the shelves in the kitchen had all been swept to the ground. The floor was covered in Sugar Puffs. When our tour reached the kitchen door I turned to Rachel saying, "Right, you hang on here and make sure that nothing gets in while I find something to block this hole in the glass."

Whoever had broken in had done so by smashing the glass panel in the back door. I say 'whoever' instead of 'whatever' because I had decided, eventually, after a lot of persuasion from Rachel, that the Undead wouldn't need to break glass to get in.

There wasn't really any way out of the situation. We were miles from everywhere and we couldn't contact anybody to help us – the stray end of the phone line still lay anchorless on the hall floor. Besides, we didn't know anybody in the area well enough to wake them up at one in the morning. Even my mother, with her great networking talent, wouldn't have been able to help us on this one. We'd had no choice but to move indoors and search the house. The west of Ireland in February is very cold at night when you are just standing about outside for hours waiting to be attacked by the unknown.

I was freezing. Even now that we were indoors I was still freezing. The bitter little winds that always lurked about the house had been joined by their cousin, a great big tough no-nonsense solid cold that was obviously a professional squatter. I'm sure that this unwelcome guest had been greatly encouraged by there being no glass in the back door and the front door standing wide open for hours. Even the moon, which only a few hours before had been a magical friend, had turned into the solitary eye of a nocturnal Goliath who scowled down at us. Rachel didn't seem to be at all as cold as I was. There's a lot to be said for excess alcohol, really.

I could find nothing in the house except some boxes with which to patch the hole in the back door. They had been left over from my mother's shopping spree. I wedged the cardboard into the frame, crushing Sugar Puffs into my knees as I did so. It seemed a good idea to leave the rest of the cereal on the floor so that I could hear the warning crunch of footsteps crossing the kitchen if the intruder came back.

You see? Sugar Puffs aren't just comforting, they're protective as well.

As we stood in the hallway surveying the damage Rachel said, "There really is some bad energy around here. I don't know if it's you or the house." She looked around drunkenly. "You know, this house doesn't conform to Feng Shui requirements. All the doors are in the wrong place for a start. Mind you, no Irish house has anything in the right place but I don't hear of anybody else finding dead bodies in their garden or their house getting hit by some sort of private hurricane." She looked at me accusingly, her gaze unfocused.

"Oh, for goodness' sake, Rachel," I said angrily, "it's not my fault. I have no idea why anybody would want to trash the house."

Rachel raised her eyebrows, swayed forward slightly and shrugged her shoulders. "I don't know," she said, leaving the accusation hanging between us.

I said nothing. It was difficult to deny that certain unfortunate things seemed to be happening in my house and garden but, as far as I could tell, they didn't have anything to do with me. And if they did why wouldn't anybody tell me what it was? It's hard to continue believing that you are the centre of a flourishing conspiracy when you haven't an idea what's going on. I sighed. Then, looking around me at the mess, I sighed again. This was going to take a lot of clearing up.

Rachel yawned. "Well, I think I'll go to bed."

I nodded in agreement and went to my room. There,

all my clothes had been tipped out of their plastic bags on to the floor. I grabbed the stray garments and piled them on top of the already well-blanketed bed. The house temperature was at an all-time low. That night I slept with the bedroom door ajar, alert to the warning crunch of Sugar Puffs.

I woke in grey light to the sound of rain lashing against the window. It came in waves, running down the glass in uneven streams. When I opened the curtains I groaned at the view of grey sky sitting on grey rock, and even that disappeared every few seconds as another sheet of drizzle swept in from the sea. In the kitchen the incessant rain had melted the cardboard that had been covering the hole in the back door, so the floor was awash with Sugar Puff slush.

So much for the warning crunch!

As I swept a river of Sugar Puffs out of the door I cringed at the idea of the daunting clean-up ahead of me. I hated kitchen cleaning. I'd always hated it. I'd never had to do it until I'd left home, and since I'd started working I'd always had a dish-washer. In fact, one of the first things that Niall and I did when we moved in together was buy a dish-washer. We had a lot of fun shopping that day, getting things we would need for our life together.

Oh, no! As if things weren't bad enough with the whole world having turned into a watery mess, depression was settling its heavy bottom on the cushion of my brain. Niall memories were marching their way across my mind, taking no prisoners, respecting no borders.

Cereal Lover

It was just after we had moved in together. I was still at the stage of trying to impress him with my cooking talents. As I had lived at home with my mother almost exclusively up to this point, I hadn't had much practice. Not only did she have an aversion to cooking but she also disliked anybody else cooking in the house. She said that the smell would put off her bridge friends when they came for coffee, or whatever they came for. So the chance to cook in my own home without being nagged by a frenzied mother was something I was really looking forward to.

My first attempt at cooking wasn't very ambitious. I made potato chips. Niall and I had had some real chips at a family-run café and really liked them. Besides, the cooking process seemed idiot proof. So chips it was. I shooed Niall into the next room and prepared my potatoes. Then I poured all the oil in the house into a saucepan but discovered that there wasn't enough. I would have to nip out and get more. The shop was quite near so I thought that there would be no harm in letting the oil in the saucepan heat and then add the new oil to it when I got back from the shop. I picked up my purse, closed the kitchen door and shouted from the hall, "I've just got to go to the shop, Niall. I'll be back in a minute."

I heard the television volume go down as he yelled, "OK."

I ran to the shop and back, thinking how clever I was that some of the oil would be preheated and I would have dinner ready in record time. When I got in I yelled, "Hi, I'm back," and headed straight into the kitchen. When I opened the door I noticed with amazement that

Niall must have come in and closed the blinds. The room was pitch dark. I couldn't even see the outline of the window and it was still fairly bright outside. I reached for the light switch and turned it on. Nothing happened. It seemed a strange coincidence that the bulb shouldn't work also. I didn't understand how any room could be this dark, and it smelt odd.

It was really spooky. It occurred to me that our new flat might be haunted by a darkness ghost who could remove all the light from chosen areas. I backed quickly into the hall, pulling the door shut. "Niall, Niall," I yelled, "there's something really wrong with this kitchen. It's gone completely dark and the light bulb doesn't work."

Niall wandered out of the living room. "What's up?" he asked, stretching and yawning.

I pointed mutely towards the kitchen. Niall walked in and immediately started coughing. Nevertheless he slammed the door shut and stayed in there. I could hear him wrestling with saucepans and fumbling with the window. While I was listening to this I noticed that some of the 'darkness' had escaped from the kitchen. Like a small, heavy dishevelled cloud it floated slowly downwards towards the hall floor.

"Niall, are you all right?" I yelled.

In response he burst out of the kitchen door, covered in what looked like soot with a teacloth held over his mouth. He slammed the door shut and stood panting in the hall, his face streaked black. "That was a close shave," he said. "All that 'dark', as you called it, is carbon particles burnt off heaven only knows what." He paused for breath. "I couldn't see a thing in there but if we leave the window open we should be able to assess what damage has been done in about an hour."

We got a takeaway, sat in the living room and ate in silence. Niall didn't say anything about it but I could see that he was annoyed. I couldn't blame him. I mean, if he hadn't come to the rescue the place would probably have burned down.

When we went back into the kitchen everything was covered in a layer of thick black dust. The bottom of the chip saucepan was completely burned through. The fuse box, which was above the cooker, had melted so that it looked like solidified molten magma. Although it was dark outside by then, I could see that even the window glass was covered in black. No wonder the room had been so dark when I'd come back from the shop!

"Wow!" I said.

Niall still said nothing. I figured that he must be really annoyed. I felt so stupid at not realising what had been going on. How could I not have known that the flat was about to burn down? It hadn't even crossed my mind. Niall must have noticed the stricken look on my face because he reached out and put his arm around me. "Ah, come on, Val, it's not the end of the world. We'll get it cleaned up. A good scrub should get rid of most of that black stuff."

"I suppose so," I pouted, "but you shouldn't have to clean up my mess."

He turned me around to face him and looked into my eyes. "I wouldn't have it any other way, Val." He kissed me and rubbed his blackened face against mine. "I'll race you to the shop for the rubber gloves." He laughed and ran towards the door.

It took us six hours to get the kitchen back to a reasonable condition. It was almost fun, with Niall supplying a constant light-hearted banter. We borrowed a lamp and some electricity from the other room and Niall moved his music system in. Half-way through the evening he produced a tape of songs from Walt Disney fairy-tale films. He put it in the machine and fast-forwarded to 'Whistle while you Work' from *Snow White and the Seven Dwarfs*. Then he danced around the kitchen mimicking the dwarfs.

"That's brilliant, Niall," I gasped between giggles. "Where did you get it?"

"Somebody at work gave it to me ages ago." He shrugged and spun me around the room as though I was a princess at a ball. A princess in pink rubber gloves.

I frowned as I thought about this and swept the last of the Sugar Puffs from under the fridge. I paused and leaned on the handle of the brush, remembering how I'd noticed that there had been an inscription on the tape cover that read 'with love from Sally'. At the time I hadn't paid too much attention to it. Now, with all the enlightenment of hindsight, I suspected that 'Sally' might have been more than a friend.

More than just 'somebody at work.'

More than I knew.

And I had a feeling that if that was the case he had certainly whistled while he worked, all right. I started sweeping furiously, waiting for the dam-burst of anger and hurt.

None came.

All I could think of was my lunch invitation and the memory of Dara's lingering kiss from the night before. I'd found some insulation against the biting pain. Some way of easing the memory.

Oh, joy!

I set about the restoration of the kitchen with a new energy. When I was nearly finished I looked at the time. Oh, no, only an hour to get ready for The Lunch.

An hour! How was I supposed to get ready for the most important moment of my life in an hour? I threw myself into a delirium of passing between the bathroom and bedroom, fighting to attain the perfect 'lunch' look from my exclusive bag-lady collection. When I stood back to add the finishing touches, the image was suspiciously like the perfect 'party' outfit I'd invented the night before. Still, that hadn't served me too badly, had it? By the time I was ready to go there was still no sign of Rachel. Not surprising, really, given the condition she had been in the night before. While I had been cleaning up I'd found some painkillers that my mother had included in her charity buy. I also found quite a good bottle of wine that would now do nicely for The Lunch. No doubt she had optimistically assumed that the combination would dull my pain.

I carried two of the painkillers and a glass of water to Rachel's room, knocking gently before going in. A stale, bitter stench of morning-after alcohol rushed at me, swearing that it still had enough strength to intoxicate me if only I would open my lungs to it. "Ah, come on," it cajoled in a slur, "just a few little breaths there now, it'll

203

do you the world a good, a gran' girl like ya, sure ya won't know yourself after it, come on."

Quickly I stepped outside the bedroom door, avoiding the most pungent burst. I inhaled and, holding my breath, ducked back in and left the medicine on the bed-side table. I dashed to the window and flung it open. A particularly aggressive sheet of rain lashed at me as I breathed in the fresh air.

I turned back to Rachel, wiping my face, and said, "I'm off now, Rach, I'll see you later, OK?"

Rachel groaned from under the blankets, pulling them down far enough to uncover one eye. "Eh?" she croaked.

I repeated myself, handing her the painkillers and the glass of water.

She swallowed them gratefully, peered bad-tem-peredly at the window and disappeared back into her lair, grunting a non-committal "Uh." At least she was alive.

Dara's place was on the other side of Ballinacarrig so I decided that I had better pop into the police station as I was passing through the village. I thought it might be best to report the midnight raid and maybe persuade the guards to reveal if the Dead German had broken out of his cold room. That way I could confirm that I had been foolish to listen to Rachel's reassurances about the intruder not being one of the Undead.

It wasn't until I reached the door of the police station that I realised it was locked. I knocked loudly, then peered through the window at its emptiness. The inces-sant rain spilled down the back of my neck as the wet wind fumbled at my clothes. I paused for a moment in front of the green box. A small sign asking me to speak into the speaker section did little to encourage me to pour my heart out to this inanimate piece of metal.

I squinted about from the shelter of the doorway. The only sign of anybody ever having been there was a soggy lump of dark material sitting in the middle of the path leading to the door. It could easily have blown in off the street. Then again, maybe it was a simple case of water-soluble guards. Maybe this was all that was left of Guard Séan. Maybe only an hour ago he had put on that over-coat and headed out into the community to do his duty. Then, no sooner had he stepped into the rain than he had dissolved, melting and steaming gently into the rivulets of water that ran down the gutters towards the gate and out on to the road. There was no way of knowing where he was now. I'd probably just parked on top of him.

Oops!

But they couldn't all be water soluble. There was, after all, only enough material on the ground for one guard's coat. I shortened my neck into my collar and ran across the road to the shop, thinking that maybe somebody there would know where the guards were. There was a short queue of people waiting to be served so I moved down the shop, waiting for them to go before making my inquiry. That way the whole village wouldn't know my business. Bad enough being the local murder suspect without drawing further attention on myself. I gravi-tated towards the Sugar Puffs. With my run of luck I might need them later. I had to say, though, that besides the Niall business, the Dead German affair, the break-in, the missing guards and the storm, life wasn't really all that bad. I was, after all, on my way to visit the sexiest man in the world.

I was smiling seductively at the box of Sugar Puffs when a surprised voice with an American accent sounded behind me. "Val?"

I swung round and came face to face with Ashling. Or should I say very-made-up-face to very-pretty-face with Ashling? No prizes for guessing which was which. Even with wet hair she glowed.

"Hi," she said, glancing sceptically at the cereal box. "How are you?"

"Fine." I smiled, holding the box closer to my coat and wishing she was anybody but this flawless slim creature. You see, it's doubly unpleasant being caught clutching unacceptable food by flawless slim creatures. Their pity-thoughts are almost tangible. They go something like, "Poor Val, here on her own buying Sugar Puffs/crisps/deep-frozen pizza. As if she hasn't enough problems with the way she looks besides making it worse by eating that rubbish." Oh, yeah, I knew pity-thoughts all right. I had a whole file of pity-thoughts. All the same, Ashling was disguising them very well – probably comes of having such a perfect face: she had no facial expressions.

"I was just over at the police station," I said casually, keeping the conversation going, "but there's nobody there."

I paused. Damn, I could feel a bout of sarcasm coming on. I could hear the distinctive creaking sound as Sarcasm's sealed tomb slowly opened. My nostrils caught the escaping whiff of years of decaying Sarcasm. I could see the clawed hand reaching out of the vault to take control. I was powerless against this possession. I became Sarcasm.

"You don't by any chance know if they occasionally grace the station with their presence, do you?"

Ashling was obviously immune to demons. She looked at me dumbly for a moment.

Oh, great, I thought, she's stupid. Beautiful, but stupid. Maybe there is a God, after all!

"Aam," she said, hesitating. "Like, ah, it's Sunday, Val. They never really open the station on a Sunday."

She must have seen the stricken look on my face because she quickly went on making small-talk. "Most places around here seem to close on Sunday. Except this shop of course." Her voice trailed off.

Sunday! Of course it was Sunday. Why wouldn't it be Sunday? It had to be some day of the week, why not Sunday?

I felt like such a fool! Was I the only person in the whole world who didn't know what day of the week it was? So much for sarcasm! "Oh, yeah," I said, my colour rising. "Of course. Silly me. Well. 'Bye now. See you."

I moved rapidly down the shop away from Ashling's puzzled gaze. I so wanted to put the Sugar Puffs back on the shelf and just run, but I couldn't, really. Besides, I might need them for security floor-coating later. I was still blushing when I emerged from the shop.

Dara's place was down a maze of country lanes, the condition of which got worse as I got nearer the house. The continuing rain and wind made it impossible to know where I was until I had driven through the gate into the yard. I parked the car near the entrance and went towards the house, sheltering the bottle of wine, my head down against the rain. I heard a door opening above me and his voice said, "Val, up here, the steps are just to your left."

As I struggled up them I realised that the house was built of timber – the first three feet or so were made of stone but the rest was timber. Typical, I thought bitterly, as yet another raindrop with no respect for its safety snuck down the back of my neck. A timber house that's probably going to leak all over me.

As soon as I stepped through the door all my bitterness disappeared. The house was deliciously warm and beautifully decorated, from what I could see in the tiny space inside the door. After he had kissed me softly but briefly on the lips Dara took the wine bottle out of my hand and held me at arm's length. He gently moved a lock of sodden hair out of my eye and said, "You look lovely. It's so nice to see you – I was afraid you mightn't come, you know, with the storm."

Mightn't come!

If I had drowned on the way I would still have arrived. And a bit more of that mouth-to-mouth would have been just the thing to revive me.

"I didn't have your phone number," I said coyly, hoping that he would understand that I wanted all his personal details, not just his phone number.

So what if I didn't have a phone? That was just a temporary handicap. Besides, I can operate a public phone. If I really want to.

Dara laughed. "We'll have to rectify that, won't we? Come on in and dry out."

He led me into a high-roofed, spacious room with a glass gable at each end. On one wall a bright fire burned, throwing a red glow on to a little table on which stood two glasses and an open bottle of wine. Silently he went to the table and poured the wine. The only sound in the room was the noise of the rain lashing against the windows and the occasional crackle from the wood on the fire. Still not speaking Dara handed me a glass of wine. Then, clinking his against mine, he said quietly, "To us."

I breathed a sigh of delight as I met his gaze and took a sip of wine. This was so romantic! Here I was in the middle of nowhere, more or less stranded by a dreadful storm, alone with an exceptionally handsome man who seemingly found me very attractive, sipping wine in front of an open fire and anticipating all sorts of untold pleasures. And there were no unsightly hairs on my legs. What had I done to deserve such luck? I glanced around the room, looking for any possible signs of a set-up, but there was nothing, just the rain falling in waves down the window and the red light from the fire playing on Dara's face as he gestured for me to sit on the sofa. "I hope you're hungry," he said, now sounding almost bashful compared to his debonair opening performance. "Lunch is almost ready, just needs another few minutes."

I nodded enthusiastically. "I'm starving."

I was. I had completely forgotten to eat while I was tidying the kitchen. That's the thing about kitchens: they really put me off my food. At the same time, I didn't want to appear like some sort of savage who had only come for the grub so I tried some small-talk. "This is a really nice house, Dara, very, ah, original. The gable windows are amazing. When was it built?"

Dara looked pleased. "Last year. We finished it about seven months ago. They don't take long to build, these timber houses. It's a modified version of a Scandinavian design. They didn't have the glass gables, but that gable there," he indicated the one with the heaviest rain, "looks right out on to the bay, and through the other one there's a great view of Moneen Mountain. Of course, there are shutters but I just couldn't cover that view with anything." He paused and laughed. "Though on a day like today it doesn't make much difference, does it?"

I looked at the expanse of glass. "What if somebody decided to throw a stone?" I asked imbecilically, regretting it the moment I had said it.

Dara laughed again, this time kindly. "Nobody's going to throw a stone. I'm miles from anywhere." Then, frowning he continued, "The only problem that the architect was concerned about was this sort of weather, something about the pressure being too much. She recommended keeping the shutters closed during storms. But I couldn't . . . today." He looked at me almost shyly and smiled. My heart skipped and gambolled inside my chest, causing my breath to come unevenly. Dara glanced at the seaward window and concluded, "Besides, this is the worst weather so far and they seem to be holding up fine, nothing to worry about. Except, that is, getting you fed."

He stood up, managing as he did so to kiss my forehead. Then he disappeared into what I assumed was the kitchen. I leaned back on the sofa, gazing at the fire and sipping my wine. This was the life. This was the way it should be, not living, bereft and in a state of permanent stress, in a refrigerator that looked like a house but which was really a depository for Dead Germans.

Dead Germans!

He was back. How dare he? There was certainly no place for him in this house. Not as long as I was in it anyway. This was my escape world and all that nasty reality just wasn't welcome. I supposed I should try to find out if there was any new information about him. I could do that when I reported the break-in tomorrow. Oh, no! Now the break-in was on my mind, jostling for space with the Dead German. I was going to have to introduce a serious reality ban.

Before I could get heavy with the mental intrusions, Dara burst into the room carrying an array of delicious-smelling food. He had prepared a whole selection of stuffed baked root vegetables and it looked very impressive. "If Madam would care to help herself," he said, handing me a plate. I certainly did care to, and while we ate Dara explained that all the vegetables were from his farm. I tried to look as impressed as I could with my mouth full.

"I have a couple of boxes of vegetables for you in my car when you're leaving," said Dara between bites.

"Great," I said, "thanks," thinking that it was about time I improved my diet. Maybe I'd even throw away that latest box of Sugar Puffs, especially if I was going to be seeing a lot of a man who could handle a vegetable like Dara did. I could feel myself veering towards lust-thoughts so I corralled my mind on to more mundane issues. "Did the party go on much longer last night, then?"

Dara raised his eyes towards the ceiling. "For ever," he exclaimed. "Dad eventually called the guards."

I must have looked downright surprised – after all, who'd call the guards to their own party!

Dara saw my expression and raised his hands, shaking his head. "No, no it's not like that. It's a way of unoffi-cially declaring the party over – they'd be insulted if they weren't called. You see, it gives them a welcome and interesting break. They'd even be in the neighbourhood waiting for the call. They get to have a chat with every-body they know at the party, and it gives people a chance to get home without fear of meeting the guards on the road, so everyone's happy. Dad declares the party over without having to say so, the guards get to socialise and the roads are clear of the strong arm of the law – perfect arrangement."

I smiled at the ease with which things operated in this rural community, but secretly resented the guards who had been off socialising while Rachel and I, just a few miles away, fought against the unknown with no chance of uniformed intervention. In my mind I had an image of Séan, his hat well back on his head, leaning against the bottom of the stairs in Terry's house chatting and nod-ding to the departing crowd. No blushing or stuttering there. But I wasn't about to reveal my little bitternesses to Dara – it would probably turn him right off me.

I stuck to the party topic. "So, does Terry often have parties like that?"

"No, not now. Very few, really, since he and my mother separated," Dara replied.

I could feel a sort of personal question coming on but it was personal about Terry, not about Dara so it would probably be all right to ask it. "He didn't take the break-up very well then. Was he very upset?" I asked, wondering how Terry managed to hide such a sensitive nature so well. I suppose you never can tell.

Dara burst out laughing. "Upset? My father? Not a chance. The only time he gets upset is if he loses money, and that happens very rarely. No, he had to curtail his flamboyant lifestyle because it was my mother's money that bought the property. She comes from quite a wealthy family in Chicago. When they split up and he decided to keep the place he had to pay her back everything, including their joint investments. Her lawyers were smarter than Dad so he's been paying through the nose ever since. He must be nearly paid up by now, but I know that his one fear is that he won't have enough money to retire into the style to which he intends to become accustomed," Dara finished with another laugh.

I must have looked a bit concerned because he continued, "Oh, don't worry, he's not poor, he's a very rich man – he's just not as rich as he'd like to be. I suppose it's all relative. But why are we talking about my father when I'd much rather talk about you?"

I was startled by such a direct change of subject, afraid that he was going to make me confess to being a jilted lover running away from a painful situation. But this wasn't the case, as he deftly turned the conversation to families and we ended up telling each other 'most embarrassing' childhood stories until well after we were finished eating.

Finally Dara made a move to clear up. As he returned from the kitchen for the last time, instead of sitting down, he leant over the back of the sofa, gently lifted my hair and kissed my neck. A shiver of excitement ran through my body, ringing its bell and yelling, 'More, more!' so loudly I was afraid Dara would hear it. It would be too compromising for me to let him know just how much I wanted him. After he had kissed my neck until it tingled with a life of its own, he knelt in front of me, held my hand and gazed into my eyes. "Val," he said, "I'm not sure how this has happened to me. I didn't think I'd ever feel like this again. But with you, I just . . . Val, I really like you and I need to know if you feel the same way. Just being near you drives me crazy, I don't think I can see you anymore if you don't feel the same."

Wow, he was dramatic as well as handsome!

I paused, wanting the moment to last for ever. He started to look distressed, so I threw my arms around him, laughing and kissing him at the same time. He laughed, too, and almost simultaneously we started to tear at each other's clothes, giggling and falling on to the rug in front of the fire. Each new area of flesh I uncovered was like piecing together an amazing, sensuous jigsaw. He was incredibly, unbelievably beautiful.

Finally we slowed down and just gazed at each other. Above us the wind and rain tore at the windows. We were both naked – well, mostly: Dara was naked and I was wearing underwear. We were a little shyer now, but each of us could read the desire in the other's eyes. Very gently he started to caress my buttocks, working his hands to remove the last of my clothing.

Suddenly there was a loud crack and an explosion. Water spattered across us, razor sharp on the face. It bounced and ricocheted until it sprayed on to the fire, causing it to hiss loudly and die. Around us glass tinkled against any hard surface it could find, shattering into dangerous splinters. The freezing Atlantic breeze roared across the room, smashing against the opposite window. I screamed and looked up at the sea-facing window. There was an enormous gaping hole in the glass gable. The evening darkness whistled into the room. I bit my lip to hold back tears of fright and anger.

This was definitely a conspiracy. Definitely an elaborate anti-Val plot. But it wasn't one I could uncover or indeed defeat.

This was a conspiracy of the gods.

Bastards!

Post-noncoital conversations

Chapter Eleven

"Here, just let me make sure that there's no glass in it," Dara said, taking my slightly damp coat from me and examining it.

"It's OK," I sighed, taking it away from him. "It was over the back of the chair, so it would all be on the outside anyway."

Look, Val, I'm really sorry about this, it was just such a freak accident. I should have listened to the architect," Dara repeated.

Oh, was that what it was? A freak accident? And there I was, thinking it was just another form of contraception. The best method of contraception of course, being not to have sex at all. And we certainly didn't have sex.

Some chance.

Naturally, as soon as the window had blown in all the love making had stopped. It had to stop with that intrusive wind whipping papers and any other portables about the room like something out of *Poltergeist*. Besides, it's difficult to make love when the object of your desires is tiptoeing butt-naked through gale-force winds across

acres of broken glass. Had I not been in shock I'd probably have enjoyed the scene. After all, a naked Dara is a
naked Dara, even if he is engaged in an Action Man routine.

As he fought his way towards the window, he had
shouted at me over his shoulder, "You couldn't ever try to
close the shutters on the other window, could you, Val?
I'm afraid it will go too if I don't get this shut immediately. But the lever seems to be stuck." He grunted with
the effort of trying to release the catch. I set off dutifully
to find whatever device he was talking about that would
save the day. So there we were. Like some macabre piece
of modern theatre, both of us nude and demented with
lust, thrusting away at levers at either end of the room.

Ah, romance.

Eventually Dara had to go outside to release the
shutter while I remained inside responding to shouted
commands. I actually thought that we worked very well
together, you know, as a team, Dara outside doing all the
hard work, me inside moving a handle from right to left
on command. Well, all right, then, maybe 'team' is the
wrong word, more sort of leader and follower. I could be
a very good follower.

It took almost two hours to secure the window and
clear up most of the glass. The whole area inside the window was soaked so we relit the fire in an attempt to dry
it out. Throughout the operation Dara, who seemed to
have had all his usual smooth charm shocked out of him,
continued to mumble, "I'm sorry, I'm so sorry, I'm so so
so sorry."

So was I. Mostly because I felt really awkward now

that the moment had passed and nothing had really happened. Nothing, that is, except that Dara probably now reckoned that I was easy. No doubt he figured that anybody with a few organic vegetables and some sweet talking could get me on to the rug in front of the fire. Naked.

I mean, when I thought about it, this was only the fifth time I had met Dara. One of those times had been by accident because he'd spilled a pint on me and another had been by chance in a restaurant. If I really looked at it, his coming by to pick up his sweatshirt didn't count either, and as Terry had already asked Rachel, my mother and myself to go to the party, that was out as well, because I'd have been going anyway. So what I'm saying is, lunch was our first real date and you know the rule – never do it on your first date. It seems that the gods had just been making damn sure I stuck to the rules. Working that out didn't make me feel any better, though. And there was more to it than that. I felt a bit exposed, emotionally that is. Exposed and sort of raw. Worst of all, for some bizarre reason I felt that I had been unfaithful to Niall. That I had, without proper consideration for the man I loved, almost made love to a stranger. In fact, *had* made love to a stranger, except for the consummation bit and that had only been prevented by faulty house design. Yes, of course, every second guilty thought was interspersed by a rasping voice that throated indignantly, 'Unfaithful? How can you be unfaithful to someone you don't go out with anymore? Someone who is, as we speak, being unfaithful to you?'

And then, on cue, the image of Niall with the other woman would rise out of the blur of my confusion.

It's night, Niall and his blonde are embracing, she with one leg wrapped around his waist. Niall's arms support her in this position as he moves against her. They are on a balcony high up above the city, which for some reason is New York! Their kisses are intense and passionate and there is champagne and romantic music, and her floaty white robe-type dress billows gently over the edge of the balcony . . .

No! This wasn't Niall. It couldn't be – he'd never do something like that. It was an illusion, induced by speculative gossip. And to think I had almost been unfaithful to him, here in this house, with this man!

All in all, the best idea seemed to be to get out of there. "I really should be going," I said, in a cheery voice, trying to hide my rising hysteria. "Thanks for a really lovely lunch." I struggled into my coat while backing towards the door.

"Look, Val." Dara stepped towards me. "I'm really sorry about the window and this mess." He inhaled deeply. "It doesn't change what I said about, you know, how I feel."

I stared intently at the floor. I'd forgotten how strained these post-coital, or should I say post-noncoital, conversations could be. I smiled a bit, hoping that would ease the situation. Everything in me wanted him to put his arms around me and say loyal, reassuring, loving things. But the outside me, the street-wise one, chewed a cigar, looked down at its spats and muttered, 'Hey, get the hell outa here now, sugar. A broad like you don't need this sorta scene. Split while you're ahead, babe.'

Ahead! I didn't think being caught in a gale-force

Atlantic wind with my pants down was necessarily ahead! Still, at the moment, running away was a much more attractive option than staying.

"I'll see you soon, OK?" I said rhetorically, avoiding his gaze and reaching for the door. He stretched out his arm and opened it for me.

"Yeah," he said, in a disheartened tone.

I stepped out into the blustery evening. It had stopped raining and all that remained was a confused and bored, directionless wind. It howled around the house, banging at the windows, tugging at the shrubbery, tormenting the plastic of a few storage bags that were outside the door. It immediately caught my hair and swung it across my face. I stumbled, half blinded, down the steps. As I crossed the yard I heard Dara's voice carried irregularly on the wind.

"Val, Val!" he shouted. "Hang on! I forgot to give you your vegetables."

My vegetables!

What did I want with vegetables? After this afternoon's experience I could feel a major outbreak of Sugar Puffs coming on. Vegetables were the last thing on my mind. Maybe I could pretend I was unable to hear him over the wind. No, that wasn't going to work: he was already at the bottom of the stairs, running towards me. "Val, hang on, it'll just take a minute. There are only a couple of boxes."

Dara ran up behind me and slipped his arm around my waist. He guided me towards his car, which was parked on the other side of the yard. His touch and his physical strength electrified and disconcerted me. I could feel my breath becoming shallow as heat rose up to my face from somewhere around my lower chest area. This proximity business wouldn't do.

As we drew nearer to his car I eased myself out of his range. Dara either didn't notice or pretended not to notice this move as he busied himself opening the back of his Land Rover. Inside there were two boxes, the largest of which he picked up and started to carry towards my car, calling to me as he did so, "That other one's very light, if you wouldn't mind carrying it for me."

Mind? Me? Of course not. The sooner I could get the vegetables into my car the sooner I could leave. The sooner I could leave, the sooner I could get home to lick my wounds and make some sense of all this emotional chaos.

I leaned into the Land Rover and grabbed the box. I tried to slide it towards me but it stalled half-way, wedged against something I couldn't see in the half-gloom of the car. I reached in and swept my hand along the floor to dislodge the obstruction. I obviously used more strength than I intended. Something very light and small flew out of the back of the Land Rover and skated across the wet surface of the yard. I peered at it in the dim light as I crouched down to retrieve it. It was a little book lying open, face down in the dirt, and as I touched it I realised it was a passport. I thought it was an odd thing to have just lying about in the back of a Land Rover. I looked towards Dara, who was hidden behind the open boot of my car. It struck me that maybe I could have just a quick look inside. I could find out how old he was and maybe see what he looked like when he was younger.

I know that I was supposed to be getting away as fast as I could and that the likelihood was that, if I thought about it, I shouldn't be interested anymore. I shouldn't have anything to do with a man who tried to have sex with me on a first date, especially one who made me feel as though I was being unfaithful to my boyfriend, my ex-boyfriend. All the same, I didn't think a little peek would do any harm. I mean, for one thing I was sure Rachel would like to know his star sign: then she could reassure me on how unsuited we were. I turned my back on Dara and peered at the open passport in my hand. In the semi-darkness my eyes focused on the photograph. I stared in alarm. I think I may have shouted but I couldn't hear myself over the wind.

It wasn't Dara's.

But there was something about it. The face that stared at me was vaguely familiar. The hair was slightly longer, the colour somewhat deeper than the last time I'd seen him, but there was no doubt that I knew him. And then it struck me, in as near as I get to divine inspiration, that there was really no doubt about who he was.

No doubt whatsoever.

It was the face of the Dead German.

I froze.

Time stood still as I stared at his picture. The wind bullied and tugged at the little book and swept my hair in mad patterns around my head, but I was unable to move.

What did this mean? How come Dara had the Dead

German's passport? Somewhere in my brain there was an answer to this question, but I couldn't find it. The answer-to-question elves were missing some vital transmission equipment. They were scrambling about in bewilderment, lost creatures in a sea of missing links. I struggled to make the connection. Suddenly I started out of my daze as a hand touched my arm and a voice said, "Val, are you all right? What's the matter?"

It was Dara.

Big blinding flash!

The elves had made the connection and they were force-feeding it into my consciousness. It had something to do with Dara and the Dead German.

Something bad.

Something bad enough for me to be afraid.

Really afraid.

I swung round to run to my car but found Dara barring my way. I dipped my shoulder and rammed him with all my force. I caught him off-balance and he reached out to steady himself. I was the nearest support and his hands scrabbled frantically towards mine. I stepped hastily out of his way but not before he had grabbed my fingers and with them the passport. I let go of it and he fell sideways on to the wet, muddy ground, clutching the little book.

Seeing my opportunity I leapt around him and ran to the car. As I drove at speed out the gate I saw his bent figure silhouetted against the yard light, staring after me.

When I grasped that I was safe I broke into uncontrollable shuddering. I started to acknowledge what I had just discovered. There was really no way around it, no question whatsoever.

Dara knew the Dead German. In fact, Dara had killed the Dead German. How else would he have had his passport? And imagine just leaving it lying around in the back of the Land Rover. That was very careless, unless of course he hadn't realised it was there. After all, the Dead German had been moved, and maybe Dara had used the Land Rover to shift the body and hadn't known about the passport. It had probably been lying on the floor since whatever day last week he had dumped the corpse at my house.

Yuck.

To think I had kissed and cuddled a guy who, less than 168 hours ago, had killed a man. Worse than that, he'd had his hands all over me.

Everywhere.

And I'd nearly . . .

I'd nearly . . .

Had sex with him!

My skin felt like it was covered in crawly things. I was suffocating with a huge, choking revulsion. I felt sick. You know, like you'd feel if you had just found the head of a rodent in your cream bun before you started eating it. It wouldn't have actually done you any harm, but you'd feel dreadful.

I remembered feeling the same once after I'd gone out with an embalmer. I didn't know he was an embalmer when I went out with him. He told me that he was an artist. Now I'm not saying that embalming is not an art or anything like that. It's just that it wasn't quite the art I had in mind. Well, it's not really Picasso, is it? Anyway, we'd gone out a few times before he let something slip. I think it was a quick sentence about somebody dropping by with their dead husband.

I freaked. It wasn't the lie. I could get over that. It was just the idea of being touched by hands that were touching dead things all the time that they weren't touching me. And I mean, what if he got a bit strange – bound to being with all that death about all the time – and decided to embalm me? I could just see my mother accepting delivery of me in a glass mummy case for the corner of the living room. I would stand there for eternity, my shoulders hunched and my hands in my pockets – she hated that pose – staring at her and her bridge friends through beady little glass eyes that followed her everywhere.

No!

The relationship with the embalmer came to a pretty swift end. I left him sitting at the corner of the bar, my half-finished drink beside his, almost weeping because I was the only woman who had gone out with him for over three years. He'd been truthful with the others. A big mistake. I think he went for a career change soon after.

This thing with Dara was much worse of course than an inappropriate career. I found it difficult to accept that he could be a murderer. I mean, he just didn't fit the part: he had no scars, he didn't walk with a limp, both his eyes seemed to be in perfect working order, he didn't speak with a funny accent and, though I hated to admit it, I found him extremely attractive. What was it with me and men? I spent years going out with one who had proved himself a cad and now I'd just fallen for a murderer. It was no surprise that my life was a mess: I had absolutely no talent for character judgement. I wondered what I should do. I couldn't really report it to the guards as there weren't any about. Sunday, remember? And I wasn't at all sure that I wanted to. What was I going to say?

"Yes, Sergeant, I did spend the entire afternoon alone with the suspect on the day in question. And, yes, we were more than appropriately intimate. Sorry, Sergeant, what's that you said? Evidence? No, Sergeant, I have no evidence. The passport remained at the scene."

If only I'd managed to keep the passport. At least I'd have some proof. As it was I still didn't even know the Dead German's name!

I decided I'd go straight home and talk to Rachel. Not that she was a rock of common sense or anything but at least she was there. Not for long as it turned out.

As I drove the car into the little parking place in front of the of the house Rachel bounded out of the door. When she came into the glare of the headlights I saw that her face was contorted in some sort of shouting fury. The wind tugged at her hair and clothes so that she looked demented. Afraid that something even more terrible had happened at the house while I was out cavorting with a murderer, I wound down the window. "What's up, Rach?" I asked, sticking my head out.

"What's up? You're asking me what's up? I was supposed to be at Jamie's place an hour ago and you ask me what's up?"

She was screaming. Not a lot of inner peace going on there at the moment. I decided not to antagonise her by mentioning this. Besides, it couldn't have been easy to be that angry and have the mother of all hangovers.

The truth was that, in all the mayhem, I had entirely forgotten my promise of the night before. I was supposed to give Rachel the car to go and visit Jamie.

"God, I'm sorry, Rachel," I mumbled, confident that when she heard my story she would forgive me and maybe not go to visit her ex-girlfriend at all. "You see I . . ." I didn't get any further.

Rachel was really annoyed and not prepared to listen to any excuses. "Excuse me," she said, really politely, in a forced voice, "do you or do you not intend to give me your car to go to Jamie's?" She stared at me stonily.

I was a bit caught on that one. "I, well, I, you see . . ." I mumbled.

"Yes or no?" she interjected in a demanding tone. Maybe she was pre-menstrual as well.

"Yes." I decided on the easiest solution to this checkmate.

"Right, then," she replied, in the same polite voice. 'Why don't you get out of the car and I'll get in and I'll go and visit Jamie before she finds something more amusing to do for the evening besides wait in for me."

Aha! Now I recognised the symptoms! She was suffering from a rather violent bout of 'insecure lover'. The symptoms evolve from a feeling of insecurity about your lover. Circumstances and the world conspire against your solving that insecurity, so you shout at everybody, except, of course, your lover. To them you are sweetness personified.

I got out of the car without even turning off the engine. Rachel climbed in immediately.

"But, Rach . . ." My only confidante was about to disappear into the night.

Rachel looked at me through the open window of the car and held up one hand in 'hush' gesture while thrusting my new box of Sugar Puffs at me with the other. "Val," she said, more calmly now, "I know that my behaviour is inappropriate and I do apologise. I realise that if I am destined to meet Jamie today it will happen. The Higher Being always knows what's best. But it's just sometimes very difficult to put so much absolute trust in the universe. Please don't take it personally. 'Bye, see you later . . . maybe."

She raised an eyebrow, pressed the accelerator and left me wind-whipped, staring after the disappearing tail-lights.

Alone.

I reminded myself never to read whatever self-help book she'd been working from.

I shivered, it was very dark and very cold outside my house in the middle of nowhere. I scuttled towards the light streaming from the open door. I needed to put something between me and this infernal darkness. I went in and closed the door firmly behind me.

Then I remembered. Well, I had to, really: the house was still a complete mess. Not only was the man I had recently lusted after a murderer, but my house had been broken into the night before and there was a gaping hole in the back door. Taken as separate issues, these were already pretty much beyond my coping capacity. Taken together . . . well.

What was I going to do? What I wanted to do was cry. After all, things couldn't really get any worse for me. The list of bad things about my life just seemed to be getting longer. At least before they had just been insurmountable emotional problems, now I had a distinct feeling that I was in danger. If Dara had killed the German and I was the only person who knew about it, what was to prevent him from trying to shut me up? He had already attempted to stop me leaving when he had seen that I had the passport. What was to stop him coming after me? He would know there were no guards on duty in the locality and that I didn't really know anyone in the area. He also knew that my phone was broken. The only advantage I had was that he had no way of knowing that Rachel was out. He would think he had to contend with two women. Mind you, what were two women to a man with a well-toned body like his and a conscience that had already allowed him to murder? He would probably kill us in such a way that it would look like a suicide pact. Neighbourhood gossip would have told him by now about my broken relationship, and Rachel had blurted out her story at the party when she was drunk. He could make it look like we had vowed eternal friendship in death instead of being unloved in this world. Oh, he would be very cunning, I didn't doubt that.

I mean, it was very likely that his interest in me had been solely because of the Dead German. I had no idea why, but it was the only reason that made sense. Why else would a gorgeous guy like him pay so much attention to me? He would come after me, it was inevitable. I'd better make sure that all the doors and windows were fastened and I'd have to block the hole in the door. If I kept the light off in the rooms at the back then it would be too dark to notice that the lower part of the door was broken. Unless he had a torch! Do murderers have torches?

As I stood in the kitchen assessing the situation something moved sluggishly in my mind. It was the answer-to-question elves again. They had found something and were trying to feed it into the system.

I resisted, I didn't like all this information, it was upsetting me. Suddenly the fact, now too obvious to be ignored, clattered into my mind. What if everything was connected? What if it wasn't just bad luck? What if the break-in, the Dead German and Dara were linked? That leaving the German in my garden was more than just a random body-dumping. And that the break-in had not been done by some misguided burglar who broke into nearly empty houses and stole nothing. What if Dara, for reasons unknown but now undoubted by the answer-to-question elves, had ransacked my house?

Aha, but he couldn't have! The presupposing elves blasted skywards, slamming against the ceiling of my mind in the force of my explosive discovery. Dara had been at the party all night. He had either been with me or looking for me. He couldn't have broken into the house!

Relief washed over me, leaving a trail of flailing, gasping elves in its wake. There was no big mystery. Chances were that there was even a simple explanation for the passport being in his Land Rover. I couldn't think of one but, then, I had just had rather a traumatic day. The struggling elves, abandoning their usual form of contact, were shouting at me from the sea of relief. I ignored them, I was busy working on excuses.

Unsuccessfully.

Eventually their shouts broke through my denial. Carrying across the ocean I heard the word 'accomplice'.

All my relief vanished into the great big fear vacuum that had silently crept in and annexed the house. An accomplice! There was somebody else around who could and would kill. Even if Dara was out of the picture there was someone else who could take up where he had left off. What chance had I? Some total stranger not only knew his way around the house but also that there was a gaping hole in the back door!

I shuddered. The kitchen was tidy from my morning's work but even colder than the rest of the house. Rachel had wedged a box against the lower part of the door but the wind still drove cold draughts into the room. I set about cutting up cardboard and plastic bags until I had created a barrier that was at least windproof. I stood back to check my work. There wasn't a hope that it would keep anything more than the rain out. I was still completely at the mercy of anybody who just wanted to crawl in my back door. Not good! I was frightened. Not as frightened, mind you, as when I had thought that the Dead German was after me. That was horrible because I didn't even know what form he would be in. And I wasn't saying that the Dead German might not still want to get me. It was just that now I knew who had killed him I felt less like a target. Come on, if you were murdered who would you go after? The person who murdered you or the total stranger who had only found your body? Things had moved on. Now I was only frightened of the mortals. The one advantage to being frightened of mortals was that they were, after all, just that: mortal. That meant that if I hid from a mortal he wouldn't necessarily know where to find me. Yes, of course, that was it, I could hide – or at least pretend I was out. If I made it appear that I wasn't in the house then Dara, or whoever he sent looking for me, would go away and look for me somewhere else. Why hadn't I thought of that before? It was the perfect solution! The car was gone, the fire hadn't been lit so there wasn't any smoke, and if I left the lights off it would appear that there was nobody at home. It wouldn't be easy to stay in the frightening dark indefinitely, and I wasn't confident that the supernatural might not still try to take advantage of me, but the chances of being murdered would be substantially reduced.

I turned off the lights. I was a genius. I was also freezing, alone, and in danger of injuring myself if I continued to stumble around in the dark. I went to bed, not to sleep or anything: I was far too nervous for that. No, I climbed under the covers for warmth and an imagined protection. Then I stared in the general direction of the ceiling and listened to the weather-beast prowling around the outside of the house looking for cracks and crevices. It was almost human. It even seemed to be knocking on the front door.

What? It *was* knocking on the front door.

It couldn't be.

No.

Unless it wasn't the wind. I sat bolt upright and threw off the bedclothes in one movement. Everything was quiet again. Had I imagined the knocking? I stayed very still, listening. I could hear nothing above the sound of the wind. Then I started violently. Something or somebody had thumped my window. Then the sound came again. And again. It was definitely somebody hitting the window but it didn't sound as if they were trying to break it. It was strange. Suddenly I knew what it was! Whoever was there was pushing their hand against each section of the glass to see if any of the window latches would give. They were hoping that one would be unlocked and that they could get in without causing any damage. That made a change!

The sound stopped. Then I heard it in the next room. Whoever it was was going to each window. Of course they were locked, but if they were going to be this meticulous they would easily discover my makeshift repair job on the back door. Dara hadn't wasted much time in coming after me. He must have thought nobody was home and was breaking in to 'fix' some domestic accident involving electricity or poisoned food. I knew all the tricks. It would be like something from *Murder She Wrote* only I didn't have any little old lady friend to solve the crime.

My mother didn't count.

I'd just be dead with no questions asked. I hadn't heard a car so he obviously didn't want anybody to know he had come visiting. Very clever. I followed

Dara's progress as he moved methodically from one window to the next. He wasn't giving up so I figured the best thing to do would be to get a weapon and lie in wait by the back door.

A weapon. Not an easy object to come up with in that house, in the dark. There was only one thing: it would have to be the top of the toilet cistern. After all, the intruder of the night before had already moved it for me. I groped my way to the bathroom and found the ceramic lid on the floor. I hauled it through the hall and into the kitchen. Dara was now thumping on the kitchen window. I climbed on to the edge of the sink, dragging the cistern lid with me. In this situation my legs dangled well above the ground but very near the door. I had found the perfect defence position. I reached behind me into the cutlery drawer and gently pulled out a knife – my back-up weapon. If I didn't kill him by dropping the slab on his head, I had, with the assistance of the knife, a few questions that I wanted to ask Mr Dara O'Neill.

By now he was trying the door; he rattled the handle impatiently. He had no torch so perhaps he wouldn't notice the patched area. Maybe he would just go away once he realised that it and all the windows were locked!

Maybe not.

He thumped the upper glass pane then the lower. He let out a grunt of surprise when he hit the plastic.

This was it, then: it was him or me. And for once I felt at an advantage. Dara tore away the covering, making no attempt to be quiet. He was definitely confident that nobody was home. This was all the better for me. I nudged the block to the edge of my knees. I couldn't see anything, but now I could feel the breeze coming through the broken door. I could hear heavy breathing as Dara crouched down to crawl in. When the noise was directly below me I extended my arms to full length, balancing my missile in mid-air.

Then I let go.

He wasn't finished yet

Chapter Twelve

"Get up," I commanded the groaning figure lying face downwards on the kitchen floor. "Come on, get up."

I pushed open the door behind me so that my getaway into the dark hall would be easier if he attacked. In my hand, poised well away from my body, I held the knife, its tip pointing at the intruder. Even though I hated and feared them, part of me wished it was a gun. Some chance.

I felt very vulnerable. The truth was that I just didn't want to be there in that situation. What I wanted was one of those transporter machines they have in outer-space movies that would whisk me off instantly to the mother ship, to safe security. But it was probably for the best that this wasn't the scenario. I'd invariably have had to wear a tight-fitting, unflattering uniform that would have looked out of place in rural North Clare.

After dropping the ceramic lid I had thrown myself at the light switch on the other side of the room where I now stood, unsure what to do next. In front of the back door, arms moving across the floor as though he was doing a very jerky breast stroke, his legs still partially outside, lay the trespasser. He was wearing a somewhat familiar jacket and a thick knitted hat on his head. That hat, I decided, would account for his still being conscious. That and the fact that I had been a little off-centre with the cistern lid. My intruder was alive and well and probably about to work out that somebody had just dropped something heavy on him. I figured that he wouldn't be pleased with that. What on earth was I going to do? I mean, it's all very well thinking, Oh, I'll just knock him out and then everything will be all right. I forgot about, What if he's not unconscious? What if he's just lying there raring to go and I haven't a Plan B on hand?

It never happened like that in *Magnum P.I.* The baddies always crumpled with one deft blow, which was followed by the welcome shriek of police sirens. Maybe I just didn't have the knack! There was really no maybe about it. I didn't have the knack. And I was totally panicked. So I got aggressive. "Come on, I know you're not hurt, get up."

I didn't want him to get up. I wanted him to curl up and go to sleep, right there on the floor – I'd even have thrown a blanket over him. The idea of stabbing Dara or anyone was unimaginable. I wasn't a killer. I wasn't even a maimer. It was one thing to drop a heavy object into the dark, quite another to look somebody in the eye and . . .

The figure on the ground regained control of his arms. He pulled them underneath his body to raise himself up. Maybe I should just hit him over the head again. That idea didn't appeal to me. Besides, it was too late now, he was already kneeling up with his head in his hands. So there was just me and the not very vicious steak knife.

I was practically jogging on the spot with fear and indecision. Maybe I should just cut my losses and run away. I could easily get out of the door now and at least have a headstart before he figured out I'd escaped. I thought of the miles of dark rural road that lay ahead of me if I took this option. I would be defenceless against 'things' that lurk in the night. Anyway, what was to say that Dara's car wasn't parked somewhere nearby within easy reach for him to follow me? I wouldn't stand a chance. No, I was going to stand my ground.

I stopped my indecisive shuffle, clutched the knife more firmly and stared at the kneeling figure. There was definitely something very familiar about that coat. The answer-to-question elves, disorientated, rubbed their eyes and yawned, furious at being woken up from their much-needed sleep. They knew that there was something they should be working out, but before they could come round fully, the man shook his head as though trying to clear away imaginary flies. Then he raised his face towards the room. Towards me.

And it wasn't Dara.

It was Niall.

I gasped and dropped the knife. All my preservation instincts crumpled in confusion. My eyebrows, like they do, formed a huge puzzle on my forehead.

Oh, no! What had I done? I had just tried to kill the man I loved. I know that over the last few days I had wanted him dead, even to the point of believing I could kill him myself. But now he was here I knew that this simply wasn't true. But what was he doing here? Was he part of this Dead German murder thing?

"Val, is that you?" Niall squinted and, sitting back on his heels, rubbed his eyes. "What happened? Why were all the lights out?"

No! I just wasn't prepared to believe that he had anything to do with the Dead German case. All my instincts begged and pleaded to be let go to him and caress him, ask him where it hurt most and kiss it better. Like a house-trained dog wanting to go outside to relieve itself, the instincts ran impatiently up and down inside the door of my will, whining to be released. Only my confusion prevented me from giving in.

This confusion was complex. And it wasn't relieved by the tidal wave of joy that swept over me at seeing Niall.

If he'd come to visit me it meant he cared.

If he'd come to visit me it must mean he loved me again.

All sorts of happy possibilities were opening up in my mind. Also, if Niall was my intruder then it wasn't Dara or his accomplice. And if Dara and his accomplice did decide to come now, I wouldn't be alone. There was also the fact that somewhere in the rumpled mess of my mind I figured that if Niall was kneeling on my kitchen floor he couldn't be somewhere else with another woman.

That was the one fly in the ointment. How was I supposed to react to Niall? How was I supposed to behave since he'd told me he didn't love me? How was I supposed to act now that I knew he had been with another woman – women, even – since I had last seen him? I was so baffled that I remained motionless, staring at him.

Niall had stopped rubbing his eyes and was now look-ing at me. "Val, it is you. What's the matter?" He grabbed the side of the sink and pulled himself upright. "Val," he repeated, more gently this time, "are you all right? I'm sorry if I frightened you but I thought there was nobody in because all the lights were out."

I was still unable to move. I wanted to cry, I wanted to laugh, I wanted to run away. I wanted my heart to stop beating like it was training for the Olympics.

Niall pulled off his hat and, rubbing his head, pointed at the cistern lid. "I gave myself an awful wal-lop off that thing." He looked more closely. "Isn't that a piece of the toilet? What's it doing in here?" He paused, then shrugging his shoulders he walked towards me. "Say something to me." He stood in front of me with an irresistible pleading look in his brown eyes.

I wanted to grab him in a tight embrace and kiss him until he and I had dissolved into one person. I wanted to break his teeth and beat him until he was nothing but a mass of swollen bruises. My emotions were a minefield of contradictions. I tried to get them under control. I took a deep breath. "Niall, what are you doing here?"

My voice sounded a bit odd but I thought that might have been because I hadn't heard it for a couple of hours. Niall didn't seem to notice but, then, he hadn't heard it for weeks.

Bastard.

The more aggressive emotions were moving ahead of the others.

"I saw your picture in the paper and I was worried, I

thought maybe you might need a . . . friend." Niall reached out and touched my arm.

I blinked back tears, accusations clamouring at my throat, choking me. "Oh, really?" I replied, with what I hoped was a heavy serving of irony.

Niall either didn't notice or chose not to. "Yeah, I tried to phone but it was engaged or off the hook all the time. I'd have it checked if I were you."

He stopped talking, seemingly unable to think of anything else to say. I couldn't think of anything to say either so we just stood there in silence for what seemed like an eternity. Over the sound of the dying storm I could hear the beat of my heart and I wondered if Niall could hear it too. Suddenly he spoke. "Your mother asked me to tell you to phone her."

"What?" I was a bit taken aback at the mundanity of what he was saying now that he had spoken. I hadn't seen him for weeks, before which he had decided that he didn't love me, rumour had it that he had been seeing another woman and all he did was deliver a telephone message as if I had gone out for an hour and my mother had rung.

"Your mother. I spoke to her earlier and she seemed to think you should phone her every day and she just asked me to remind you."

This normal conversation was becoming too much for me. It was so like Niall just to turn up and be casually and infuriatingly charming, even after I had just tried to kill him. Luckily he didn't know that.

I decided that I'd better get the conversation back on track. "What are you doing here, Niall?"

He looked at me, aware now that he couldn't fob me off with general statements about friendship or messages from my mother. He focused on his feet, shuffling them from left to right. He always did that when he felt awkward. I knew him so well. My heart ached with regret and longing. Niall looked at me, squinting slightly, his head tilted to one side in one of his I'm-so-irresistible poses, and said, "Could we sit down? I walked all the way here from the village and I'm really knackered. There's some stuff I want to say to you."

I beckoned towards the kitchen table and reached for a chair. Niall looked around the room, staring for a few seconds at the remains of the door-covering flapping noisily in the wind. Then he said, "Val, it's freezing in here. There's a gale-force wind coming through that great big gaping hole in the door. Don't you have another room? Maybe with a heater?" To emphasise the point, he rubbed his hands together and pulled his hat back on.

A gush of anger burst through my composite of emotions. How dare he waltz, or crawl, as the case may be, into my house and start complaining about it? It was my house and I could have a freezing kitchen if I wanted. Besides, the kitchen was tidy. I didn't want him to see the mess that the rest of the house was in. I wanted him to believe that my life had improved since we'd been apart. I didn't want him to think I was living in a slum. I felt trapped and that made me angry. My anger escaped, spraying directionlessly at Niall.

"Well, if you hadn't put a great big gaping hole in the door it wouldn't be so cold in here, would it?"

I immediately regretted what I had said. After all, he

had travelled a long way to put that hole there.

Niall looked stunned. He obviously hadn't known he was passing comment on my lifestyle. It didn't take him long to spot the contrite expression on my face, though, and he regained his confidence rapidly, becoming cajoling. "I'm sorry about that, I'll fix it for you, no problem, but you have to agree it's cold in here and I for one could do with thawing out. You don't look too warm yourself."

He reached out and put his arm around my shoulder. It took all my self-control not to burst into wild, abandoned sobbing and throw myself into his arms, blurting out all the fear and trauma I'd experienced since we'd split up. Instead I walked determinedly out of his reach through the door into the hallway, turning on the light as I did so. Niall, following close behind me, whistled when he saw the devastation. As we went into the living room he stopped dead, folded his arms and demanded, "What on earth's happened here? The place looks like it's been hit by a bomb."

"Somebody broke in last night while I was out."

I kept it simple. I'd like to have lied but I couldn't think of any other explanation for the condition of the house. I didn't mention who I thought had done it or anything. Getting into all that might have meant him figuring out that I'd dropped the cistern lid on his head.

"Have you reported it?"

Again I was tempted to lie. I knew, though, that if I did, Niall would inadvertently find out the truth and I would look like an awful fool. I mumbled something about leaving it until the next day as there didn't seem to be anything missing.

Niall gave me a look that said plainly, 'how on earth would you know in this mess?' and changed the subject. "At least it's a bit warmer in here. Is there a heater?"

"No," I said despondently, all my defensiveness draining away. "There's only the fire."

"Right, then," Niall said, kneeling in front of the fireplace. "You sit down and we'll have some heat in no time."

I sat down. As I watched his familiar back the depression metamorphosed into the regret and longing I'd had earlier. With this came all the unanswered questions, pushing, jostling and complaining at being ignored for so long. I decided it was time to have another go at getting to the point.

"Niall, why are you here?"

Niall sat back, leaned against one of the chairs and lit a cigarette. He inhaled deeply, fixing his gaze on the fire. "I've missed you, Val." He glanced up at me, a pained expression in his eyes, then looked away again. "I've missed you a lot and I've come to see if . . . if we could work something out."

I froze. Not so much froze, maybe, as everything in my body stopped. I was suspended in time, afraid to breathe, afraid to think, afraid to believe that Niall was saying this to me. I was silent for so long that he looked up at me questioningly. He must have taken my blank expression as incomprehension because he reiterated, "I've missed you, Val. I'm sorry it's taken me this long to say it to you but . . . I had to be sure."

Sure? What's this sure business? He had to be sure he missed me? Was that it? Or he had to be sure that he preferred me to another woman? He seemed to be forgetting that this was no longer just a simple break-up. He'd been with another woman – women, maybe. But of course! He had no way of knowing that I knew about the other woman. Or else he just thought that I was really stupid. Was that it? Did he think I was really stupid? I didn't have the courage to bring up the subject. Besides, maybe he still intended to tell me about her.

"Sure, Niall? Sure about what?"

He bit his lip, his eyes soft now, in the way that used to make me catch my breath.

My breath caught, I found it difficult to speak.

"Sure that I love you, Val." His voice was gentle. He paused, reached towards me and took my hand. "I had to be sure that you are the person I want to be with." This was amazing. It was more than amazing, it was flabbergasting. I don't think I had ever heard Niall talk like this before. He hardly ever used to say, 'I love you,' without making some joke. And now here he was making whole sentences full of emotional vocabulary one after the other without even a suggestion of facetiousness. And he wasn't finished yet.

I expected that, at this point, he would get on to telling me about the other woman. I didn't want to hear it but I needed to know, and I wanted him to tell me without my having to ask. I wanted to believe I could trust him. He tightened his hold on my hand, his expression earnest now. "There's something I want to say to you, something I need to say to you."

This was it, then. He was going to tell me all about the sex-machine blonde. I could feel the pain starting already.

He paused and took a breath, then, like someone taking medicine, he inhaled quickly and said, "I want you to marry me."

A whitewater, flash flood of confusion thundered through my brain, leaving in its wake a stillness never before experienced in my mind. Across this calmness floated images of our wedding, our life together, all the little special events that I had always thought would be our future. I was cocooned in a cloud of white as I floated back down the aisle on Niall's arm. We gazed into one another's eyes. The air was thick with confetti and the congratulatory clapping of our friends. Then, in the same dancing blizzard of coloured paper, Niall and I waltzed in slow motion round and round a gilded room, still drowning in each other's gaze. The birth of our first child, swaddled and peaceful, as Niall held my hand and looked lovingly, admiringly and gratefully into my eyes. The whole future I had dreamt of glided, wavered, wisped its way about my head.

And melted.

Niall was staring at me expectantly. My dazed eyes caught his and as I looked into them I realised that they weren't the eyes of the man in my dreams. Oh, they were Niall's eyes, all right. It's just, to me, they were different. I was staring into the eyes of a man who was lying to me. No, lying was the wrong word. I was looking into the eyes of a man who wasn't telling me the whole truth. So my dreams melted.

But maybe Suzy had been wrong, maybe there never had been another woman! It was no good: the moment was ruined. The image of Niall and the other woman rushed into my mind, vaudeville-style, stamping and kicking about to fill the place where my dreams had been. An enormous aggressive pain crawled out of my heart spitting and biting like the creature in *Alien*. It lunged at my rational mind devouring it and its placatory little ideas in one mouthful.

And so I became the *Alien* monster.

I started to breathe heavily. The words I was about to say fitted into my throat at all the wrong angles. They were like the pieces of a jigsaw being crammed into place by a two-year-old. Niall was still staring at me, waiting for my response. He hadn't noticed that I'd turned into the *Alien* monster. I dropped my hand so that he was forced to release his hold on it. I resisted the urge to snap off his head with one bite and instead hounded some words into a sentence.

"Did you? . . . Were you? . . . That is . . . Look, Suzy said she saw you with somebody else."

Niall looked taken aback. I'd go as far as to say that he looked shocked. So he didn't know that Suzy had spotted him. His expression changed to remorse, shame, even. He sighed and stared down at his hands. "Yeah, I did see somebody else. She didn't mean anything to me, though. Not like you do."

He was staring at me wide-eyed as though he was telling me a simple fact. It was the type of expression you would have if you were saying to someone, 'No, honest, eggs really do come out of chickens.'

It just didn't seem all that simple to me. I felt like I was in a shower in which the water kept changing from extremely hot to extremely cold in rapid succession. Had it stayed at one temperature I could at least have got used to it. Niall had said the one thing to me I had hoped and dreamt he would say, and in almost the same breath he had told me that he had been with another woman. This didn't sit well with my view of a marriage proposal. I was still angry, I was still hurt.

"Is that why you said you didn't love me? Because you were seeing this other woman?"

It killed me to have to talk about her. It was one thing when she had been free-floating in my head but now she really existed and I was referring to her as if she was just another fact of life.

Niall looked shocked. "Of course not. I told you – I said that because I needed to be sure."

We were back to 'sure'. Well, I wasn't 'sure' I understood.

Niall sighed and clasped my hand again. "Val, I don't know any other way to say this. I love you."

The angry *Alien* monster got the better of me. I was infuriated by the way the conversation was working in dizzying little nose-dives, the driving force of which was Niall's petulant need to be 'sure'. I had to get some facts.

"Niall, did you sleep with this woman?"

I couldn't believe I'd asked that. I could hear the sound of tearing as a piece of my heart rent with the effort. Right at this moment it did seem that the easiest option would have been just to accept what he said and not probe anymore. But I couldn't. I had been too hurt.

Niall looked about the room as though searching for the right answer. His gaze ended up focused defiantly on the leg of my chair. He sat like this for a few moments, motionless, a yellowish glow from the weak fire playing on his face.

"Yes," he said.

He didn't try to justify it.

He didn't offer any explanation.

He didn't make any excuses.

I suppose I'd asked for that. I wanted to cry. Anger was the only dam trapping the Niagaran deluge that was building up behind my eyes. I knew that if I started to cry I would lose track of what was going on and we would probably get married or not get married without ever finishing this discussion. I inhaled, holding my breath to the count of ten, so that my voice wouldn't shake when I spoke.

"Niall, how can you sleep with another woman then straight afterwards ask me to marry you?"

My voice was becoming a little shrill with hysteria. Oh, why couldn't I be one of those calm, cool, collected women who cut through and shape conversation like a talented ice sculptor?

Niall looked up at me sharply. It seemed that I had finally asked the question that was going to get us out of these endless circles. I could see that it would be an effort for him to answer it. He couldn't go for the quick yes or no option. His face became troubled as he searched for the words.

"We'd been together for ages and it'd been great. I never thought when we started going out that we would last so long."

I must have looked a bit indignant at this point because he added hurriedly, "Don't get me wrong, it was the easiest thing in the world. At the beginning I used to go off and do things just to prove I could but after a while all that didn't matter anymore. Maybe I matured or just started appreciating what I had. Whatever the reason, I was really happy and time just whizzed by. Do you know what I mean?"

I nodded. I understood the words but I didn't have the faintest notion where he was going with them. He took a deep breath. "In the past year or so you've started dropping hints about getting married." I opened my mouth to say something. However, realising that what he had said was true, I closed it again. Niall held up a placating hand. "Please, just let me finish, this isn't easy for me."

I nodded, pursed my lips and stayed quiet.

"I knew that you were disappointed at Christmas when I didn't propose."

Damn right I was: the least a girl could expect is that she be proposed to before she's thirty. I didn't say this aloud, though, because I figured it might just prove his point.

He went on, "I also knew that you thought I was holding out until Valentine's Day and I suppose I was. But I panicked. I suddenly began to wonder if we were right for each other." He paused. "What I wondered was if you were right for me. Do you understand? It's like, out of all the women I know or would know were you the one I should spend that rest of my life with?"

He directed a questioning gaze at me. I didn't change my facial expression to accommodate his. I knew that I looked like a rabbit that had been caught in the headlights, but I didn't care. He was saying things that even if I had thought them I could never say to another person, especially not the person about whom I was having the doubts. I had to confess, grudgingly, that I sort of admired his honesty. It made me wonder if I shouldn't come clean about Dara. I knew nothing had happened but it would have if the window hadn't blown in. Niall was being honest with me and maybe I owed him the same in return. But I couldn't bring myself to say it – after all, I had been on the rebound, what excuse had he? He had cast me aside and gone hunting . . . practically.

No, I'd let him finish first, he owed me that much. I continued to stare at him.

Getting no response, Niall decided to plough on. "I was scared, it was as if all my feelings for you went dead with the fear of that life sentence of a commitment."

I didn't like his choice of words but it made what he was saying very clear. What I didn't understand was why he was saying it about me. He wasn't making the commitment to just anybody, he was making it to me, the woman he loved. I wasn't just some strange objective commitment.

Before I could get angry Niall continued, "So when I said I didn't love you it wasn't really true. What I meant was that I was afraid to love you, in case . . . in case I was wrong." That part seemed reasonable enough. But he was still nowhere near explaining to me how all this had led to him sleeping with somebody else. I mean, we all have doubts but it doesn't mean we rush off into the arms of the first person who'll have us, does it?

Niall seemed to be having difficulty getting on to that bit. And I wasn't going to help him. He wasn't exactly saying things I wanted to hear. Now he was looking about him like a haunted man. He started speaking again, haltingly. "I decided . . . well, I thought I could maybe be as happy with somebody else. Anyway, when you left, there was this girl at work. She'd fancied me for ages – she was always hinting that we should go out. So I took her up on it."

My heart-rate had just gone way beyond the legal speed limit. A feeling of unfathomable dread pursued it. I didn't trust myself to speak. Besides, I didn't know what to say. I figured he was probably about to tell me that she was much better in bed than me. Or that they had a fabulous time but, really, he needed some mundanity in his life. Or that she had refused his marriage proposal so he had decided I'd do. I folded my arms and looked at him, waiting for him to continue.

"Val, don't you see what I'm trying to say? I've been an awful eejit, you're the only woman I want to be with, I was stupid to think anything else." He leaned forward on to his knees now, clasping both my hands in his. "Please, forgive me, I was really scared that things would go wrong. That you'd get bored with me or someday I'd meet somebody else and realise I'd made a mistake. I was . . . afraid." He stopped talking and looked at me, his eyes brimming with tears.

I'd never seen Niall cry. It came as a bit of a shock to find out that he could. I couldn't find my anger anymore. All I could see was Niall in pain. I reached out and touched his face. The by-now familiar feeling of regret and longing rushed in, overpowering all my other emotions.

Niall took my hand in his and kissed it. "I'm sorry Val, say you forgive me."

I wasn't sure I *could* forgive him. The regret and longing faded and now I found it difficult to forgive him for something I couldn't have done, no matter how afraid of a relationship I was. Besides, it crossed my mind that the last man who had said he was sorry to me that day had turned out to be a murderer. But Niall wasn't a murderer. He was just confused and insecure. And he loved me. He'd said so. My life was suddenly in an upright position again. Very dented and misshapen but no longer topsy-turvy.

All the same I still couldn't bring myself to lie and say I forgave him, so I simply nodded and shrugged. Niall's face broke into a smile. It was that happy, mischievous smile that had tortured my memory when I thought I had lost him for ever. He got up, dragged me out of my chair and threw his arms around me. "Oh, that's great! I knew you wouldn't let me down. Now you can leave this freezing hell-hole and come home to me again. It'll be just like it used to be."

I buried my face in his shoulder, inhaling his smell, closing my eyes as I felt his body against mine. An enormous sense of relief immersed me in its soothing warmth. Niall was back. It had all been a horrible misunderstanding. His lips brushed their way from my forehead down my nose to my lips where they remained, our kiss reminding me of how things used to be before my world had fallen apart. In his embrace I had no memory of my afternoon with Dara, or of the litany of misfortunes that had plagued me since I'd left Niall.

Everything was going to be OK.

I did notice, though, that I didn't hear him rushing in with a repeat of the marriage proposal, but that would all settle itself with time. He had just overlooked it because of the difficulty he had in talking about emotions. The important thing was that he had proposed, and that meant he did want to spend the rest of his life with me. Besides, we'd need a little time to get over this before we could get married. I knew it could all be sorted with a bit of compromise, a bit of give-and-take, that we'd be even closer once we'd worked through this.

I smiled up into Niall's face and he bent his head to kiss me again. All the emotion, angst and turmoil that I had been storing for weeks suddenly snapped free and tears streamed down my face. Niall stood back and, laughing, wiped them away saying, "It's all right, it's all right, everything is going to be all right."

That's when we heard the knock on the front door.

He would probably pick on my
furry-face slippers

Chapter Thirteen

"Are you expecting anybody?" Niall asked, in a con-
tented voice, from somewhere slightly above my head.
He mustn't have noticed how I had stiffened when I'd
heard the knock.

"No," I said, feigning slight surprise.

No, I wasn't expecting 'anybody'. Not just 'anybody'.
I was expecting a murderer.

And not just any murderer. I was expecting the murderer I'd nearly had sex with that afternoon. But this
wasn't something I wanted to explain to the man whose
arms were around me, the man who had just proposed to
me, the man whose proposal I had every intention of
accepting if he ever got round to repeating it. I thought
that 'no', while feigning slight surprise, was a very good
response.

There was another knock on the door, louder this time.
Niall lifted his head and looked out towards the hall, "I
think whoever it is wants to come in."

Of course they wanted to come in. How else were they
going to kill me?

I broke into a stage whisper. "Maybe we shouldn't answer it. It must be some sort of weirdo to call by this late. If we stay quiet they'll just go away."

Niall looked puzzled and spoke in a normal voice. "It's only eight o'clock." His look changed to pity. "Don't be afraid, you're not on your own anymore, I'll be right beside you when you open the door."

I had to think very fast to come up with a feasible excuse. "Niall, the guards said I wasn't to answer the door for anybody, what with the Dead German and the break-in and everything."

Niall scratched his chin. "I thought you said you hadn't reported the break-in."

Who was he? Bloody Sherlock Holmes? Can't a girl even tell a simple lie now without some smart-ass taking her up on it? I back-pedalled. "I meant with the Dead German . . . if they knew about the break-in they'd have said the same thing . . . I'm sure."

I was jabbering now. Niall hesitated for a moment.

The knocking started again, and then a man's voice shouted from outside, "Val, are you there?"

It was Dara.

Niall smiled and said, "See? It's no weirdo, it's somebody who knows you. Do you recognise the voice?"

I shook my head. I now had the feeling that no matter what I said we would open that door.

"Come on, we'll answer it together."

Niall took my hand and led me towards the hall. He was quite determined to answer the door. I still couldn't come up with any acceptable reason not to. Besides, Dara was hardly going to kill both of us. As soon as the door opened he'd see that I wasn't alone and he'd go away. I hoped.

Niall reached for the latch, pulling the door towards him so that he was momentarily hidden. I was left standing in the doorway facing Dara. He looked untidy and distressed but even handsomer than I had allowed myself to remember. A swarm of confused emotions smothered my fear. I was glad that Niall was behind me and couldn't see the expression on my face. I noticed a mudstain down one side of Dara's jeans, a result of his fall in the wet yard, and I reminded myself that he was here to kill me. Before I could react to this he declared, "Thank God you're here, Val! I've got to talk to you."

"I don't have anything to say to you," I said shortly, reaching for the door.

Dara stretched his hand forward as though to prevent me from closing it and gasped, "But, Val . . ." He stopped dead; he had just noticed Niall and, not recognising him, obviously thought the better of voicing his threat.

"Go away, Dara," I said flatly. I could feel Niall moving behind me. Dara's hesitation indicated that he wasn't about to slaughter us on the spot. I felt greatly relieved by this. All I needed now was for him to get out of the doorway so that I could close the door and go back to where Niall and I had left off.

Dara, however, had no intention of collaborating. He glanced swiftly from me to Niall and back again then fixed his eyes on mine. "We can't just leave it like this. I don't know why you ran away but I'm sure we can work something out." His gaze became beseeching. "Please Val."

He didn't know why I'd run away! God, he had nerve. As if I'd still be alive if I hadn't run away.

As if I wouldn't be lying on my back somewhere, staring at the night sky through dead, glassy eyes if I hadn't run away.

As if the Dead German and I wouldn't be discussing whose shift it was for Undead hauntings of the Burren if I hadn't run away.

Oh, he was very cool. He was also pretty perceptive because he noticed the look of disbelief on my face. "What have I done?" he burst out in astonishment.

I made a God-you-must-think-I'm-so-stupid gesture with my eyes and tried to close the door. It bounced back on making contact with Dara's raised arm.

"Go away, Dara," I shrieked, a little afraid now.

Niall moved swiftly into the doorway. "You heard what she said, pisshead, beat it," he snarled.

Dara raised his hands and backed away from the door. "I just want to talk, that's all," he said calmly.

"Well, nobody here wants to talk to you so why don't you fuck off?" Niall had never been one to beat about the bush.

Dara now had the look of a man who had grasped the situation. He cast a hurt look at me and turning away said, "I'll call round tomorrow. OK, Val?"

Before I could nod or shake my head he had moved off into the darkness towards his car. I closed the door, breathing a sigh of relief, turned to smile at Niall and said, "Thanks, you were great."

But Niall wasn't looking too great. In fact, the expression on Niall's face reminded me a lot of the dark sky that had shrouded the stormy coast all day.

He was scowling. It was one of those great big irreversible scowls that turns your whole face downwards. The type of scowl that if you'd made it as a child your granny would have told you that the wind was going to change and you were going to be left with that face for ever.

"Niall, what's the matter?" I asked, genuinely puzzled.

"What's the matter?" he demanded, his eyes flashing into life. "You ask me what's the matter? Who the hell was that guy?" He glared at me.

Oh-oh, Niall seemed pretty put out by Dara's visit. He didn't seem to have warmed to him at all. It just proved that he was a better judge of character than I was. All the same, I thought it might be better if I didn't blurt out everything about Dara in one go. It would be best if I just presented a rough idea of who he was, sort of brushed over things, maybe give a general all-round impression to start with. Then, after a while, I could tell him about Dara being the murderer.

"Aam, he's . . . he's the son of the solicitor who dealt with my case . . . sort of. He has a farm on the other side of the village," I said, matter-of-factly and, I think, informatively.

Niall snorted. "I don't want to know what he bloody does – he could be the Yorkshire Ripper for all I care. What I want to know is what's he to you? What the fuck's he doing coming around here talking to you like that?"

He stood in the hall in front of me, shoulders hunched,

fists clenched, his face contorted with anger. I'd seen him like this before, but only about things that had nothing to do with me. He'd get this mad if somebody lied to him or something. I'd never seen him so angry with me. It was as if he'd changed personality or was lost in an impenetrable fog of fury. I couldn't figure out why he was so angry at Dara. I mean, yes, he had been a little persistent, but he'd only been like that because he wanted to kill me. That shouldn't have affected Niall because he'd had no way of knowing.

"He was a bit out of line, wasn't he?" I said doubtfully, not sure what sort of answer Niall was looking for. I'd picked the wrong one, and as his expression darkened I thought he was going to burst with rage.

"Stop trying to make excuses, just stop now! Is he your lover or not? Yes or no?"

Oh-ho!

Now I understood. Niall was jealous. That was very sweet. I'd never seen him this jealous before – it was so flattering. I laughed and held out my arms to him. "Ah, come on, Niall, you have nothing to worry about. I thought he was a nice guy but nothing really happened."

It was true that nothing had really happened and, anyway, Niall and I had split up so it wasn't like I had been unfaithful even if it had felt like that.

"What do you mean 'nothing really happened'? What exactly went on between you two?" His fury was almost tangible.

I paused for a moment before answering. He seemed to have really gone off the rails about this. Maybe the best way to handle it was just to be gentle and reasonable and then he would understand that he had nothing to worry about.

"Look, I met Dara last week, we got on very well, we had a couple of dates, but now I know that he isn't my type and that's really all there was to it." I shrugged my shoulders and smiled at him cutely – at least I hoped it was cutely.

He looked down at his feet and thought about what I had said. He seemed to be a bit more in control, more like the Niall I knew and loved. Then he raised his eyes and looked straight at me. "So when did you see him last?"

Now, that was an awkward one, wasn't it? My change of heart wouldn't sound too credible when he heard that our last date had been only that afternoon. But I wasn't going to lie. Besides the fact that my lies always went wrong, I didn't want to lie. Niall would just have to accept that when he and I were apart I had moved on a bit. It didn't mean that I loved him any less, it had just been a temporary lapse. "This afternoon," I said a bit defiantly. "We had lunch at his place."

"And how long did this lunch take exactly?" Niall asked, with a sort of suspicious sneer.

This conversation was starting to feel uncomfortable. It was like the first time you wear your new little black party number. The day you bought it, you see, you had optimistically got it a size too small because that morning you had started a new diet and you were feeling promisingly slim. However, by the time you got to wear it several diet-forgotten dinners later, it was feeling uncomfortably tight. That's what this conversation was like: uncomfortably tight. Indignation was trying to burst through the seams. I thought Niall was taking this whole issue a bit too far. I mean, it wasn't as if his recent record was squeaky clean! I felt like pointing this out to him in no uncertain terms, but I held back. The poor guy was probably still feeling insecure because he had been completely honest with me and now he was sensitive and vulnerable. I decided that all he needed was a bit more reassurance.

"Niall, I thought we were finished. If I'd known you still loved me I'd never have gone near him. Honest."

"Oh, sure," Niall spat. "You love me so much you don't see me for a couple of weeks so you have to go off with the first stud you meet. You just want to have a man around and it seems any man will do."

Damn, I was getting angry. I could feel the anger steadily edging its way across the decision to be reassuring. He was pushing me so far that I was going to topple right over the edge. I was aware that he was hurt and insecure and all the rest of it, but now I was mad. He hadn't even given me an opportunity to tell him that Dara was a murderer. And now I didn't want to tell him, because now we had moved on to the Planet of Principle.

On Principle he shouldn't talk to me like that.

On Principle I could see somebody else if Niall was seeing somebody else.

On Principle I could have whoever the hell I liked calling to my door.

So, I lined up my Principle army and attacked.

"What's it to you, anyway?" I said shortly, afraid to show my anger because, despite my principles, I didn't want to lose Niall again.

"What's it to me?" Niall barked. "I'll tell you what it is to me. I just asked you to marry me and I have no intention of becoming engaged to someone who goes slutting about the country as soon as I leave her alone for a moment."

I felt like he had just slapped me. I also felt like I needed a reality check. This couldn't be Niall speaking: his mind didn't work like that and, if it did, how come I wasn't finding out about it until now? It seemed that the only correlation between my reality and his was that he had proposed to me. At least he had admitted that much. Even if it had been just to unpropose. I didn't have the slightest idea how to argue against Niall's seeming irrationality. I decided to try and do a bit of clarification to see if he was really saying what he seemed to be saying.

"Just exactly what do you mean by that, Niall?"

"Oh, you needn't bother coming over all innocent with me, Val. I've known what you're like for years."

Now I was genuinely surprised. I had no idea what he was talking about.

"What?"

"You must have thought I was an awful eejit," Niall sneered. "Do you think I didn't notice? I'd leave you alone at parties just to watch you try to hit on other men and you'd have a go every single time. And if things weren't going your way you'd come and check up on me just to be sure I was still on standby."

This was incredible. I had thought I understood at least partially what he was talking about, that we were having an accusatory, jealous confrontation, but now it was more than that. Niall seemed to be saying that I had some sort of pathological dependence on the attentions of men, and instead of saying anything to me about it all this time he had just watched and grown resentful.

"That's just so ridiculous—"

"Is it? You think back and tell me how many times you stayed with me for a whole party."

"But that's because—" I stopped. I realised that what I was about to say was an accusation about his behaviour at parties. And I knew that it would get us nowhere. I knew that this wasn't really the issue and I didn't want us to tumble into a festering quagmire of old resentments.

I changed tack. "Niall, you don't know what you're saying, you're upset—"

"Upset? Of course I'm upset! Wouldn't you be upset if you had just swallowed all your pride and come grovelling to tell someone that you loved them, only to find that they were involved with someone else?" Niall was almost shouting by the time he got to the end of that outburst.

I was resolute. "I'm not involved with someone else . . . and, besides, you and I had split up."

"Split up? Is that what you call it? You just walked out – packed a bag and off you went, as if I didn't matter a damn. We probably hadn't been to enough parties over Christmas for you to flirt at, so you ran off to see what you could pick up here."

"Hang on a minute, Niall, you said you didn't love me, that's why I left. The next thing I heard you were with somebody else. I'd call that pretty split up, wouldn't you?" Now I was shouting.

"Oh, yeah, you'll call it anything that suits you."

This conversation didn't seem to be going anywhere. I decided I would try to make one last inroad into logic. I took a deep breath to quieten my voice. "Niall, you were going out with somebody else so why shouldn't I? Even if we ignore what you said about not loving me, why should it be all right for you to see someone else and not all right for me?"

"It's completely different," Niall growled.

Obviously logic wasn't good for Niall. In fact it seemed this whole conversation wasn't good for Niall. Come to that, it wasn't very good for me either. I started to wonder how it had begun, how we had got stuck on this roundabout of accusations.

His voice cut across my mental back-tracking. "How was I supposed to react? Just sit at home after you left? No, I got on with my life. And, believe it or not, women do find me attractive. They always have. It's not just you and your men, you know."

I didn't know. "What men, Niall?"

"Oh, don't start that again. Wasn't that scene at the door just now proof enough? What men!"

"Niall, I was never once unfaithful to you through all our relationship. I just don't know what you're talking about."

"That's the problem with you, isn't it? You come over all dumb whenever something you don't want to talk about comes up. Well, I'm sick of it. Sick of it, you hear?"

I couldn't not have heard at that volume. Niall was talking like somebody who didn't like me – in fact, he was talking like someone who hated me. And while I could accept someone not liking me, I didn't understand why Niall suddenly hated me. It didn't seem to be something I had done that was bothering him: it seemed to be me, the way I was. Whatever way that was.

"Niall, what are you saying?"

" 'Niall, what are you saying?' " he mimicked. "What do you think I'm saying?"

I thought about that for a second but I couldn't come up with an answer. "I don't know."

"What I'm saying is that if you want to continue with our relationship there will have to be a few changes. Right?"

"Like what?" I genuinely wanted to know how I could make things better between us.

"Well, for one thing I don't want you quizzing me every time there's a minute in my life that you can't account for. My life is my own, not some sort of appendage to our diary." He paused for breath. "And I won't be treated like some sort of meal-ticket-gigolo who escorts you to and from parties . . . Or is wheeled out when you want to show your single friends that you have a boyfriend."

I didn't say anything. I was trying to figure out this view of our relationship, trying to understand what he meant.

Niall wasn't holding back. "And another thing, you can stop hassling me about your bloody wedding. You haven't a hope in hell of snaring me. You're just like all the rest, trying to trap me." He stopped.

I think I'd stopped breathing. He sounded like a total psycho. This was the man who had just proposed to me and told me he loved me. At any moment I expected him to take out a knife and start a frenzied stabbing attack – you know, a succession of those really short fast stabs to the chest – or he might even resort to the *Fatal Attraction* option and boil my pet rabbit. But, then, I didn't have a pet rabbit so he would probably pick on my furry-face slippers.

That last outburst had really hurt. One question emerged through the smarting pain. Who were 'all the rest' who had tried to trap him? What 'all the rest' was I 'just like'? Somehow without me forming them the words popped out – well, fell out, really. 'Popped' would have required some enthusiasm and all mine had been trampled under the stampede of Niall's attack.

"Who are 'all the rest'?"

He didn't answer. I waited. Niall still didn't answer. He stared blindly at the phone connection lying on the hall floor, his head tilted to one side as it always was when he was thinking. I closed my eyes to resist the feeling of regret and longing that this familiar pose would provoke, but all I felt was a tight feeling in my heart and a sense of detachment. The detachment came as a relief. It would hold the hysteria at bay.

"Niall, what 'rest'?"

Niall breathed out heavily and moved his fixed gaze to the kitchen door. His mouth was twisted downwards in a bitter line. "See? That's more of it. Everything I say you pick into tiny little pieces. You can't let me be myself, can you?"

It seemed to me that we were clean out of straight answers. All I could think of now was what he wasn't telling me. All I could think was that this woman he had just been with hadn't been the first, that at various times during our relationship there had been others. Of course, I had no proof of this, he might have been just saying it to annoy me.

I resented him wanting to annoy me.

I resented him accusing me of constantly flirting and looking for men.

I resented him reducing the life I dreamt we would have together to a trapping exercise.

We were standing opposite each other in the hall. I was staring at him but he refused to meet my eye. He must have been able to feel my anger and hurt but he stood as though he had been turned to stone. He was blocking me out, just as he had the day we broke up, only this time I knew it wasn't that he didn't love me, it was that he disliked me. No matter how many conditions he imposed and I met, it would never alter the fact that he didn't like me.

I'm not saying you have to like the person you love, far from it, but I wasn't even sure that Niall loved me and if he did I'd have to figure out if that was the type of love I wanted.

I knew that getting angry with Niall wouldn't make any difference. Anything I said now would just make him more annoyed.

What I really wanted to do was close my fists and beat him with them until he begged for forgiveness at having hurt me.

What I really wanted to do was put my head on his shoulder and cry soft tears, just as I had in the kitchen earlier, and forget that the last half-hour had ever happened.

What I wasn't going to do was stand in this unfriendly hall any longer. I turned away from Niall to move towards my room. "I'm going to go to bed, Niall. I'm tired."

He didn't look at me or move until I tried to walk past him. As I did so he reached out his hand and grabbed my arm roughly, swinging me around to face him. "That's right, walk away. Ignore it and it will disappear, that's your theory, isn't it? Well, you can't walk away from the truth. I don't need you, I've never needed you. There have always been others and there always will be. You're not that precious!"

I inhaled sharply, frightened now by his angry hatred and his seemingly threatening proximity. He stood gripping my arm, his teeth gritted, daring me to respond. Seconds passed slowly. I had no answer. All I had was information I didn't want and an overwhelming desire to get away from Niall.

Silently I tore myself from his grip, ran down the corridor to my room, threw myself inside and closed the door. I leant my back against it and screamed silent tears at the ceiling. Earlier that evening I had been afraid of being murdered, now all I could think was how much less painful it would be if I were dead. I knew that I would never have the courage to do it myself but a nice neat little murder would do the trick. It seemed a reasonable idea now to go out and offer myself to Dara for assassination. It would solve both our problems.

So there had been other women, not just now when

we had split up but all along, and I had never noticed. Was something wrong with me that I just didn't see things? Why was it that everything I touched seemed to turn bad? I got a glimpse of how things could be and then they would disintegrate. Even Niall, who up until today had simply been indecisive and maybe unfaithful, had turned into the boyfriend from hell. Only a short time ago I had been happily immersed in our getting back together and planning how to cajole him into reproposing. Now my wedding dream had been revealed as 'trapping.'

Was it? Had I been trying to 'trap' him? I mean, if he had told me that he was completely anti-marriage I'd have dropped the subject, but he'd never said a word. He always behaved as though that was what he wanted as well. He'd joke and drop hints and make references just the same as I did. He could have mentioned that marriage was a problem. To me it was just the thing you do at around a certain age, like learning to drive or wearing your skirts a bit longer. I didn't even have an opinion on it. If I had known he had one I would gladly have taken it into account. Instead he had waited until now and just vomited all this gall on my dreams.

But it wasn't just my dreams he had sullied. It was also my self-esteem. And there was something far more fundamental than that. He had made me doubt the very image I had of myself. Was I really the type of woman who queried and pursued him so that he had to account for every moment of his time? Was that what had driven him to other women? Was my world so uninteresting to me that I needed another person's life to fulfil it? I walked away from the door and threw myself on the bed, my eyes fixed on the ceiling. Outside in the hall I heard footsteps and the clink of glass against glass. Niall must have got bored with his own company in the living room and decided to go to bed with whatever bottle he had selected. I hoped he would realise that Rachel's room was occupied and go to the other bedroom. Mind you, telling occupied from unoccupied would be no mean feat in the condition those rooms were in.

But he could sleep in the sock on the clothes-line for all I cared. I lay on my bed going through every party we had ever attended, trying to unearth evidence of the flirtatiousness Niall had spoken of. At the same time I tried to think what other women he could possibly have been with and when.

I couldn't find any.

That wasn't just me avoiding the truth. On the one hand I genuinely couldn't find any other-man-intent at all – I had been totally devoted to Niall – and on the other I found it difficult to accept that Niall had either the time or the inclination to be with other women. Maybe I was too trusting, too devoted, and now it seemed that my devotion had grown and matured into my own private little monster. I had pampered, nourished and cared for the beast until it had turned on and devoured me. Remembering Niall's words and the expression of violent anger on his face brought on a fresh bout of crying.

Just when I thought all the tears had stopped.

Just when I thought my life was going to get back to normal, it had all fallen down in pieces again.

I couldn't go on like this. I had to make some sort of decision. I had avoided decision-making up to this. When I had thought that there was something between Dara and me it had been easy. I could just move from the loss of Niall to the excitement and distraction of a new love with Dara. I hadn't had to think. Life had just carried me along. Now that I didn't have anybody else to run away to I would have to consider where I stood with Niall. And it would appear that I didn't stand anywhere with him, and if what he said was true I'd never stood anywhere with him. So, even if he hadn't blown my romantic notion of our perfect union in marriage out of the water, was there really anything in our relationship on which to build a marriage? I was wading knee-deep in this stark realisation when I heard a car pull up outside. Before I could work myself into a Dara-panic I heard a key turn in the front door.

It was Rachel. Things mustn't have gone too well with Jamie if she was back. I couldn't muster enough interest to go and inquire. She stumbled about the hall, went into the kitchen briefly, then headed for her room and closed the door.

Seconds later she burst into my room. With a startled look on her face and indignation in her voice she proclaimed, "Val, there's a man in my bed."

Love was just another
four-letter word

Chapter Fourteen

"But what has he done to upset you so much, Val?" Rachel's face was almost comic in her concern.

"He, I, he—" I burst into tears. Rachel moved from her position at the end of the bed, put her arm around me and stayed there rocking me until my breathing settled.

It hadn't taken her long, after she burst into the room with the scent of male on her nostrils, to realise she was in a casualty zone. She took one look at my tear-stained, stricken face and forgot all her indignation. She quizzed me gently until she found out, if not the cause of my grief at least the source.

When I was calmer she said, "Well, it does seem as though he's been with other women but he must care about you if he came all this way to see you, mustn't he?"

I shrugged my shoulders, too exhausted from crying to work my way through the maze of contradictions that had made up my evening. "I don't know, Rachel. You know, he said things that only someone who hated me could say."

Rachel nodded, "I don't want to sound repetitive, but

you remember I've always said that Niall is undeveloped? I mean, with the amount of drink and drugs he takes it's obvious he doesn't want to develop either. Saying vicious and hurtful things is a symptom of that. He'll even tell lies to hurt you more. He may not have been with other women, except that recent one, but he knew it would really piss you off if you thought he had. He'll strike out if he feels threatened or hurt. Did something happen to make him feel bad about himself?"

Big question. Well, no. Not so much a big question as a very big answer.

I sighed and told her the story of Dara's visit. She was dying to know why Dara was so determined to see me but I just hinted at a disagreement and left it at that. I'd fill her in later. The last thing I needed just then was her outbreak of shocked disbelief if I told her that Dara was a murderer. Even I had to admit that my having a romantic lunch date with a killer was much more interesting than my boyfriend – my ex-boyfriend – being hurtful. I mean, given the choice, which would you choose as a topic of conversation?

Rachel nodded and tutted as I he-said-I-saided my way in more detail through my encounter with Niall. By the time I got to the end Rachel was incensed. "He is so spiritually bereft, so out of touch with his inner self. Anybody who wants to hurt someone else that much is completely scrambled. You really should pity him."

Yeah, like I'm going to pity somebody who picks on me just because they've had a bad day. I don't think so! Besides, if there was any pity going around why didn't Niall keep a bit for me instead of attacking with such precision? I didn't see why I had to be the 'big' person all the time.

Rachel could see I wasn't convinced. "Val, it's not just him. You have to have pity for yourself as well, and I don't mean self-pity, I mean a healthy compassion. After all, there must be something in you that's drawing all this dysfunctionality."

Great. I was just a maladjusted magnet. I'd forgotten that with every dose of sympathy I received from Rachel I'd get a triple serving of her take on life. And while it was a relief to pour my heart out it wasn't like she was giving me any concrete advice, was it? I still didn't know what to do about Niall.

But Rachel wasn't finished. "You have to learn to respect yourself more, Val. You mustn't be afraid to ask for what you want and the universe will provide. But you have to get out there and ask. That's what I did with me and Jamie, and things have turned out fine." She smiled at me, her eyes shining with happiness.

Oh, my God, Jamie! I'd completely forgotten. I hadn't even enquired about it. I felt so selfish. There I was wandering on about myself and Niall while Rachel had probably just gone through a similar experience . . . Maybe not, though, judging by the expression on her face. "Oh, wow, I'm sorry, Rach, how did that go?"

"It went really well," Rachel said, with a look of dizzy happiness. "We've decided to get back together."

What? Get back together after all she told me about that cheating wagon? After all she had said about feeling like she was just a stop-gap until someone more interesting came along? I didn't say that – I had enough bother without Rachel hating me as well. What I said was, "Well, that's nice, I'm really glad . . . but I thought you said that . . ." I had to be careful here because what I wanted to say was, ". . . you couldn't stay with her if she was always being unfaithful. Aren't you afraid you'll catch something?" or ". . . I thought you were tired of being a filler-in between her other relationships. Does this mean you like being second best?"

What I actually said was ". . . that you weren't entirely happy with how things were when you were together."

Rachel smiled. "Yes, that's true, I had allowed myself to become very angry because I had lost sight of my own inner strength. I had forgotten that all that really matters is that we love each other."

Yeah, that was a fairly basic requirement, all right, but what about all that infidelity stuff? I mean, having an open relationship either bothers you or it doesn't, and the last time we had discussed it, sharing Jamie with other people had really bothered Rachel. "But Rachel, I thought you said that Jamie seeing other women was the reason you split up. Is she going to stop doing that?"

Rachel looked a bit perturbed. "Aam, no, but that's not the point. The point is, she loves me, she has always loved me and she has always told me this. And I love her. I can't just not love her because of what some might see as an imperfection. To be loved is one of the greatest gifts of the universe. I'm not going to just throw that away. Look at me! Now I'm happy, yesterday I wasn't happy. Being with Jamie makes me happy."

There was no denying she seemed happy.

Cereal Lover

I remembered happy. Happy was what I had been earlier that evening when Niall had said he wanted to marry me and everything looked as though it was going to be all right. Happy, mixed with an enormous dollop of excited, was what I had been that afternoon when Dara had started kissing my neck. I'd been happy twice that day. That was a record. Maybe I'd used it all up, all the happy. That was it for the year, probably for life, because I certainly wasn't happy as I sat there listening to Rachel's theories on love. And I couldn't envisage ever being happy again. Maybe I should take a leaf out of Rachel's book and be more accepting. Why couldn't I just kiss and make up and get on with life?

But now that I thought about it that's exactly what I had done. I had completely forgiven the break-up, the other woman, the length of time it had taken Niall to get in touch. I'd overlooked the whole lot. I had done exactly what Rachel had done, except, of course, that I didn't for a moment expect Niall to see other women again. I'd been prepared to let it all go but he had moved the goalposts. Damn it, he'd moved the playing-field. And I was left standing on an unmarked patch of naked wasteland. And another thing, a big thing that I had overlooked. He'd said he didn't love me.

Now, I know that I'd been prepared to ignore that earlier on when he had proposed and said he loved me. But since then he had taken all that back. And that was the difference between Rachel and me. Jamie had always said that she loved Rachel. She hadn't woken up one morning, savaged all the toast, and declared she didn't love her. That was a big difference. Jamie loved Rachel and didn't try to change her. Rachel loved Jamie and had now decided that she wasn't going to try to change her.

I loved Niall just the way he was or, rather, had been, but Niall wanted to change me. Maybe he had been telling the truth when he said he didn't love me. What he loved was somebody he wanted me to be. Somebody completely different. Perhaps he had reached the point in our relationship when he wanted me to become Grace. Amazing Grace. Manifestation of man's fantasies.

I couldn't accept Niall because he didn't accept me. Reaching that conclusion brought back the dark memory of all the things he had said to me in the hall after Dara had left. The tireless class of tears were nipping daintily from behind their desks, slapping each other on the back at the idea of going out to play. At the same time the skin on my cheeks tightened in protest at the very suggestion of more crying.

Rachel sensed the oncoming outburst. "Oh, come on, Val, let it go. Imagine you're surrounded by a white light that is all-loving. Immerse yourself in that love. Things will look much clearer and much better to you if you do."

Love!

I might as well immerse myself in boiling oil.

Damn.

Fuck.

Love was just another four-letter word.

Rachel knew I wasn't taking the bait. She sighed and shook her head. "Let it go, it's not going to do you any good if you hold on to it. Storing that sort of hurt and hate only attracts more."

She paused to think for a moment. "Maybe your time with Niall is over."

Yeah, she would say that because she didn't like him. It was all right for her to bitch and complain about her partner then go running back, but it wasn't all right for me!

I fumed a bit. I didn't say anything to Rachel, though, because somewhere in whatever part of me worked these things out a flag was flying. Well, it wasn't so much flying as being waved feverishly above the trenches by an apprehensive hand. And I suppose it wasn't so much a flag as a small rag of indefinable colour tied to a stick. But I saw it. And I knew what it meant. It meant that I felt that what Rachel had said was true. Maybe my time with Niall *was* over. Maybe all the hurtful things that he had said, along with his claim about the other women, was the death-blow to my feelings for him.

Ah.

Now it was my turn to sigh. "You're probably right, Rach, and I don't even know how it happened."

Of course, it killed me to have to admit to Rachel that she was right. But, then, it always killed me to admit to anybody that they were right and that I, just perhaps, hadn't been 100 per cent right.

Rachel brushed back a strand of stray hair that had been hanging unattended over my face. "That's better," she said. "Now open yourself up to the positive. Only let positive thoughts into your mind and good things will happen to you."

Her expression changed and a flash of inquisitive interest came into her eyes. "So, tell me, what happened with you and Dara?"

She was finally getting back to the topic that really appealed to her. I groaned. It all seemed so ludicrous now, so removed from the situation I was in. It was as though Dara had been whisked away in the gale-force wind of Niall's emotional turbulence. My belief that he was a murderer had faded because the whole Dead German situation had paled into unimportance.

"Come on, Val. You've got to tell me, you were gone for ages. And when you got back here you looked like something had happened!"

Oh, something had happened, all right, but not what Rachel thought. And certainly not what I had hoped for. I outlined to her in rapid detail the events of the afternoon, glossing over the more intimate moments in the lead-up to the window blow-in.

When I got to that point, she gasped, her face wide-eyed disbelief. "I don't believe it!" Her hands shot up to her mouth. "I really thought he was the one for you. Especially as he communed with nature and all. Well, you just can't tell, can you? You either have some very bad karma or you're being well protected. Which is it?"

What a question. It was like asking a child immediately after birth whether it was better to be in the womb or out of it. Besides the fact that the child would not understand the question, there was also a strong element of powerlessness involved, definitely a no-choice situation. On those grounds I refused to answer.

Rachel didn't seem to notice, and ploughed on with her theorising. "You didn't get cut or injured physically so even if it is bad karma there's someone watching over you."

I held up my hands in surrender before she analysed the smashed-window incident to death. "Hang on, hang on? Rachel. Wait until I'm finished before you decide whether I'm doomed or blessed."

Rachel frowned a little at my lack of reverence for the mystical but made no comment. She didn't want to put me off telling the rest of what had happened between Dara and myself by protesting too loudly. I went on with the story. When I got to the part about the passport Rachel looked shocked. She was speechless with disbelief as I concluded with my late arrival back at the house. I sprinkled this part of the history with just a gentle helping of guilt-inducing poor-me-isms to make her look ashamed. "Val, I had no idea. You should have told me. I'd never have left you here all on your own if I'd known. You know that, don't you?" I shrugged, throwing a little cloak of doubt over her affirmation.

Much to my gratification she almost broke into a wail. "You must believe me! I never intended leaving you all alone in that situation. I had to see Jamie but I'd never have gone if you'd told me what had happened." She looked as though she was going to cry.

That was the last thing I needed. If she started crying I'd have to comfort her and I wasn't yet ready to relinquish my spotlight position as the centre of attention. "Forget it, you weren't to know. Maybe I could have explained better or something."

My voice trailed off and Rachel looked relieved. She took a short breath. "I don't know what to say about Dara being the murderer. It's incredible!" Then she looked puzzled. "But you said he called by here tonight, earlier on, that he met Niall. What did he do? How did he act? What did he say to you? He must guess that you know he's the murderer."

I nodded. "I'd say that he came here to sort me out, kill me, you know, but he changed his plan when he saw Niall. Said that he'd call back tomorrow."

Rachel looked as if somebody had just tried to steal her underwear while she was still wearing it. "He never. Can you believe the cheek?" Her expression changed. "You're going to have to do something about your karma. Maybe some aura manipulation would help, I know this great woman who could probably fit you in at short notice."

I ignored what she said. The only thing I was going to manipulate were my movements so that I didn't bump into Dara again while he was head-hunting me.

I still hadn't worked out what I was going to do about him. At the moment I felt safe because Rachel and Niall were in the house but what about tomorrow? Rachel would inevitably want to dash back to Jamie as soon as she had packed her bag and Niall . . . I had no idea what Niall wanted to do but I had a feeling that it wouldn't include me.

And it wouldn't include me because I didn't want it to include me. Had I just made that decision? Oh, no, I was getting a bit ahead of myself. What was I thinking? I knew what I was thinking but I wasn't at all sure that it was what I should be thinking. It frightened me.

With one deft sweep I shoved that entire subject to the back of my mind where I locked it up. Then I was just left with my original worry.

"I don't know what to do about Dara. I don't really

want to go to the guards but even if I did go I don't have any proof."

Rachel looked a bit disconcerted that I had totally ignored her karma-manipulation suggestion, but she didn't get annoyed. She was too delighted with her decision to go back to Jamie for that. Instead she looked at me pessimistically and said, "You're going to have to do something, because if what you say is correct the sooner Dara gets you out of the way the better for him."

I felt sick. It's one thing to think that the man you nearly had sex with wants you dead but it's quite another thing to hear somebody else say it. "Maybe I should just leave. If I get in the car and start driving now I'll be back in Dublin in a few hours and I could hide out there. Or I could go to London . . ." I was panicked. It looked like I had to plan a whole new life. Incognito.

I could see myself in fifty years' time in some hot, sprawling city in South America. I'd be a little old lady using a walking-stick like a crutch as I shuffled fearfully the few metres from my apartment to the grocery. My dark glasses would hide my eyes, now faded with age, which would dart watchfully towards every doorway and stranger. I would mumble to myself in English broken by decades of Spanish speaking. Suddenly I would jump at the sound of a dog barking nearby and, clutching my cane tighter in my bird's-foot hand, I would turn and limp back to my apartment. Later, in the cooler, emptier, safer darkness, I would come out to do my shopping.

Alone, destitute, in an alien land that was never home. *Nemo.*

I was *really* panicked. I didn't want to spend the rest of my life being someone else. Well, to tell the truth I wouldn't mind spending my life being someone else, as long as I could pick who to be. Like, let's say Athina Roussel, heir to the Onassis fortune, or Kate Moss, supermodel – anybody rich and famous really. Oh, yeah, and beautiful as well. Then I could afford loads of plastic surgery and stay beautiful for ever. At my age I'd probably have to start right away at the plastic surgery if I were to salvage anything.

Oh, no! At this stage of my life, if Dara did kill me, I wasn't even going to die young. The news reports would say that a 'woman's' body had been found. A 'woman'! I wasn't old enough to be a woman, I hadn't done enough to be a woman, I couldn't be a woman. And if I wasn't a woman I was definitely too young to die. I must have been hyperventilating at this point because Rachel grabbed my arm and said emphatically, "Breathe. Come on, inhale and exhale slowly, come on, come on, you can do it, breathe, breathe. It's not going to do you any good getting so uptight."

Uptight? What did she mean uptight? I wasn't uptight, I was concerned, and justifiably so. It was all right for her: she wasn't next on anybody's hit list. She wasn't facing years in exile separated from her loved ones. And even if she was at least she had loved ones to be separated from. So maybe I was a bit uptight, I had things to be uptight about. Nevertheless I listened to her advice and took a few deep breaths. It didn't alter reality but at least I stopped gasping.

"That's better," Rachel said, patting my shoulder.

"Breath is the source of life. Let it flow through you. It will bring you comfort and strength."

"What am I going to do, Rachel?"

All that breathing had calmed me enough to ask questions.

"I don't know," she replied, her face glum. "We need to talk to someone who knows about this sort of thing, somebody who could advise us."

I blinked and wiped my sleeve along the line of my chin to soak up tears that had come seemingly from nowhere and were dangling there. There had to be somebody I could ask who wouldn't have me committed immediately for one paranoia problem or other. I folded my arms and chewed my lip in a concentrated thinking pose.

Meanwhile, Rachel sat with her eyes closed, her face towards the ceiling and her hands upturned on her lap. I expected her to start humming in a monotone any second. She was distracting me. "Rachel, what are you doing?"

"I'm opening myself to the Higher Being so that we will be guided in our search for wisdom."

She tilted her head even higher. I shut my eyes so that I wouldn't have to watch her. Great, I thought, from behind my closed eyes, I'm about to be murdered and my friend is worshipping the roof. The reminder that Dara wanted to murder me made my eyes shoot open again. My heartbeat started to increase. "Maybe we ought to wake Niall and just tell him," I said to the meditating Rachel.

She didn't move or open her eyes. "I don't think saying

anything to Niall would do you much good," she said, with a tone of finality.

"Ah, come on, he's not that bad. You're just saying that because you don't like him. I'm sure if he heard about the danger I'm in he would do something to help me."

I felt suddenly resentful of Rachel's dislike of Niall. She must have sensed my anger because she opened one eye slowly and tilted her head towards me. "I'm not saying he wouldn't help you, Val. It's just I'm not so sure he'd hear you. The vodka bottle is beside the bed, empty, and he didn't budge when I walloped him with a pillow. No, I wouldn't say that Niall is going to be much good to you for a while." She closed her eye again and redirected to the ceiling.

"But there isn't anybody else," I said hysterically. "I'll just wait until he's sober and then tell him."

Rachel opened her eyes, clasped her hands in her lap, looked at me and sighed. I was obviously coming between her and the Higher Being big-time. "I have a better idea," she said calmly. "Why don't you ask Terry?"

Terry!

I looked at her in stunned silence.

Why on earth would I ask Terry? He'd probably take it as some sort of come-on. He'd laugh, cross his legs in that short-man way and say, "Tell me that little story again, but this time could you do it in a French accent? Oh, and by the way I have a little black and white outfit here that I'd like you to wear while you're doing it, if you don't mind."

"I'm not positive that Terry is the best idea," I said,

through gritted teeth, unsure whether to laugh or be appalled.

"Oh, but he is," Rachel said brightly. "He is. Don't you see? He's a solicitor so he'd know about the legal side of things. He's Dara's father so he will naturally be interested in anything that concerns him and his office is a ten-minute drive away. He's the one."

I thought about what she'd said. She had a point. If I set aside the fact that I believed he was, well, 'romantically' interested in me, he was the perfect choice. And if what Dara had said was true about how he always tried to help him out, then he could probably solve the dilemma without anybody getting hurt or having to do a long prison sentence or anything. And, besides, it was either him or Niall, and I really wanted to avoid giving Niall the opportunity to tell me he'd be glad if someone murdered me, and that he really had to be going as he had all these other women to entertain.

Yeah. Terry it would be.

I nodded my agreement at Rachel, who smiled back. "See? The Higher Being does know what's best, after all!"

Rescue remedy

Chapter Fifteen

"Christ almighty!"

The volume and proximity of the man's voice startled me out of my sleep.

"This is bloody unbelievable!"

I squinted bleary-eyed in the direction of the voice and saw Niall standing in the doorway of my room. His hair was tousled. His brown eyes were set deep in a face that was bloated from too much alcohol the night before. His expression was angry.

"Yesterday you had some total stranger sniffing around and now you're sleeping with a woman! And after all I said to you last night!"

He stormed out of the room. The bed shook gently and I turned round to see Rachel laughing silently into the pillow beside me.

"He thinks we . . . he thinks you're sleeping with a woman just because I crashed here last night. And I wouldn't mind but it's his own fault."

"What do you mean?" I asked, hardly listening to her, I was so upset by Niall's reaction.

"Well, if he hadn't hogged the only bed with blankets on I could have stayed in the other room," Rachel replied indignantly.

This was all I needed. As if things weren't bad enough, now Niall thought that I was a lesbian. I tried to sort things out in my head before I drove myself into a panic.

Last night I had been annoyed and hurt because he had accused me of trying it on with every man I met. Then, for good measure, he as good as admitted that he had been with other women during our relationship. It shouldn't really matter to me what he thought and he had no right to comment on my sleeping arrangements after yesterday's revelations.

"Bet you're glad you don't have to ask him to save you from any murderers," Rachel teased as, still laughing, she climbed out of the bed. She tugged open the curtains to reveal a bright, frosty morning and turned towards me jumping from one foot to the other on the cold floor. "Can I use the bathroom first?"

I glumly agreed. Why not? With the way things stood between us I wouldn't need to have make-up on or, indeed even wash my face to talk to Niall. And I did need to talk to him. I needed to know if what he had said about the other women was true. I needed to know if our whole relationship had been based on deceit or if he was just trying to be hurtful. I quickly pulled on my clothes and stepped into the hall. The smell of fresh cigarette smoke hung in the cold air. Niall was having his morning nicotine hit. He was most probably standing at the kitchen window alternately glowering at the view and tipping ash into the sink, waiting for me to come and talk to him. He would be in exactly the same position I had been in when I had spotted the Dead German.

Well!

It has been a while since we heard from the Dead German, hasn't it? My finding out who had killed him must have exorcised him. Or maybe he had gone off to haunt Dara and, even as I thought about it, was clawing at the shutter that covered Dara's broken window, pleading to be let in. The flesh on his grasping fingers would fall off, the more vigorous his efforts became, until eventually he would be merely tap-tapping with bony talons, his voice now a whisper on the wind as he implored, 'Let me in, let me in.'

Boy, was I glad he wasn't hanging around my place anymore. All I had to worry about now was a bad-tempered ex.

I'd said it! Without having to think about it I'd called Niall my ex, just straight off, with no hesitation. Was this progress or regression, I wondered. I'd soon find out.

I forced a smile on to my face and stepped into the kitchen. Nobody was there. All the cupboards were open, shouting their emptiness at the room. Niall must have been looking for food to nurse his hangover. Well, he'd come to the wrong kitchen. The box of Sugar Puffs stood untouched by the fridge. Niall didn't like Sugar Puffs. I walked back into the hall and called his name. There was no answer. Maybe he'd been struck dumb. Oh, bliss, not to have to talk about the night before or better still, not to have to make small-talk to avoid talking about the night before, or his outburst in the bedroom that morning. If he was struck dumb maybe he would become all passive and loving, and be grateful to have someone like me to look after him. I mean, if he was struck dumb I could go out with him again, I'd totally forgive the nasty things he'd said to me and we could live happily ever after as long as he just looked at me adoringly all the time. Come to think of it, maybe what I really needed in my life was a dog. But in the meantime I'd better find Niall and get this over with.

I knocked on his bedroom door and opened it gently. "Niall, are you in here?"

I peered around in the untidy, pungent gloom. The room was empty. Well, if he wasn't in the bathroom with Rachel, and I didn't think that was likely, he must have stepped outside. I went to the front door but as I reached to open it I realised it was already ajar. So Niall had gone outside! I stepped out into the crisp morning and looked around. He was nowhere in sight. I walked out on to the road and scanned the flat countryside. In the distance I saw a figure getting steadily smaller on the Ballinacarrig road.

So he was gone, just like that.

No goodbye.

No tears.

No kiss.

Just gone.

All the energy I'd been storing for our conversation evaporated like condensation clearing from a window. Life without Niall stood out more distinctly than it ever had when I was fuming and hurting. I could almost hear the desert wind whistle over the empty wasteland of my emotions. Tumbleweed moved unevenly across the picture. My entire future was an empty prairie.

I now saw I had never acknowledged that we had broken up. I had seen it more as a minor outbreak of war, dangerous and life-threatening but nevertheless engaging and engrossing. Hearing that he was with another woman, other women maybe, had added indignation and hurt, but I still hadn't accepted that we were finished. Last night had sorted things out for me, though. I stood motionless on the road, my eyes fixed on the view. The bright morning shone happily on the limestone hills, mocking my misery. I stared blankly ahead of me as I remembered how I'd thought that Niall and I would last for ever. How we would never disagree or squabble like other couples. How if we ever had a problem we could overcome it by talking and working things out.

There had been one occasion when we were living in London and had decided to get out of town for New Year. Despite heavy snow warnings we headed for Cornwall and stayed on the Lizard peninsula. Contrary to the reports the weather was beautiful, unlike the guesthouse we had booked. Although originally a Victorian building, it was trapped in a 1970s decorative time-warp – the nastier sort of 1970s decor. Everything was Formica and plastic in the worst possible taste. The wallpaper and the carpet were of contrasting swirly patterns and the lights, pinned to the wall behind miniature elaborate fringed lampshades, were far too bright. The music, from the 'elevator' collection, came tinnily through small dusty speakers on the walls. Visually and atmospherically it was the guesthouse equivalent of Fawlty Towers.

Joan Conway

There were four other couples staying there and each of them was driving a Capri or a Vauxhall or some other hideously go-faster striped seventies car.

We were the only couple under forty-five. At dinner we sat quite near to the couple who had arrived in the Capri. We had already worked out earlier in the day that they must have been together a long time because they now looked alike. Have you ever noticed how couples who have been together for years eventually start to look alike? I've noticed the same with dogs and their owners. But back to this couple. At first we thought they were being really nice to each other, but a bit into their meal the woman made a jerky, irritated movement, so we started listening to their conversation rather than to the tone.

They were fighting like two thirsty people discussing the last drop of water left in the world. But they were doing it in really sweet voices, smiling and laughing all the time as though they were having a great time and getting on marvellously. Niall and I listened, enthralled, as they accused and castigated each other, dredging up twenty years of remembered injustices and hurts. We wanted to laugh but, of course, we couldn't, not without giving the game away. So we stayed eating calmly until the end of the meal, then got out of there as fast as we could.

Later in the pub we laughed until tears were streaming down our faces.

"Did you see . . . did you see the way he kept putting his knife down like as if he would stab her with it if he didn't get it out of his hand?" Niall gasped.

"And the way she kept smiling, even though she was

306

calling him 'bastard' through her teeth," I squealed, hardly able to talk I was laughing so much.

"I'll bet they didn't have a very happy Christmas. I wonder why they stay together if they hate each other that much?" Niall said, sobering slightly.

"I don't know."

I was starting to get depressed at the idea of two people fighting all the time, but staying together anyway. "Will we end up like that do you think, Niall?"

"Of course not, silly, we never fight, and I can't think of any reason why we should start, can you?"

I thought for a moment. "If there was a problem we would talk about it, wouldn't we? We wouldn't just let it fester until we hated each other, would we?"

"No. Now, stop fretting. We don't have any problems and we could never hate each other. And, anyway, if we did we wouldn't get into bitter arguments like that, we'd go for the jugular, we'd be like Michael Douglas and Kathleen Turner in whatever that film was called. Ah, you know, where they start murdering each other when their marriage doesn't work out."

"*The War of the Roses*?"

"Yeah, that's the one. I'd just strangle you in a crime of passion – serious passion!" Niall said, grabbing me by the throat and kissing me at the same time. We relapsed into helpless giggles.

Now that we had reached the end I was glad he hadn't decided to kill me instead of being bitter and leaving. Two people out to murder me in one day would have been a no-win situation. So much for never fighting and not letting things fester.

I put my hands up to my face to warm my freezing cheeks and went back into the house. In the kitchen I reached for the Sugar Puffs.

As I did so Rachel breezed in. "Hey, save some for me," she said, pointing to the cereal. "Where's the homophobe this morning? He doesn't seem to be getting into the spring spirit, does he?"

I looked at her dejectedly. "He's gone."

Even Rachel was a little surprised. "What do you mean?'"

"I mean he's gone, Rachel. He just walked out and left the door open. I saw him in the distance going towards the village."

Rachel made a fancy-that face and said, "Maybe he'll get some healing from the limestone and it will ease his anger." She put her arm around me. "Look, it might be for the best. Perhaps you two weren't meant to be together."

I sighed and looked at the colourless lino. Rachel must have thought I was going to cry – couldn't blame her, I'd been making quite a habit of it recently.

"Hey, it's not that bad, Val. It's a bit of a shock, that's all. I'll get you some Rescue Remedy. It'll make you feel better." She left the room to unearth whatever potion she was going to administer which would miraculously cure my impending emotional breakdown.

Before I had time to finish my cereal she was back. "Here, open your mouth." She was standing beside me poised with a drop dispenser.

"What?" I looked from her to the tiny bottle in her hand.

"Rescue Remedy. Great for conditions like this. A few drops and you'll feel much better in a while. Come on, open your mouth."

I did. And the few drops I swallowed tasted so strongly of alcohol that it made me long for more. I wanted to find a bottle of whiskey and drink until I felt no pain. I'm sure Rachel didn't know what I was thinking but nevertheless she behaved as though she was determined to keep me focused.

"If you feel OK after you get yourself ready we should go. My bus is at ten thirty and if you think you'll be OK without me I'd like to catch it. Besides, you'd better contact Terry. The longer you leave it, the more chance there is of Dara calling around again."

Oh, no, she was right. I still had to sort out the Dara thing. All I wanted to do was curl up under the bed, preferably drunk, and never see anybody ever again. "But what if we meet Niall on the way? I'm sure he's walking back into the village – there isn't anywhere else he can go." I was hoping to gain immunity somehow from the day's duties by coming up with as many obstacles to starting it as I could.

"No, by the time you're ready, Niall will have had over an hour to walk to Ballinacarrig. That's plenty of time. He'll probably be on the same bus as me but I don't have to go very far so I won't have to resist the anger vibes for too long."

Rachel ushered me out of the room. In the cold bathroom I looked gloomily into the mirror at my unhappy face and decided that if I was going to be begging favours from Terry I had better make myself presentable.

Though short of painting a clown's smile on to my face I wasn't sure what I could achieve.

Getting myself to look half decent took ages so that by the time I reappeared in the kitchen Rachel was pacing impatiently. "We're cutting it a bit tight, Val. Come on, let's go."

"Sorry, yeah, I lost track. Ready?"

"Yeah."

I hadn't even time to cover the ill-fated lower back door. I rationalised that, as my efforts so far hadn't prevented anyone from breaking in, there wasn't much point in covering it.

We reached Ballinacarrig in record time, but even so the bus was already set to leave. All the passengers were on board and the engine was running as the driver waited the last three minutes until the scheduled departure time. As soon as I had parked Rachel leapt out of the car, waving frantically at the driver. I grabbed one of her bags and we scurried towards the waiting bus. Before she climbed on, Rachel turned to me panting and said, "Are you sure you wouldn't rather I stay?"

Yeah, I was sure I'd be very popular keeping her away from her beloved Jamie for one moment longer. "No, Rach, thanks, but I'll be fine. Terry will sort things out for me," I said with more confidence than I felt.

"OK then," she replied, looking relieved. "Promise that the moment I leave you'll go straight to Terry's office. Everything will be OK. Just think positive." She hugged me and disappeared into the bus.

I stood back as it pulled away and looked along the window at the other passengers. Niall was sitting on my side of the bus in the window-seat about three rows from the back. My heart jumped. I felt as though I should do something – throw myself in despair against the side of the bus or, indeed, under the wheels, anything to prevent him from leaving. But I didn't, even though only yesterday I had wanted to marry him. How quickly things change. I felt sad.

Niall stared blankly out of the window in my direction, his face an impassive sulk. As he passed me I raised my hand in a half-gesture but he didn't respond. My last image of him was one of dark immobility, his brown eyes dead in his tired, ashen face.

He was gone. My heart contracted and my throat grew tight but before I could get too involved in whatever emotion was about to engulf me I heard my name being called.

"Val, hey, Val, hang on a minute, Val."

I swung round, afraid, for a moment, that it might be Dara. It wasn't, and I didn't recognise the person calling to me. The cloth-capped man coming towards me looked familiar but I couldn't say who he was. Then he was standing in front of me. "Hi, Val, glad I caught you, it'll save me a trip out to the house."

As he continued to speak I realised it was Séan the guard. He wasn't wearing his uniform but I recognised him because his ears were still doing their duty of holding up his hat. They were any-hat-will-do ears. It must be great to have auricles like that, working even on your days off. I didn't say that to him.

"Oh, hi, Séan, you're up early."

He blushed slightly and looked at his watch, probably

surprised that I thought it was early. "Have a few things to do at the station," he said quickly. "There was a message from your mother on the answering machine this morning." He stopped and creased his brow trying to remember it. Then he spoke as though repeating by rote: "She said you are to phone her. That you were suppose to phone her every day and that you haven't and that she's worried. She phoned the garda emergency number as well but they assured her that a girl had to go at least two days without phoning her mother before they could arrest her." He laughed heartily at his joke and only stopped when he saw my polite, unamused smile.

It was a wonder my mother hadn't called out the air-sea-rescue crew because I hadn't phoned her. She was such an embarrassment. Talk about parental pressure!

Séan coughed uncomfortably. "Well, you might give her a bell," he said, to prove that he was serious now. Then he looked as though he had suddenly remembered something. "Did I hear you were looking for us yesterday?" he enquired, in a tone that seemed to suggest I had been looking specifically for him.

Well, it didn't take long for no-news to get around! I didn't want to tell him about the break-in now that it all seemed to be tied up with Dara and I hadn't yet spoken to Terry. I groped for a feasible story. "Ah, aam, a glass pane on the door blew in at the start of the storm yesterday and I was . . . I was just wondering if it was safe to leave it like that for a couple of days, you know, around here."

Séan ran his fingers across his forehead as though this

was a matter of the utmost gravity and looked at me sceptically – well it looked sceptical to me, OK? But it turned out that he was only thinking. "I'd say it would be all right maybe until tomorrow but try to get it fixed as soon as you can. There was a lot of damage done yesterday. Dara O'Neill, that's Terry O'Neill's lad, lost an entire window, and it's the sort of window that will take a lot of fixing." He nodded knowingly.

I froze at the mention of Dara. Maybe they had already caught up with him and I wouldn't have to go to Terry after all.

"Any news about the, ah, the body?" I asked diplomatically.

A baffled look crossed his face.

"Nothing yet. Very unusual, I hear, not to have at least a suspect within twenty-four hours in a rural crime like this." He sighed heavily. "Of course, he was a foreigner," he added almost as an accusation, seeming to forget that I was there.

I decided to grab the moment while I could and moved away slightly. "Well, thanks for the message, Séan. I'll talk to you again soon."

"Eh?" he said, startled from his reverie, and looking as though I had just pinched him.

"I said, I'll talk to you again soon," I reiterated, more loudly, in case he hadn't heard me the first time.

"Oh," he said, as if he was in pain. "I, aam, yes, well, ah . . ." His eyes, which met mine for a split second, held a look of helpless panic as he searched for something more to say. I moved impatiently from one foot to the other. This jolted him into timid speech. "Is everything else all right out at the house?" he stuttered. Before I could answer he had rushed on. "Like, I could call out later and . . . ah . . . you know, make sure everything is all right." He paused, smiled nervously, then added, "All in the line of duty, of course."

I had a feeling that his interest went a little beyond the line of duty but I didn't want to get into dealing with that right now. I needed to get off the street in case Dara spotted me. I also needed to take Terry into my confidence as soon as possible to guarantee my removal from his son's hit list. All the same, I couldn't really say no to Séan or he might become suspicious and start his own little local-hero investigation.

"Yeah, yeah, sure," I said, neutrally, figuring that I could arrange to be out that evening when he came by. I would work out some excuse later when things were less hectic. I turned away.

"Great, I'll see you later, then," Séan said after me, in a tone that suggested we had just arranged a date. Then he back-pedalled a bit to reality and, raising his voice, almost shouted, "Be sure to get that door fixed, OK?"

I turned and waved, already moving swiftly down the street towards Terry's office.

So they still didn't suspect Dara. It was time to fill Terry in on a couple of details. I let myself into the heat of his reception area and waited while the woman at the desk finished on the phone. She was the same woman who had looked at me disapprovingly when Terry had asked me to the concert. Eventually she turned to me: "How can I help you?" From the expression on her face I knew that she remembered me.

Cereal Lover

"I'm Val O'Hara, and I want to see Terry O'Neill, please."

"Do you have an appointment?"

"No."

"Mr O'Neill goes to court on Mondays and is not in his office until the afternoon."

Ah, great, just my luck. I couldn't wait around. I'd have to be a bit insistent. "Look, I have to see him. It's personal and very important: where can I find him?"

She looked as though I had just told her I had soiled the carpet. Obviously 'personal' and 'Terry' weren't words she liked to hear from young women. She flicked a page and said, "He only had one case in court this morning and if it was heard immediately he could quite possibly be at home by eleven thirty."

I looked at my watch: it was just eleven. By the time I got to the car and had driven to his house it would be nearly eleven thirty. I mumbled my thanks and headed for the door.

"Oh, Ms O'Hara?"

I stopped and turned.

"Your mother, Mrs O'Hara? Left a message on our answering-machine, something about not phoning her and that you should . . ."

· · ·

Chapter Sixteen

". . . phone every day as you had promised that you would . . . something along those lines. Sheila in the office didn't know what to do with it so she included it in my messages this morning."

Terry O'Neill was standing beside his car in the gravelled area in front of his castle, his arms full of files, his breath as he spoke surrounding his head in great foggy clouds. It seemed that everybody I met that day was going to give me a message from my mother. The same message. She had tapped into her new-found County Clare network.

Terry had only stepped out of his car when he'd started to recount it. I hadn't even had time to tell him my reason for being parked in front of his house when he arrived. Now he had stopped talking and was looking at me expectantly.

I stared back at him for what seemed like an eternity, vainly searching for a sentence that wouldn't come out as, "Your son is a murderer: what are you going to do about it?" I had to say something. "Could I have a word with you if you're not too busy, Terry?"

Don't know why I added the last bit. I didn't care if he was totally run off his feet, I was still determined to offload my Dara burden on to him.

Terry's eyes lit up. "But of course, Val. I'm surprised you think you even have to ask."

He somehow managed to disengage one of his arms from the file-carrying and stretched it out towards me. "You can have a little chat with me any time you like."

Oh, cosy! Now he had the appearance of a man with greater anticipations than a chat.

His short-man's walk was even more pronounced as he swung his way towards the house. Maybe I should tell him immediately that I had nearly had sex with his son the day before, and if that didn't quench the light in his eyes I could reveal how traumatised I was at rebreaking up with my boyfriend and that any sort of relations were out of the question. I didn't say anything. I hadn't the courage. I just thought what a stupid idea it had been to turn for help to the one man in the whole county who leaned too close to me whenever we met.

And now he was doing it again. We were in the hallway, which was larger than most people's living room, and he still brushed against me as he put down his files. I wasn't going to give in to his inappropriate space invasion. I stood my ground, not moving as he leaned towards me.

"Excuse me," he said, smiling at me slightly, as he moved even closer.

This was too much. I swung round ready to say something appropriately cutting, then realised I had been standing directly in front of the table section of the hall-stand on which he wanted to put down his papers.

Oops!

OK, so maybe he wasn't 'leaning' today but he was still, well, patronising. And I could see him smiling to himself as I fluttered out of his way, embarrassed by my mistaken assumption.

He ushered me into the kitchen. "Would you like a little coffee?" he asked cordially.

I nodded gratefully, more at the 'coffee' than the 'little'. It felt like ages since I'd had my cereal breakfast and my stomach had started its lunchtime rumble. Coffee would be just the thing to kick some life into me.

While Terry busied himself we talked about the party and the weather – well, Terry talked and I listened. I'd forgotten what an easy conversationalist he was. While he was grinding the coffee I looked around the kitchen. Oddly, without all the people in it the room seemed smaller. Even the balconies appeared less grand than they had a couple of nights before. With the furniture back in place the room was a lot more homely and a lot less austere. An Aga, now boiling water for the coffee, made the room almost snug. On the walls were pictures of Dara and Ashling at various stages of growing up. I settled back comfortably into my wooden kitchen chair. The smell of brewing coffee and the soothing tone of Terry's voice had lulled me into a feeling of security. I pretended that I was just making a friendly visit that had nothing to do with accusing his handsome son of being a murderer. My pretence didn't survive long.

"So, Val, what can I do for you?" This was it, then. Time to tell.

I had no idea how to start. I'd never before had to confront a parent about their child's behaviour. Terry set the coffee cups on the table, sat down and looked at me expectantly.

"Well, aam, it's . . . aam, ah. It's about Dara."

Terry nodded wordlessly and took a sip from his cup.

I'd started, I couldn't go back now. I figured that it was better just to come clean, say it straight out.

"Dara killed the Dead German."

Terry stared blankly at me. It was that sort of blank that said a lot was going on in his head, but his face remained impassive. Then he pursed his lips and inhaled gently through his teeth. I'd seen him do that before. It was in the restaurant when we were having dinner together. He had been trying to decide what to select off the menu. His half-moon reading glasses had been perched at the end of his nose as he held the list at arm's length, his head tilted back. All the while he had inhaled gently through his teeth. Evidently it was something he did when he was concentrating.

His expression changed to one of shrewdness as he said carefully, but sharply, "And why do you think that?"

I must say that this wasn't quite the reaction I had been expecting – after all, I had just told him his only son had committed a serious crime. I mean, if I'd been told something like that about my child, if I'd had one, I would at least have leapt out of the chair and flapped around for a while, proclaiming his innocence. I assumed that it was just his lawyerness taking over. Whatever the reason, the ball was back in my court. I didn't feel inclined to tell him the whole story, you know, about being naked on the mat and all that so I cut to the need-to-know stuff.

"I was around at Dara's yesterday – he was giving me some vegetables." This last bit was supposed to explain why I'd been there, and as Terry accepted it, it must have sounded reasonable. "And," I went on, "as I was taking them out of his car I found the Dead German's passport, just sitting there in the back. Dara must have used his car to move the body and it fell out of a pocket without him knowing."

I was warming to my task now and was prepared to do a bit of descriptive enhancement in case Terry didn't get the full picture. I stopped talking and tried to work out his facial expression. I'd obviously said something to impress him: he wasn't looking quite as blank as he had at my opening statement. The thing was, though, that I couldn't work out whether he was surprised, concerned or what.

"Is there anything else you think I should know about this affair?" His tone was measured, almost calculating.

I guess he was trying to establish how much incriminating evidence I had. I told him my suspicions about the break-in and how Dara had called by the evening before. I didn't tell him I suspected that Dara might have been going to murder me. After all, I wanted Terry on my side and I had a feeling that he wouldn't stay there for long if I confessed to my belief that his son was raring to kill again.

When I had finished talking Terry got up and went to

the Aga to pour himself another coffee. I'd been talking so much I was still only half-way through mine. Instead of returning to his seat he remained standing by the stove as though the further away from me he was the less my words could affect him. Facing me, he leant his short body against the metal bar, one leg relaxed, his coffee cup nestled in both hands. He sighed. "I must confess that what you have told me doesn't come entirely as a surprise."

He paused, he was back in control, back into his usual rhythm of speech. The pause went on so long that there was a moment when I suspected that he simply wasn't going to elaborate. I struggled to adjust my average-pause-between-sentences expectation to his. Finally he continued, "I feel that I must take you into my confidence. I assume I can trust you?"

I nodded, saying nothing in case I put him off or in case he hadn't finished his sentence and I'd be interrupting.

He rubbed his chin pensively.

"A short time before . . ." he paused again and inclined his head towards me, ". . . your Dead German was discovered, I found a plank of wood on Dara's land that puzzled me."

He took another long break. Well, not long in the history of mankind or anything but an eternity when you're sitting on the edge of your chair, convinced that you're about to become the next Miss Marple – at a considerably earlier age, of course.

"It had blood on it, not much, just a little, in fact, but not what you'd expect to find on a horticultural farm."

Terry lifted his head and looked out of the window, his eyes distant. "I put it in my car and brought it home, intending to ask Dara about it, but I forgot." He glanced at me. "You know, busy time of year."

I didn't know but I nodded anyway. If nothing else it filled the time until he got on to the next sentence.

"I only remembered it when I heard about the body, and for some reason I just thought it best not to mention it. I put it in the basement and more or less forgot about it. I now realise, of course, that it might indeed be relevant, especially in the light of what you have just said about Dara."

So he believed me. I had been so afraid that he would scoff at me and demand evidence or deride me for slandering his son. But he believed me and now he trusted me to share his confidence. Whatever reservations I'd had about Terry crumbled, and a little glowing halo appeared around his head. On my first evening with him I had seen him as a fairy godmother, now I knew he was an angel. An angel with interminable pauses between his sentences but an angel none the less.

"Oh, can I have a look?" I asked in excitement, believing that once I saw it the whole murder thing would unravel. "Maybe it will help us prove something."

Yeah, prove that Dara was a murderer.

That thought hit me pretty heavily. I didn't like it and I was sure it wouldn't appeal to Terry. Still, he didn't react. Instead he put down his coffee cup and said quietly, "If you come with me I'll show it to you."

Under any other circumstances I would have looked very sceptically on this sort of invitation, especially coming from a man with a personal-space-violation record. But now I figured that I had misjudged Terry. He was being calm, supportive and trusting about the whole Dara thing, and I wasn't just going to start treating him like I didn't trust him. If it would get me out of my next-on-the-list-to-be-murdered dilemma I'd have followed him to Narnia. I pushed aside my cup, got up and followed him through one of the doors leading from the kitchen. It was the same one that I'd gone through when I'd run away from the party. Instead of going straight on as I had, he turned right immediately and in a short time we reached the top of the stairs into the basement. We didn't speak once we left the kitchen. I was too busy admiring the house, now that I could see it in daylight, and I just presumed that Terry was worried because his worst fears about Dara had been confirmed. I, of course, could never stay silent for very long, though.

"Terry, what should we do about Dara, you know, now that we know that he's probably the one who killed the . . . the man?"

It didn't seem right to call him the Dead German out loud anymore now that we knew who had killed him. Terry paused on the stairs. He evidently suffered from the affliction a lot of males have: he couldn't do two things at the same time. In Terry's case it was thinking and walking on stairs.

"That's hard to say," he said presently, and continued down the stairs.

Talking and walking was obviously OK.

"Essentially we have very little evidence so I suppose the first thing we should do is have a chat with him about it. He may not have intended for anything like this to happen. And, really, that's what would determine what we say when he hands himself in."

Hands himself in! So that's what would happen. I wasn't sure I liked it as a conclusion but it did sound remarkably easy.

It all sounded so simple.

It all sounded so sad.

Why did it have to be Dara who'd done it? He was so charming and sweet and handsome and . . . interested in me. I pulled myself up short. He wouldn't have been interested in me if it hadn't been for the Dead German. Why else would he have ransacked the house, seduced me and turned up on my doorstep determined to kill me? Just because I felt safe having told Terry about my suspicions didn't alter Dara's intent.

"Here we are," Terry said decisively, stopping in front of one of the many doorways we had passed since we had come down the stairs. This one was closed and, I calculated, locked, as Terry was searching in his pockets for a key. The door was like all the doors in the house, old-fashioned and robust, with a huge key hole.

While he was doing the key thing I looked about me. Unlike upstairs the walls of the basement were unevenly plastered, the theory being, I suppose, that the servants didn't need the same luxuries as the owners upstairs. I shuddered as a chill passed through me. The basement was cold and damp and quite spooky. In fact, it struck me as just the kind of place that would be haunted by the ghost of an unhappy serving-maid or authoritarian butler, who prowled the corridors ensuring that his rules were carried out. I was going to ask Terry about this when the lock snapped open.

"That's it." Terry breathed a sigh of relief. He swung the door open and ushered me in. "Its just there on the other side of the room . . ."

His voice followed me as I moved across the uneven floor. The room was empty except for a small chair and a pile of papers, which sat under the window. Not a plank of wood in sight.

"Where exactly is it, Terry?" I spoke politely in case I was just being really stupid in not spotting the exhibit marked 'murder weapon' that was staring me straight in the face. There was no reply. I turned around to see if Terry was all right only to find that he wasn't even in the room. To make matters worse the door was closed. And to compound everything I heard the lock snap back into place.

I was locked in! Terry had locked me in with the murder weapon! Wherever it was. I threw myself at the door handle and yelled, "Terry, Terry, what are you doing? I can't stay here, let me out."

I stopped rattling and shouting and listened. In the corridor outside I could hear the sound of receding footsteps and then, in the distance, the scrape of shoes on stone as Terry mounted the stairs, leaving me alone in the basement.

I threw myself against the door again, screaming and yelling anything that came into my head, beating my fists on the sturdy wood until my hands hurt. Then I stopped, hoarse, tired and bewildered. There was only one thing that I could work out from my present situation. It was that Dara had indeed had an accomplice, as I had suspected the day before. And that accomplice was his father.

So much for the Higher Being!

How could I have been so stupid? I'd played right into their hands. I'd even swallowed the old murder-weapon-in-the-basement ploy. Of course there was no blood-soaked plank in the basement – I'd even looked through the pile of old newspapers and there was nothing. Besides, there had been no blood on the Dead German. Why should there be any on this plank, if it existed? It was all lies and I'd fallen for it, hook, line and sinker! Terry had no intention of going to the guards. I mean, all he had to do now was get rid of me and he and Dara would be untouchable.

How could I have been so stupid? I was definitely a contender for the most gullible person in Ireland award. Indeed, I'd make it to the world finals, no problem. I could see myself receiving the trophy in a packed stadium. It would be a statue of a Wallace-and-Gromit-type man made of some horrible Plasticine stuff. He would stand one foot tall with his mouth open in a 'Dah?' expression. He'd look really stupid. And my name would be engraved on the base. I'd probably have to make a speech.

To distract myself from this horrible thought I crossed to the window and peered out. Being below ground, all I could see was the window-box. But if I bent down and looked upwards I could see about five inches of the real world. Most of that view was taken up by the wheels of my car. The window consisted of six small panes, which had been painted shut. Outside there were metal bars. Unless I turned into Tom Thumb there was no way I could get through them. I checked the door again, but even though the key was still in the lock there was no way I could get it.

I sat down disconsolately on the chair. It was very little, a child's chair probably, or a dwarf's. I manoeuvred it so that it was in front of the window, determined that if anybody moved into my part of the yard I would spot them and attract their attention. Time passed very slowly, sitting in the little chair with my neck twisted to look out of the window. I wondered if this was it for me. Would I sit in this chair until the O'Neills came for me? Maybe they wouldn't come. Maybe they would just leave me here to die. They would get some bricks and mortar and build over the door and window so that I would be sealed in for ever. I would starve to death in this little chair in this little room. The flesh would gradually deteriorate until there would be nothing left but bones and the musty smell of crypt, eternally trapped in this dark, airless cavern. Of course, if that happened I'd have to haunt the place. A solitary figure in turn-of-the-century clothes oooooooohing my way along the gloomy passages, endlessly searching for justice but never finding it.

Justice, after all, is for mortals.

In about a hundred years when they were renovating or knocking down the castle they would uncover my grey, cobwebbed skeleton and wonder . . . But the O'Neills wouldn't want a ghost in the house so they'd probably kill me and make it look like suicide. They would throw me off the nearby cliffs of Moher. I've heard they're very popular for suicides. I'd be found a month later nibbled and battered after weeks of the wild Atlantic's hospitality. Barely recognisable, just another statistic.

I didn't want to die. Especially if it was because I couldn't think fast enough.

And I definitely didn't want to die while I still hadn't a notion what I was dying for.

Why on earth would Dara and Terry want to kill a well-built German? At least now I knew who'd ransacked my house. It had been Terry. When I had met him on the corridor during the party he'd been wearing his coat. Why would he wear his coat to fetch a bottle of wine from his own cellar? If only I'd known it, I'd caught him coming back from breaking into my place. Dara taking us upstairs to the get-away-from-the-party room had simply been a decoy, just in case we might have noticed that Terry was missing from his own party. That had been done very smoothly. Most probably the only reason he'd asked us to the party was to get us away from the house. Very clever plotting by Terry and Dara.

Oh, I must have been such an easy target, the betrayed, lonely woman just looking for someone to 'love' her. I might as well have had a 'come and get me' label tattooed on my forehead. Maybe I had.

With that thought in mind I was about to settle into a savage self-pity frenzy when I heard the faint crunch of footsteps on gravel. There was somebody in the yard! As long as it wasn't Terry I'd try to attract their attention. But unless they stepped into my tiny range of vision I had no way of knowing who it was. Should I take a chance?

The indecision as I crammed myself against the dusty window for a better view was unbearable. I could hear the footsteps more clearly now but they didn't seem to be getting any closer. Oh, no! Whoever was in the yard was going straight to the front door. They weren't going to come near my basement window at all. Time to start yelling. It was a risk but I'd have to take it.

"Help, help, someone! I'm over here!" I banged on the window. "Help, let me out."

With all the noise I was making I couldn't hear what the footsteps were doing. Had they gone into the house? Had they stopped? Were they coming over to investigate what all the noise was? I didn't pause to find out. The shouting and hammering were a glorious release from the horrible tension that had built up during the hour of my imprisonment.

Suddenly a pair of feet appeared beside my car wheels. They were wellingtoned feet with clay on them and they didn't stay long. A head of blond hair flashed briefly to the level of the boots then disappeared. In an instant the wellingtons spun round and ran away.

I stopped yelling and banging. The wellingtoned feet and blond hair could belong to nobody but Dara.

I kicked the wall below the window in frustration. I'd miscalculated. I'd lost my only chance of freedom. I'd just put paid to my only means of raising the alarm. They would probably come and board the window or kill me immediately or do whatever it was they were going to do to me.

Well, they wouldn't get me without a fight. I scoured my tiny cell for a weapon but there was only the little chair. Great! That meant me and a child's chair against a grown man or two. I was frowning quietly at the chair when I heard the shuffle of rubber shoes on the corridor. I listened closely to what sounded like only one set of footsteps.

Maybe it was just Dara. Perhaps there was some hope for me and a little chair against one man. I had to at least try.

Silently I grabbed it and stood behind the door. I was doing far too much of this lying in wait inside locked doors lately. But this time I'd get the right person. The shuffling stopped outside the door and somebody wrestled with the lock, panting slightly with the effort. A moment later accompanied by a final grunt the lock gave way and the door was flung open. There was a pause. Whoever was standing there was obviously surprised to find the room empty.

"Val?"

Dara's voice was almost a whisper. My jaw tightened in anger to hear him speak my name so softly. I dared him to step into the room. Dared him to come into range.

He did. He walked straight to the middle of the room and before he had a chance to look around I ploughed at him with the chair. I caught him in the side and he fell against the opposite wall in a pile of arms, legs and chair. Without stopping to see what damage I'd done I turned and ran out the door in the direction of the stairs, exhilarated by the success of my attack but frightened that he wouldn't stay down for long. I threw myself on to the stairs but stopped dead as a voice above me said, "And just where do you think you're going?"

I looked up and there, standing a few steps from the top, filling the stairwell, was Terry. And in his hand he held a gun. A gun!

I stared in disbelief.

He couldn't have a gun. This was the west of Ireland, for God's sake. I mean, yeah, there might be the odd murder but people didn't just go around brandishing guns! Terry was a rural solicitor, not some Chicago mobster spoiling for a kill. Where did he get a gun? I had the distinct feeling that he wasn't going to answer this question, if I'd had enough wit about me to ask it. I didn't have enough wit. Instead I stood at the bottom of the stairs, clutching the rail, my mouth open in amazement, my eyes locked on Terry, who stood staring back at me, his eyes hard and piercing in his expressionless face.

I was afraid. Very afraid.

Guns just did that to me. I was the sort of person who got frightened if I heard there was a gun in a glass case of a museum I was visiting. When I visited my brother in New York I would go to the other side of the street if I saw a policeman coming because I knew he would be armed. The only place I could tolerate any sort of firearm was in the cinema, on screen that is, and then only if it was a very little one for self-defence. Guns petrified me and I was sure that Terry could see it in my eyes.

Abruptly Terry broke our eye-lock. He stared behind me at something, a vaguely helpless look crossing his face. Then he returned his gaze to me. I heard the soft shuffle of wellingtons on the corridor.

"Val, Val, what's going on?"

Dara's voice came from behind me, sounding bewildered.

I didn't answer and I didn't turn. I couldn't take my eyes off Terry. Dara mustn't have seen Terry until he was almost beside me and then his voice sounded surprised. "Dad, what are you doing?"

Terry looked stricken but he kept the gun and his gaze focused on me. His mouth worked as though he was speaking but no sound came out. Dara made to brush past me and go up the stairs. Terry stiffened but didn't move the gun from me.

"Stop!" he shouted. "Don't come any further! Step back and stay behind her where I can see you. This is pointing straight at her heart."

My heart didn't like that at all – it tried to leap out of my throat, its frightened scream vibrating through my body, but it didn't succeed.

Dara stepped back. "Dad, what's this all about?"

Now I was a bit confused. Why was Terry threatening Dara? I mean, after all, they were in this together. Maybe I was witnessing a mutiny – yeah, maybe they'd had a disagreement. This might work to my advantage.

Terry didn't answer Dara's question. He'd regained the composure he had momentarily lost when Dara had appeared.

"Have you got the passport, Dara?"

"Of course I have. You know that's why I came by. But please, Dad, you've got to tell me what this English guy's passport's got to do with anything? And, Jesus, whatever it is, put the gun down and let's talk about it."

He sounded close to tears. Now it was my turn to be bewildered. Well, even more bewildered than I already was. I tore my gaze from Terry and swung round to Dara. "English?" I snapped. "That's the Dead German's passport." Dara, fishing in his pocket for the little book, shrugged and looked puzzled.

"You and your bloody Dead German," Terry barked, from the top of the stairs, making me refocus immediately on the threat of death, which I'd forgotten for a split second. "He's not bloody German. Where did you get a stupid idea like that, anyway?"

At this point I didn't know whether to be more astonished at the Dead German's change of nationality or at Terry's cursing. He was the sort of man who never swore and to hear him do so sounded all wrong. I went for the Dead German astonishment. "I thought he was German because he was carrying a German guidebook," I said indignantly, forgetting that if I annoyed Terry he'd shoot me.

He didn't shoot me. Instead he threw his eyes to heaven. "The guidebook has nothing to do with where he's from. That was something else entirely." He didn't add 'you stupid eejit' to the end of that sentence but it was there, unspoken. And, I must say, he wasn't being very informative.

"Did you have something to do with this guy's death, Dad?"

Dara was standing beside me now, the passport held out in front of him like he didn't want it anywhere near him.

"I told you not to move, Dara. Get back." Terry took

another step down the stairs.

Dara moved behind me again. "Did you, Dad?"

For the first time since Dara had arrived Terry took his eyes off me. He looked at his son with an expression of torment on his face and lowered the gun. "Yes. But it was an accident. I didn't mean to . . ."

Terry never finished that sentence. Instead he lurched forward and the gun flew out of his hand as he grasped in mid-air for support. In his scramble he missed the banister.

Terry tumbled headlong down the stairs, landing motionless where Dara and I had been standing seconds before.

"Are you all right, dear?" A woman's voice came from the top of the stairs.

My mother!

I swung around and looked up the stairs to where she stood, legs apart, her hands still clinging to the door jamb. "And he seemed like such a nice man!"

Would this mean no more Sugar Puffs?

Chapter Seventeen

"It's all rusty and it doesn't open, it's completely useless." Dara peered at the gun in the half-light at the bottom of the stairs. "It doesn't even count as a weapon, Dad. What were you at?"

Terry shook his head. For a few seconds after he had crashed down the stairs and landed motionless at the bottom I'd been afraid that he was dead. I was afraid that, on top of everything else, my mother was a murderer. I mean, after all, Terry had only been holding a 'pretend' gun and he had lowered it before my mother had sent him flying. That would be classed as murder, not self-defence, wouldn't it?

Fortunately, with a little help from Dara, Terry managed to sit up. Then he promptly burst into tears, babbling remorsefully about never having wanted to hurt anybody. At this point my mother, having assured herself that everything was under control, hushed him and said, "Well, I'm going to make some tea. It's the best thing when people are upset." She cast a disparaging glance at the sobbing Terry and continued, "My advice to you is that you get out of this cold, damp cellar as soon as, well, as soon as you're all . . . when you're all a bit more composed." She disappeared up the stairs on her tea-finding mission.

I stood quietly in the dark corridor, debating whether I should have gone with her. Terry was starting to pull himself together and it seemed to me that I might become a voyeuristic presence at a private moment between father and son. What was I thinking? Up until a few minutes ago I had thought that these two were collaborators determined to kill me. Of course I wasn't going to leave them on their own. Besides, Terry was starting to become coherent and I was entitled to know the details of whatever it was that had turned my life into a murder mystery.

Dara spoke gently to his father. "Dad, what's going on?"

Terry had one last shudder, took a deep breath and raised his head. "You know that land deal I've been doing at Gleninagh?"

Dara nodded. "The German syndicate one for the shoreline? I thought that was all finished."

Terry shook his head despondently and raised his clasped hands to his forehead. He didn't say anything more. In fact, he looked as though he had given up completely on the conversation. I moved the weight of my body from one leg to the other and folded my arms impatiently, using all my will-power not to bark questions at him: He seemed oblivious to my presence and my speaking to him might startle him. I kept quiet.

Dara, though he didn't show it, must have been feeling

a little impatient as well because eventually he asked, "What about it?"

"The dead man, the man whose passport you have, was sent here to put pressure on . . . things . . ."

He paused. I knew it was a pause because he kept staring into mid-air as if he was looking for the other bit of the sentence. I was getting good at this!

Finally he continued, ". . . to put pressure on me." He paused again. Then, snapping into concentration, he looked directly at Dara. "He was an international thug. The Germans hired him to threaten me because I refused to . . . well, to get rid of old Mrs O'Loughlin."

This puzzled Dara. "Mrs O'Loughlin?"

A look of impatience crossed Terry's face. "Yes, yes, you know she's out there by the ruin. She's right in the middle of that tract of land and none of the property development can go ahead while she's still there."

Understanding dawned on Dara's face. I fidgeted: this conversation was going far too slowly. I didn't want geographic details, I wanted the abridged version as it related specifically to me. Still, I held back and the conversation trawled on.

"How did they think you were going to get rid of her?"

Dara was obviously on rewind, not fast forward.

"They wanted me to get a doctor to certify that she was incapable of living on her own or something like that. In fact, that's what we argued about."

Terry was losing his attention to detail. He was drifting off into the ocean of even bigger pauses. Dara tried to reel him back in.

"Who?"

"What?"

"Who 'argued about'?"

Terry looked at Dara as though he thought he was a bit dense. Mind you, Terry looked at a lot of people like that. "Myself and the thug, of course. Who else? He said he was going to guarantee that she wouldn't be able to live on her own. When I objected he grabbed me by the collar, I hit out and he fell against the Aga. He twisted his neck. It was horrible . . . I think he died instantly."

Things were getting clearer, much clearer. But there were still a few things I didn't understand. I glanced at Dara to see when he was going to get on with the questioning, but he was immobile, his mouth hung open and there was a look of shock on his face.

But of course! Poor guy! I'd had an hour to get used the fact that Terry was a murderer, but Dara had only just found out. He blinked. "But . . . but why didn't you just go to the police?"

Terry became adamant, almost defensive. "No matter what way you look at it, I killed a man. That, plus the fact that my planning permission for that land wasn't strictly by the book, would have caused a huge scandal. All my retirement money is tied up in this."

By the time he had finished this explanation it was as if he was pleading with his son. Dara rubbed his hand across his forehead in disbelief. It didn't look like he was up to the job of inquisitor anymore and I needed to get a few answers while the truth was flowing. I spoke for the first time since the shock of seeing my mother had silenced me. "Why did you leave him at my house?"

Terry looked at me as though he'd never seen me before. Then he turned away. "I didn't know it was your house. It's not your house. As far as I was concerned whoever had been staying there was gone and nobody would be about again until the summer when the Johnstons came back for their usual summer spell. I left him on a property with no resident owner, a holiday home, so as not to get anybody into trouble. I left his passport on him so that he could be identified."

Oh, yeah, wonderful! Acres of land in the county and he had to leave the body on my patch! Maybe Rachel was right about my karma.

Dara moved. He was coming out of whatever shock-induced coma he had fallen into. His colour had risen and even in the semi-darkness of the basement he looked good enough to distract me from any further questioning. But now he was starting to work things out for himself. "So when you borrowed my jeep last week that was what it was for! And that's how the passport got in there."

In fairness to him at this point, Terry looked a bit shamefaced. "Yes. I didn't know that's where it was. I thought someone at Val's had found it and had it in the house."

Yeah, like, if I found a passport I wouldn't hand it in. What did he think I was? Some sort of criminal? He'd obviously been spending too much time with his clientele – he thought everybody was a crook.

Dara, for no immediately apparent reason, was looking disgusted. My guess was that he was thinking about all that dead meat in his vegetarian four-wheel drive. But

I may have been wrong. In fact, I was wrong.

"Dad, how could you do all this? It's so – so dishonest."

Don't you just hate it when a child starts to nag a parent about their behaviour? I'd always associated it with self-righteous sixteen-year-olds. Now I was amused to see Dara doing it. Before this could develop into an interactive guilt trip, my mother appeared at the top of the stairs. Well, actually her legs did, a bit like those old Tom and Jerry cartoons where you only ever saw up to the knee on humans. "I've found the kitchen and the tea. Why don't you all come out of there into the heat? You'll feel a lot better if you do. Come on now, dear, bring everyone along."

As we obediently climbed the stairs I remembered one thing that still puzzled me. "Terry."

He stopped and turned. Evidently listening was also a bit of a problem for him when he was on the stairs.

"If he was English, why was he carrying a German guidebook?" OK, call me nit-picking and tenacious but I just had to know.

Terry shrugged. "I didn't know he had that. It's their password – their mark, so to speak, for the Gleninagh project. The guidebook would accompany any correspondence that the investment group didn't want to put their letterhead on. There's an aerial picture of the land in question on page seven."

My mother was gone. I could still smell the exhaust fumes from her car, which by now was out of sight. She'd headed for Dublin, determined to get there before dark. I knew she wouldn't.

Cereal Lover

I stood outside my house in the empty world of flat rock and watched the crisp cold air play with my breath. It seemed incredible that there could be so much quiet in the world, after all the excitement of the afternoon. There was also a certain welcome vacuum with the departure of my mother's ceaseless chatter.

Tea prepared by my mother in Terry's kitchen had been a strained affair. Only she spoke, encouraged by an occasional monosyllabic response from Dara. I was too embarrassed to say anything and Terry had fallen into a pensive depression. I finished my tea and left Dara and his father to work out the logistics of their decision to go to the police. I knew it wouldn't be easy for Dara but I didn't have the courage to go to him and say so. I didn't even have the courage to squeeze his hand in a gesture of understanding. Instead I caught his eye for an instant before I left with what I hoped was a look of support and sympathy. With my luck, he'd probably take it as a look of loathing and contempt. Once outside, whatever reserve my mother had previously shown, disappeared. "Imagine, just killing a foreigner in cold blood like that, and then trying to put the blame on you!"

"Mum, I don't think he was."

"Well, what else was he doing, dumping the body at your house and then making sure he was there while you were being interviewed by the police in case you had actually seen anything? I call that an abuse of his position as a respected member of the professions in the community. Imagine if your father went about doing that sort of thing."

I tried to imagine it, but it's a bit difficult to create a

347

scenario in which a dentist can be less than honest. How about the dentist who removes all your teeth without telling you then sells them to another client who wants real teeth in his dentures? Or the dentist who takes all the painkiller out of his injections then sells it to punk-rockers so that they will feel no pain when they crash into one another while dancing? Somehow I think the punter would be very quick to notice what was missing and probably take immediate and violent action.

"Mum, I really don't think . . ."

"And I thought he was such a nice man, asking us to his party. I was even feeling a certain sympathy for him because of that son of his."

"What? You mean Dara? Why?" I was rather taken aback by this turn in the conversation. What did she know that I didn't?

"Well, really, you know what I mean. To raise a fine-looking boy like that and then have him become some sort of small farmer. That's really more than any parent should have to bear. If I thought . . ."

"Mum, Mum, hang on . . .!" I had to stop her. If she got on to careers I was finished. Time for a change of subject. "Before we start that would you please tell me what you're doing here? How on earth did you turn up at the top of the stairs when you did?

A little smile of triumphant pleasure played on my mother's lips. "Well, it was easy, dear. When you didn't ring I knew there was something wrong, especially after I had left all those messages. So I gave you until this morning and then at eight thirty on the dot I left, and you know the rest."

I did not know the rest. There were huge great gaps in any logical succession of events I put together. "But I could have rung after you left and you wouldn't have known and how did you find me once you got here?"

"Mobile phone, your father's mobile phone. Sally in the office did some diversion thing that meant all calls to the house went to the mobile phone. Marvellous inventions, I must get one myself. I hear you can get them in red and blue and any colour, really, and much smaller than this one." She pulled an enormous old mobile phone out of her pocket and dropped it into my outstretched hands. It was lucky she hadn't decided to hit Terry with it or the results might have been fatal. "And as for finding you? Simple. I went straight to the police station. After all, it is their job to find people, and that nice guard I met while I was here said he had seen you go into the solicitor's some time before. He seemed very concerned – he even wanted to come along but he had to mind the office. He assured me repeatedly that he had delivered my message so I knew for certain that something was amiss. Well, they told me in the solicitor's office that you had gone to Terry's, and when I got there all the doors were open so I simply followed the voices. And just as well I did, wasn't it?"

I nodded. There was nothing I could say. She had gone to an awful lot of trouble but, really, there had been no need: everything had more or less settled itself. My mother believed that she was the hero of the moment and I wasn't even going to try to dissuade her. "I'll see you back at the house, Mum," I said, going to my car which was exactly where I'd left it that morning.

"All right, dear." Her voice echoed across the winter-sunlit castle courtyard.

I was alone.

The thing was, even though I had been on my own most of the time since I had come to County Clare I'd never really been alone. I'd always had my emotional trauma as dialogue. Now that was gone because I had finally let Niall go. And with Niall gone I had no reason to stay in hiding in Clare. I was free to go back to my own world and find my life, if I had one.

I pulled my scarf up around my ears. It was starting to get really cold again now that the sun was doing its usual February-early-retirement routine. I hunched up my shoulders and headed towards the house. I had some packing to do before I left for Dublin. Who said life couldn't start at thirty? Well, I did, but maybe if I got something done with my hair things wouldn't be so bad. I went into the house.

It was the same temperature inside as it had been outside. I kept my scarf and coat on while I packed. It didn't take long. As I put the first bag into the car I found the boxes of vegetables Dara had put there the day before. A little wave of heated excitement passed through me at the memory of our afternoon in front of the fire. That was another fine mess. Imagine what he thought of me now that he knew I had believed him to be a murderer! And a devious manipulative murderer at that, the worst sort, I'm sure! It was the sort of thing that guaranteed there would be no hope of us ever getting together again.

I had gone back into the house, nursing my bitter little

poor-mes when I heard a car stop outside. Even though I knew everything was nicely wrapped up and currently being sorted at the police station I felt a little stab of apprehension as I peeped out of the window. The apprehension changed to dismay when I realised that it was Séan the guard keeping his appointment. I had forgotten all about it. I looked around in panic, wondering if there was any hope that I could dash out the back and avoid him. The last thing I needed was a small-talk session with a guard who exhibited idiosyncratic hat habits. There was no escape: he'd more than likely seen the curtain move anyway, so he knew I was at home.

I opened the door before he had a chance to knock. He didn't seem in the least surprised at that and without any invitation from me he stepped into the hall. "Val, are you all right?" He looked at me intently, then removed his hat before it could start any of its usual antics. This was all a bit sudden and intense for me so I just nodded dumbly. "It's just, you see, I know all about it. I've just come from the station."

Oh, God, I'd forgotten he'd be there. Dara was probably still telling everybody how we had had dinner, then taken all our clothes off in front of the fire and how we nakedly tried to save the house before it blew down and how we had had to put all our clothes back on to go outside and find the passport. The whole village would know about our afternoon together by now. I blushed. "Oh, really?" I tried to sound cool and unflustered. "What's going on now?"

I thought that the broad, open-ended approach might be the best. "Well, Terry O'Neill has confessed to the murder, but you know that, don't you? Weren't you out at the house earlier, from what I hear? Do you want to press charges?"

Press charges? The thought hadn't even crossed my mind. Of course I didn't want to press charges, I just wanted to forget about the whole thing. If Séan knew that I had been in a situation about which I could press charges, what didn't he know? I had to ask. "What else did Dara say?"

Séan looked puzzled. "Dara? No, Dara didn't say anything." His face darkened slightly. "Nothing at all. No, it was Terry who said that he had falsely imprisoned you. Dara said hardly anything."

I smiled with relief and lied. "Oh, yeah, sorry, I meant to say Terry, got the names mixed up." I shrugged apologetically. "I bet you're all very happy in the station now?"

Séan nodded contentedly. "Yeah, it certainly takes the pressure off. Head office were really starting to grumble. It's a bit of a shock that it turned out to be such a respected member of the community, though." I lowered my eyes to the floor, hoping that by not saying anything and not encouraging conversation he would leave and I could get on with my packing.

Sean shifted nervously. "So, you're going to stay around a while longer then, are you?" he finally asked, looking around the dishevelled hallway.

"Oh, no. I'm leaving right away, I'm just in the middle of packing actually." Maybe a heavy hint would work. Séan looked a bit stricken but within seconds his face cleared. "Off back to Dublin?" he said confidently.

I nodded.

"Now isn't that a coincidence, Val?"

I looked at him blankly. It didn't strike me as being anything like a coincidence.

"What?" I asked shortly.

"Well, I'm in Dublin all next week on a course." He faltered, then went on carefully. "Maybe we could meet up some evening?"

What? Was I hearing correctly? Had Séan just asked me on a date? Oh, no! How was I going to get out of this one? I could just see us sitting in some place like the garda club – I'd never been there but I'd heard about it – socialising with scores of men whose hats moved erratically on their heads. There had to be an easy way of saying no. I opened my mouth to speak. "I, amm, I, I . . ." Suddenly, through the open door, I saw another car pull up outside. ". . . I see somebody else has come to visit," I finished, with relief.

Séan swung round to follow my gaze out of the door and we both watched as Dara got out of his Land Rover and walked towards the house. My heart did a little dance and I pushed past Séan out of the door towards Dara.

"Dara."

"Val." His face broke into a smile. He opened his arms and we embraced warmly as he kissed the top of my head lightly. Then he released his hold and spoke cheerily over my head. "Hi, Séan, you seem to be everywhere today."

I turned to look at Séan. His face looked as though it had collapsed. It wasn't so much tearful as hurt, dejected and broken, a sort of medley of pain. He swallowed hard, unable to meet my eye. "I'll be off now, then," he said shortly, and walked towards his car, his shoulders held stiffly straight as though denying his feelings.

"What's the matter with him?" Dara asked.

"Oh, nothing. He was just leaving," I replied, feeling a slight pang for Séan's disappointment, but nevertheless glad that I hadn't had to get into a no-thank-you-I-don't-want-a-date litany.

And now there was just Dara. After the initial warmth I felt awkward, unsure of what to say next.

"How are you?"

"I'm fine, Val, I'm OK."

Small-talk. Think small-talk. Quickly, quickly.

"How's Terry?"

"Fine, he's talking to the guards."

"Oh, good. I mean, well, it's not really, that is, I mean . . ."

"Val, I need to talk to you."

I looked at him for the first time since he'd arrived. I mean, I know we'd hugged and all, but I hadn't really looked at him, you know, into his eyes. They were full of that sort of fervour that I had seen in them the day he had asked me to Terry's party. My heart jumped faster and other bits of my insides jerked in a sort of pleasure-pain tango. I waited for him to continue.

"Val, I still feel the same way about you. I know everything's all messed up now but that hasn't changed." He searched my face for a reaction.

I didn't react, I was waiting for the 'but' bit.

There was always a 'but' bit.

And here it came.

"But I suppose you'd have nothing to do with the son of a murderer."

You must be joking. Nothing to do with . . .? Given the slightest chance I'd have everything to do with . . . Just give me the opportunity! Maybe I wouldn't have to go back to my miserable life in Dublin after all! I could buy a pair of wellingtons, just hang out here and get into some lust. I could . . .

Dara's voice broke across my thoughts. "I realise of course that you have to go back to Dublin. That's where your life is. And I'm sure there are probably other people to take into consideration." He looked at me meaningfully, and I realised that I had never had a chance to explain the Niall incident to him. And now didn't seem like the best time to get into all that. I'd have to play along. I gave a slight nod. What else was I supposed to do? Deny that there were other considerations, other men in my life, and reveal myself to be a lost soul wandering through the desolate valley of my-boyfriend-rejected-me?

The silence worked. Dara looked resigned. "But if you think I have any chance, will you tell me now? I couldn't bear the idea of you leaving without my knowing. Maybe if there's a chance, any chance, just say yes now and I could visit you in a couple of weeks when things have settled down here."

Hey, incredible.

Fantastic.

All I had to do was say yes, pretend I had a life to go to and I'd see him again. In fact, it seemed that the more

life I pretended I had the better this would work! I'd
have to go and get a life!

Dara was gazing at me earnestly.

Oh, my God, a happy ending!

Would this mean no more Sugar Puffs – ever?

I savoured the moment, taking a quick, furtive glance
around for any natural calamity that could mess things
up for me – I couldn't spot any. I gave a little mental sigh
of satisfaction.

I smiled into Dara's ardent green eyes.

And nodded.